THE SILENCER MYSTERY
THE COMPLETE CASES OF
GILLIAN HAZELTINE, VOLUME 3

BOOKS IN THE ARGOSY LIBRARY:

GOLDEN RIVER: THE COMPLETE
ADVENTURES OF BEN QUORN, VOLUME 1
TALBOT MUNDY

LADY OF THE NIGHT WIND
VARICK VANARDY

KING OF THE EXILES
THOMSON BURTIS

FOR A POINT OF HONOR: THE COMPLETE
CASES OF RIORDAN, VOLUME 2
VICTOR MAXWELL

THE DARK WATERS
WILLIAM CORCORAN

MURDER WITHOUT MOTIVE: THE COMPLETE
CASES OF SHOW-ME McGEE, VOLUME 1
FREDERICK C. DAVIS

MURDER IN THE NUDIST CLUB
FRED MACISAAC

GORILLA CARGO: THE COMPLETE
ADVENTURES OF McNALLY, VOLUME 1
RICHARD WORMSER

GREEN MAMBA: THE COMPLETE
CASES OF DAFFY DILL, VOLUME 2
RICHARD B. SALE

THE SILENCER MYSTERY: THE COMPLETE
CASES OF GILLIAN HAZELTINE, VOLUME 3
GEORGE F. WORTS

THE SILENCER MYSTERY

THE COMPLETE CASES OF GILLIAN HAZELTINE, VOLUME 3

GEORGE F. WORTS

ILLUSTRATRATIONS BY

WILLIAM MOLT
ROGER B. MORRISON
JOHN R. NEILL

COVER BY

GEORGE W. GAGE

POPULAR PUBLICATIONS · 2024

TABLE OF CONTENTS

THE SILENCER MYSTERY

*An absorbing murder mystery with a
tremendously dramatic courtroom climax,
by the well-remembered author of "Fortune,
Inc.," and "The Girl in the Blue Sarong"*

1

IN THE FEW seconds while the traffic light at the corner of Walnut Avenue and Madison Street remained red, Gillian Hazeltine saw all *but* all of the murder of Oscar Treidler. And what he failed to see was, strangely, the most important of all. What he failed to see was—the murder!

Gillian Hazeltine had, in obedience to the traffic whistle, brought his luxurious black-and-nickel coupé to a stop, the first car in the traffic line. On his right was a small grocery truck. On his left stood a yellow street-car. Above and ahead was the red light, glaring like an angry eye.

Turning his head slightly to the right, Gillian Hazeltine could see the large plate-glass window of Oscar Treidler's real estate office, so clear from a recent washing and polishing that it seemed to exist not at all.

Oscar Treidler was seated at his desk, a pasty, plump Buddha of a man who fondly called himself Square-Deal Treidler and who, as many men knew to their sorrow, was one of the greatest rascals in Greenboro, a man underhanded and oversmart. Passers-by could, by merely sliding their eyes, look in at Oscar Treidler, sitting there in plain sight of the passing world.

His eyes widening with interest, Gillian Hazeltine suddenly bent forward. A hatless young man had approached the window and was staring in at Oscar Treidler. His hair was black and curly. His face was white

as paper. His shoulders
were hunched up. His head
was thrust forward. His
demeanor was somehow
ominous. He was tugging
at something in his hip
pocket.

Gillian Hazeltine recog-
nized him as Gale Whar-
ton, a young aviator who,
because of his recklessness
in the air, was everywhere
known as Flip. He had often driven past Flip Wharton's small farm and knew that Flip's income was derived
from two sources: aerial joy-rides and the breeding of
ribbon-winning wire-haired fox terriers. He had met Flip
but once, when the aviator had come to his office for legal
advice on an invention which would do away with airplane
propellers.

As the aviator, glaring in at Oscar Treidler, tugged at
his hip pocket, the red light went dark—and a great many
things happened.

HAZELTINE SAW A flash of blue metal as the thing Flip
Wharton had been tugging at was whipped from his
pocket. Then his view was cut off by the grocery truck,
which had eased ahead.

He said excitedly to himself:

"What's that damned fool up to?"

Above the muffled exhausts of motors he heard a woman
sharply scream. The grocery truck slid ahead, and Hazeltine's view was again clear. He saw, just below the gold

Flip Wharton was sprinting across the intersection
when the traffic-officer extended his foot.
The young aviator went sprawling.

lettering on the window, a cobweb pattern with a round clean hole at the center.

His heart gave a sickening lurch. Square-deal Treidler, upright at his desk, had unquestionably been shot. From a hole in his neck blood was gushing. As Gillian Hazeltine held his breath, Treidler pitched forward across his desk.

Flip Wharton was sprinting diagonally across the intersection. The traffic-officer extended his foot; the young aviator went sprawling to the pavement, and the policeman leaped upon him.

The noses of a growing crowd were pressed against the large window. Gillian Hazeltine felt weak and ill. In the presence of death he always felt weak and ill. Although he had been, for upward of twelve years, a criminal lawyer, and had had contact with murderers with the blood of the kill fresh on their hands, he had never grown inured to the visible evidences of death.

The warmth was gone from the sunshine. The breeze drifting through his coupé, so springlike a moment ago, now seemed wintry.

But life, it appeared, must go on. Two policemen, springing magically from nowhere, were yelling at the paralyzed line of traffic. A siren shrieked behind Gillian Hazeltine. The line of cars began to move. He mechanically let in his clutch. His eyes were straight ahead. He was so weak he could hardly grip the wheel.

AS HAZELTINE DROVE on toward the fashionable residential section where he lived, his trembling stopped and his mind cleared. He was glad that murders and all that went with them were forever behind him. Only last week he had publicly announced his retirement from the bar and his entry into politics.

Until he had driven his car into the garage behind his house it did not occur to him that, although he had practically witnessed the murder of Oscar Treidler, he had heard no shot. He had been less than twenty feet away when Flip Wharton had killed Oscar Treidler; yet he was positive he had heard no shot. Why had he not?

Others were speculating on that point. Oscar Treidler's life had gushed and bubbled away through a hole in his neck. A bullet had pierced his carotid artery, letting the life out of him as quickly as the air is released from a punctured tire. Yet no one had heard a shot.

Gillian Hazeltine went into his house. His Japanese butler, Toro, met him in the lower hall and said in his painfully precise English:

"Mr. Oscar Treidler has just been murdered, sir. The district attorney is on the telephone and wishes to speak with you."

"Tell him I'm not in. Tell him you don't know where I am or when I'll be back. Tell the same thing to everybody who phones this afternoon. I don't want to be disturbed. Serve luncheon in my study."

Gillian Hazeltine went on up to his study. He wanted to think. The murder of Oscar Treidler had ruined his plans. He knew that, although that shot had been unheard, the lives of many people would be as violently affected as if a ton of dynamite had been set off on that busy corner.

SURROUNDED BY POLICEMEN and detectives, Gale Wharton was seated in a bare, glaringly lighted room in the Seventh Precinct Station-house. Two hours had elapsed since the murder of Oscar Treidler; yet, strangely, no eye-witnesses to that shocking incident had been found. There was absolutely no question in the minds of the authorities that Gale Wharton had shot the real-estate man. But on two minor points the case was somewhat mystifying. Why had no one heard the shot? Why had no one seen him fire it?

Savagely, the aviator reiterated:

"I did not shoot Oscar Treidler!" Then, with a moan: "What's going to happen to my sister? This will kill her— the poor kid!"

A glowering sergeant of detectives, seated so close to him that their knees were locked, barked:

"Then what was you doin' with this rod?"

Flip Wharton put his hands to his eyes. The detective, grasping each wrist in a powerful hand, pulled them down his face. They left trails of dirt and sweat. This was the sixth detective who had interrogated the prisoner.

"I was going to shoot him!" the aviator burst out. A murmur of interest ran through the assemblage of uniformed and non-uniformed officers. A confession!

"But I didn't!" declared the young man with the staring black eyes. "I didn't shoot him! I couldn't!"

"Oh, you was gonna shoot him, eh? You was gonna shoot him, but you couldn't, eh? Well, if you was gonna shoot him and then couldn't, why did you beat it like hell right after he was shot?"

"Because I was afraid I was going to! I didn't know he had been shot till you told me. The first thing I knew—"

"Wait a minute! You was afraid you— Say, that don't make sense. Why was you afraid you was gonna shoot him?"

"Because I hated him!"

"Oh, is that so! Oh, you did, did you? You hated him, did you? You go around like this, do you, shootin' people because you hate 'em?"

"No! I never shot a man in my life. I couldn't! No matter how much I hated him, I couldn't shoot him. That's what I'm telling you!" the young man declared hotly. "I couldn't shoot a man like that. It would be murder! I realized that when I looked in the window at him. I was going to shoot him, but I knew I couldn't. Why don't you look for the real murderer instead of wasting all this good time on me? What's going to happen to my kid sister? I tell you, this'll kill her!"

A LAMP WITH a huge nickeled reflector, not more than a foot from the prisoner's face, suddenly flashed on, white-hot. He blinked his eyes and squinted. It had not occurred to him before that he was being third-degreed, but now it did.

The sergeant of detectives barked:

"If you didn't shoot him, how come this rod's got one exploded shell in it?"

"I used that shell to kill Honey Boy Blue this morning. That was what started it. I shot Honey Boy Blue and came into town to shoot that dirty skunk. I was—"

"Wait a minute. What started what? Who the hell is Honey Boy Blue?"

"My dog. That's his name. He's—"

"Hold on. You shot your dog, eh? This is getting good. You shot your dog, then you came into town to shoot Treidler. Did you shoot your dog in the neck like you shot Treidler, or did you shoot him somewhere else?"

"I tell you, I didn't shoot Treidler!" Sweat from the heat of the glaring light was running down the aviator's cheeks.

"That's right," the big detective chuckled with heavy jocularity; "I keep forgettin' you didn't shoot Treidler. You shot Honey Boy Blue. Why did you shoot Honey Boy Blue?"

"Because he was poisoned. Treidler poisoned him. I had to put him out of his suffering."

"You mean Treidler?"

"Good God, no—I mean the dog! Treidler poisoned him because I wouldn't sell him to him. I bred him myself. He would have walked off with the blue ribbon for his class. I mean, in the dog show. Treidler wanted him because he knew Honey Boy Blue would beat his Sassy in the wire-haired fox-terrier class. And when I wouldn't sell him,

Treidler poisoned him. Anybody who poisons a friendly little dog like that deserves to be shot!"

"Sure he does! And so you shot him!"

"I did not. I tell you, you're wasting valuable time on me. Somebody else shot Treidler."

"Don't be so fast. You said you hated Treidler. Did you ever have any other rows with him?"

"Yes. Lots of them. He got fresh with my sister once."

"Did you tell him if he laid a hand on her you'd knock his block off?"

"Yes, I did."

"You had plenty reasons for hatin' him, didn't you?"

The aviator squeezed his eyes tightly shut against the dreadful hot glare of the light.

"Yes, and—"

"And so you came to town this mornin' and shot the big slob! I don't blame you! He certainly had it comin'! I'd 'a' done it myself! You did right in shootin' Treidler! Now, just sign this, which says you admit shootin' the big bum, and everything will be all right."

"My God, I *didn't* shoot him!" the aviator cried. "Can't you get it through your thick heads? Don't you realize the real murderer is getting away while you're wasting all this time on me? You've got to catch him! My sister—"

"Quit squawkin' about your sister. Wharton, if you don't come to your senses pretty soon and sign this statement, I'm gonna get rough with you. I'm losin' my temper, I am. Any jury in the world would send you to the chair without this confession, but you're gonna sign it."

"I won't sign it. I didn't kill Treidler."

The sergeant heavily and sadly shook his head. "There's

only one lawyer in this State who could do anything with a case as funny as yours, Wharton. That's Gillian Hazeltine. If you got any money, you better get busy and retain Hazeltine."

"Hazeltine's quit the law," broke in one of the policemen. "It was in the *Times* a week ago. He's gone into politics, and he ain't takin' any more cases. He's runnin' for police commissioner."

"I know all about it," snapped the sergeant of detectives. "But I'm sayin' that the only lawyer who ever could do anything with a fishy case like this one is Hazeltine."

"I didn't kill Treidler," the prisoner muttered. "I don't need a lawyer."

The sergeant of detectives snorted. "Naw, o' course not. Neither does a baby need its mother! Mike, throw this sap back into his cell. Give him half an hour to think things over, then bring him back."

2

THE OFFICES OF Mr. Adelbert Yistle, the district attorney of Greenboro, fairly hummed with excitement. The murder of Mr. Yistle's old friend Oscar Treidler was not merely a cold-blooded murder to Mr. Yistle; it was a heaven-sent opportunity.

One of the prerogatives of a district attorney is to deliver opinions, and Mr. Yistle was delivering an opinion, as he pounded softly on the edge of his desk.

A square-built man, with a strong, judicial forehead surmounted by a mop of pale-brown hair, and a massive jaw, Mr. Yistle was a commanding figure. He was an extremely ambitious man. He had entered the race for the police commissionership against Gillian Hazeltine, because he thought that the time was ripe to show up Gillian Hazeltine in his true colors. Countless were the courtroom battles the two had fought and—now—now the police commissionership! The police commissionership was a pivotal position. No matter why. It was. A groove ran straight from the police commissioner's office to the governor's mansion. In the past twenty years five Greenboro police commissioners had become governors. It was one of those jobs.

Mr. Yistle was talking to two of his assistants, Mr. Bullock and Mr. Chapman. Both were young men. Both had the same opinion of Mr. Yistle—they thought he was an awful ass. But both took pains not to let him know it. The great difference between the two assistants was that Mr. Bullock was a man who always said "Yes!" and Mr. Chapman was a man who almost invariably said "No!" Mr. Yistle went to Mr. Bullock when he wished to be yessed, and he went to Mr. Chapman when he wished to be noed. The present crisis was so vital that he had called for both of them. He wanted the yes and the no side of a problem which struck him as being delightfully simple. But no problem yet associated with Gillian Hazeltine had proved as simple as it had looked at the outset.

"Deeply as I regret the loss of my old friend Oscar," he was saying to the two attentive young men, "the fact remains that it is an ill wind that blows nobody some good. Take, for example, the police commissionership. Gillian Hazeltine is a clever man. People don't call him the Silver Fox just because his hair happens to be pointed with silver! Am I right?"

The district attorney paused. Mr. Bullock, who was a pale, thin young man with kind brown eyes, a disappearing chin and a prominent Adam's apple, said, "Yes sir!" effusively, and clinched his statement with, "You're absolutely right, Mr. Yistle!"

Mr. Chapman for one of the first times on record, did not say no. His nod was briskly affirmative. He was a brisk young man with a git-up-and-go-get-'em jaw, a strong mouth and a pair of powerful blue eyes. He would agree with anybody who said that Gillian Hazeltine was a brilliant man. More than once he had suffered mental crucifixion in a courtroom when Gillian Hazeltine was on the other side of the case.

"This—this regrettable murder," Mr. Yistle went on, glancing from assistant to assistant, "is going to kill Gillian Hazeltine's chances for the police commissionership."

"Why?" asked Mr. Chapman dryly.

"Why, dammit all, Chapman, can't we engineer things to make it a triumph for this office?"

"How?" asked Chapman.

Mr. Yistle with his big, hard hand gently but impatiently pounded his desk.

"Well, what have we?"

"A murder of prima facie evidence," answered Chapman. "It'll go to the grand jury. That aviator will plead guilty— and that's all that will happen. Where's the triumph?"

"He insists that he's innocent. And so far, you're dead wrong. It isn't a prima facie case. It's purely circumstantial. Six hours have passed since Treidler was shot down in cold blood by that ruthless murderer, and although the city has been combed, so far there isn't a single eye-witness."

"It's lucky for us," said the chronically dissenting Mr. Chapman, "that Hazeltine isn't defending that fellow. He'd make a lot of that. I've never yet seen him attack circumstantial evidence without tearing it to shreds."

"Look here, Chapman," said the district attorney sternly, "we are going to send that aviator to the chair—do you get that? It will be the last act I perform before resigning this job. Wharton is going to the chair! If the case remains circumstantial, we will send him to the chair!"

"How?" asked Chapman.

"Let us consider this murder as it happened," answered

Mr. Yistle. "It happened in broad daylight. At least a dozen people might have been looking at Flip Wharton when he fired the revolver. Well, what happened? I'll tell you. Our minds are geared to the usual, not to the unusual. Anything unusual confuses people. A man pulling out a gun and firing it at another man, killing him, is unusual. You've known it to happen time after time. Perhaps a dozen people half saw this murder. Will their testimony conflict? You can bet it will! Why? Because it always does! Of the twelve, two or three will have seen Wharton fire the shot with his left hand. Of the twelve, two or three will swear they heard two, three or four shots. In my address to the jury, I will stress that point."

"But," put in his no-man, "it is fairly well established that no one heard even *one* shot."

"He must have used a Maxim silencer."

"But he didn't. His revolver was an ordinary revolver."

"Chapman, it seems to me you are trying to befog the issue."

"That is my opinion," agreed Bullock.

"I am merely bringing up points that any good lawyer will raise when the case comes to trial," Mr. Chapman defended himself. "No shot was heard. No silencer was found. So far, no one saw the shot fired."

MR. YISTLE DID not reply at once. He frowned. He reached into his mahogany humidor, selected a fat blond perfecto and leisurely lighted it. He cocked the cigar upward, thrust his thumbs into his armpits and said:

"My motto, when I am convinced that a man is guilty of a crime, is: Interpret Justice Broadly. There is no doubt in our minds that Flip Wharton murdered Oscar Treidler—

my dear old friend. Shall we hesitate to adopt any means
at our hand to bring about his conviction? We shall not!
If we cannot find an eye-witness to the murder, we will—
find one."

"You mean," said his fearless no-man, "we will manu-
facture one?"

"I do!"

"I absolutely agree with Mr. Yistle," Mr. Bullock
hastened to say.

"The day you disagree with him about anything," said
Mr. Chapman, angrily, "I shall expect to see the heavens
crash to the earth, the rivers start to running uphill, an
army of celluloid cats to pass unscorched through—"

"Boys, boys!" Mr. Yistle pleasantly stopped him. "We
were talking about witnesses. If no one actually saw that
shot fired, it seems to me quite logical that a witness must
exist somewhere who saw Wharton throw a silencer into a
passing truck. There must have been trucks in the vicinity.
If we can't find actual witnesses—"

The ringing of the phone bell stopped him. Mr. Bullock,
nearest the instrument, picked it up, said hello and listened.

His eyes suddenly seemed to bulge. He gasped, "Is that
so! How wonderful! I'll tell Mr. Yistle!"

He hung up the receiver.

"Chief," he got out thinly, "it was the detective bureau.
They've finally got track of an eye-witness. And who do
you suppose it is, chief? Gillian Hazeltine!"

The district attorney for a moment looked at his assistant rather stupidly.

"Gillian Hazeltine *saw* the murder?" he gasped.

"He must have! His car was parked, in the traffic line

up, right beside Treidler's window. Two cops saw him. He must have seen every detail of the murder!"

The magical possibilities opened up by this information almost stunned the district attorney. He gulped.

"Do you boys realize what this means?" he demanded. "It means we've got Gillian Hazeltine with all his clothes off!"

"Why?" asked Mr. Chapman. "You said you didn't want an eye-witness."

"Why? My God, man, can't you see the triumph in it for me? He'll be *my* witness! He'll be a minor actor in the drama in which I'm playing the leading part! I'll put questions to him that will bring out certain unsavory episodes of his past! The papers will print it word for word! When I get through with him, Gillian Hazeltine won't have any more chance at that police commissionership than a cross-eyed, bow-legged girl with a hare-lip has of getting into the Ziegfeld Follies! I'll make a sucker out of him!"

"The man hasn't been born who can make Gillian Hazeltine look like a sucker," disagreed Mr. Chapman.

Mr. Bullock hit the desk a heavy blow.

"You're wrong, Chapman! The man has been born! The man is Mr. Yistle!"

"Just the same," muttered Mr. Chapman, "it's a damned good thing that Gillian Hazeltine isn't going into court to defend that aviator. He'd make suckers out of all of us. He always has, hasn't he?"

"You boys get busy," said the district attorney. "And let's pray that no more eye-witnesses are found."

3

THE MANSION IN which Gillian Hazeltine lived sat upon a gracious green hill above the Sangamo River. It was one of the show places of the exclusive Riverview development—and an eloquent testimonial to Gillian Hazeltine's success. With the reputation of being the most brilliant criminal lawyer in the State, he had, in a few fast years, acquired a considerable fortune. Still young—he was not yet thirty-three—he had devoted himself so faithfully to his career that he had missed out on a great many worthwhile things. He had not had time to go into Greenboro society. He had not had time to cultivate many friendships.

Gillian Hazeltine was, as a consequence, rather a lonely young man. He lived alone in his handsome house. And he frequently had no one to talk to. The afternoon of the murder of Oscar Treidler had not been a pleasant one. He saw what Mr. Yistle had seen: the destruction of his political hopes. He felt blue. Other men when they felt blue had some one to turn to for consolation—a wife or a close friend. He had no one.

Watching the afterglow fade from the western sky, Gillian was smoking an after-dinner cigar in his sun-parlor when his Japanese houseman, in his impeccable English, announced from the doorway:

"Mr. Norton Garth presents his compliments and wishes

to have a word with Mr. Hazeltine. I told him you were not at home, sir, but he insists that you are. He is seated in the drawing-room."

Gillian, with the cigar clenched in his teeth, a plume of blue smoke trailing out behind him, went inside. In his present state of mind, any intrusion was welcome.

A handsome man of sixty with thick, smoothly brushed white hair, a trimmed white mustache, kindly blue eyes and a golfer's tan, arose to shake his hand when Gillian entered the drawing-room. Gillian was a little surprised at this visit, and a little flattered. He had always admired Norton Garth, who had risen to his present eminence from the Greenboro slums. He was a self-made man who had acquired wisdom and culture, had softened his early harshness with kindliness. His favorite phrase was "Let us temper justice with mercy." A few years ago he had sold a lucrative commission business to enter politics. Although the two men were on opposite sides of the political fence, they had for years fostered an admiration for each other that amounted almost to affection.

Norton Garth had publicly announced his approval of Adelbert Yistle for police commissioner, but even this put no strain on their friendship. Gillian knew that Norton Garth was looking with hungry eyes at the governor's mansion. Everyone called him the Colonel, although he had never been a colonel of anything.

HIS HANDSHAKE WAS firm and warm. Toro had laid a small fire in the fireplace. As the two men seated themselves before it, "Colonel" Garth gravely examined Gillian's dark, handsome face.

"You knew, of course, that Polly Wharton's brother had

shot and instantly killed Oscar Treidler this morning?" he asked.

"I practically saw it happen," Gillian affirmed.

"Why do you say 'practically,' Gillian?"

"Because I could not go on the stand and swear that I saw him shoot Treidler. I saw him pull out the gun. I saw Treidler die. I did not actually see the murder, because a truck pulled up just when it happened and my view was cut off. I was in my coupé, held up in traffic."

Norton Garth brought his fist down with a soft thump on the arm of his chair.

"Gillian, this is very strange. I am in precisely the same predicament. I was in that line-up too! My limousine must have been two or three cars behind yours—or where was your car?"

"The first in the line, Colonel."

"Mine was, I should say, the third or fourth, but it is all badly confused now. I saw him pull the gun from his hip pocket. I knew what was going to happen, because I know Flip and his sister Polly quite well, and I was aware of the bad feeling existing between Flip and Treidler. When I realized he intended to shoot Treidler, I shut my eyes. I must have had them shut for ten seconds. I was so scared, Gillian, I almost fainted! I waited for the sound of the shot. It didn't come. When I finally opened my eyes, they were staring straight ahead into the window—and I saw that poor devil die! It was horrible!"

Colonel Garth passed a snowy handkerchief over his forehead.

"Staring straight ahead into the window—and saw that poor devil die!" Gillian repeated.

"I've been so shaken up I can think of nothing else. Gillian, is there any doubt in your mind that Flip killed him?"

"No, Colonel."

"But why was there no sound of a shot?"

"Flip is an inventor," Gillian answered. "It would be no great problem for him to make some sort of gun that worked with a powerful spring or compressed air and would make no sound when fired."

Colonel Garth shook his head firmly.

"I've talked with the chief of police. He says that the revolver taken from Flip was an ordinary .38 caliber."

Gillian shrugged. "I'm not a detective, Colonel."

"On the contrary," the Colonel disagreed, "you're the smartest detective in the State. I've sat in a courtroom and watched you make deductions that *Sherlock Holmes* would have envied."

"But I'm not in that business any more."

COLONEL GARTH REMOVED an old briar pipe from his pocket and absently filled it from a leather pouch. When the pipe was going, he said:

"Gillian, I'm here tonight because of Polly Wharton. She's at my house, waiting, with my wife. The poor little thing is at her wit's end. She begged me to persuade you to defend her brother. That's my errand, Gillian."

He paused. Gillian waited. He knew that the Colonel had befriended Miss Wharton in the past; that he had at one time secured a position as stenographer for her in the city engineer's office. He knew, too, that during a shake-up in the engineer's office, when employees were being discharged right and left because of grafting, the

Colonel had arranged a holiday in Florida for Miss Wharton and another girl, so they would escape the unpleasantness.

"The real victim of this tragedy," the Colonel went on, "is Polly. I'll put it to you bluntly: Will you take Flip's case?"

Gillian slowly, firmly shook his head. "For two reasons," he said. "The first is that Flip is guilty as hell. The second is that, as a politician, I'm still too young and tender to risk it. As it is, all my beans are spilled. You know yourself that this trial will give Yistle the chance to walk into that police commissioner's job. It's a clean-cut murder case. But Yistle will put up a big ballyhoo. He'll be washed into the police commissionership on a tidal wave of easy publicity. Damn his hide! He's nothing but a dummy, and you know it!"

Colonel Garth leaned forward and tapped him on the knee with the stem of his pipe.

"But how about the real victim—Polly Wharton?"

"What about her? I don't know her. I never laid eyes on her."

"She's a fine girl, Gillian, and game. She has red hair and green eyes. If my daughter had lived—"

"Colonel," Gillian interrupted him, "I won't sacrifice my prospects over a sentimental pity for a red-headed girl with green eyes. I feel sorry for lots of people in this world. Every time I feel too sorry, it cost money."

"You're hard-boiled, Gillian."

"I'm jealous of every inch of my future, Colonel. Regardless of what anybody else thinks, you and I know that Flip killed Treidler. I've never yet gone into court to defend a man when I knew that he was guilty."

"But wait a minute, Gillian. Politically, I'm an enemy of

"You shot your dog; then you came into town to shoot Treidler!
Did you shoot your dog in the neck, like you shot Treidler?"

yours—the most dangerous enemy you've got. I'm going
to do everything in my power to help Yistle lick you in this
election. My party wants to see you steam-rollered. Things
look pretty dark for you now, don't they? But supposing
something should happen that threw you and me on the
same side of the fence. I look on you as one of the most
brilliant political prospects in the State. I'd like to have
you on my side."

Gillian grinned at him.

"Are you selling me something, Colonel?"

"I'm saying that you and I would make an unbeatable
political team. We're both wealthy and we'll admit that
we're both clever. That is the silver side of the dark cloud
hovering over you. Think that over, Gillian. Now let's get
back to Polly Wharton. Don't you owe anything to the
sacred oath you took when you became a lawyer? Polly

insists that Flip is innocent. The police grilled Flip all afternoon. He collapsed finally—still declaring his innocence. If
there's room for any doubt, don't you owe it to your sacred
oath to defend that boy?"

"My mind," Gillian firmly answered, "is closed."

Toro came silently into the drawing-room and
announced:

"Mr. Yistle is calling on Mr. Hazeltine."

Gillian darted a quick glance at the Colonel and said:

"Send him in, Toro."

Mr. Yistle, ruddy of cheek and bright of eye, walked
energetically into the drawing-room. He was rubbing and
wiping his hands together with the air of a man thoroughly
satisfied with himself. It was Mr. Yistle's day. Triumph
sat as a mantle upon him. In response to Gillian's directly
inquiring look, he chuckled and said:

"I come to bury Caesar, not to praise him! You don't
look happy, Gillian. Has something happened to upset
you? Good evening, Colonel. Well, how are my two star
witnesses?"

Neither man answered him. Mr. Yistle pulled up a chair
and sat down between them. He extended his hands to the
glowing logs. He turned to Gillian.

"I understand that Flip Wharton and his sister are trying
to retain you. Anything in it?"

"I wouldn't touch that case," said Gillian, "with a
ten-foot pole."

"I'm told," said the district attorney, "that you saw the
murder."

"I saw enough of it to convince me that Wharton is
guilty."

"That's bully," said Mr. Yistle. "We seem to be having a little difficulty in rounding up eye-witnesses. I never heard of so damned many people looking the other way when something exciting was happening. You'll consider it your public duty, of course, to take the stand?"

"If my testimony is needed," Gillian answered, "I will take the stand."

The district attorney laughed. Gillian had never liked Mr. Yistle. At this moment, he liked him still less.

"Your testimony," said Mr. Yistle, "is indispensable. And so is yours, Colonel. With your reputation, Gillian, as a keen observer, and yours, Colonel, as a public-spirited citizen, we'll send that young pup to the chair."

GILLIAN FIDGETED. "IT looks to me," he growled, "as if you're using this murder as a roller-coaster for taking a political joy-ride."

"No," said Mr. Yistle. "I'm using it as a juggernaut to trample down a political enemy or two."

Colonel Garth looked at him sharply and started to speak, but Mr. Yistle went on.

"It's the first time, Gillian, that I've ever had you just where I want you. Pardon me if I seem to be gloating."

"I've understood," said Gillian, somehow keeping the anger out of his voice, "that the proper time to gloat is when you've got an enemy licked. Your juggernaut hasn't run over me yet."

Mr. Yistle made the mistake now of chuckling. Gillian gazed at him with eyes as cold and as hard as steel.

"I've got just enough faith in my luck," he said, "to bet you five thousand dollars that I'll somehow lick you yet."

"Adelbert, don't take it!" snapped the Colonel.

"I've already taken it," said Mr. Yistle, and he laughed again. "Why don't you take Wharton's case, Gillian?"

"If there was the slightest doubt of his guilt," Gillian hotly answered, "I would!"

"Just to spite me, eh?"

"Adelbert," said the Colonel, rising, "we're going. I have some things to say to you in private. Come along."

Mr. Yistle started to protest, but it was his master's voice. He had always obeyed the Colonel implicitly; he followed.

THE COLONEL DISMISSED his car and rode in Mr. Yistle's sedan. He had nothing to say for several blocks. Then he vented himself liberally.

"Adelbert, you're a fool! I dropped in on Hazeltine for the express purpose of calming him down and sounding him out. I helped him make up his mind not to touch this Wharton case. You crashed in there and undid all my good work. He's sore enough now to take it on the sheer speculation that, in spite of all the evidence, Wharton may be innocent."

"I wish he would!" growled Mr. Yistle. "If I could just get him into the courtroom, I'd make a monkey of him!"

"Adelbert," said the Colonel with a weary sigh, "it will be a red-letter day in your life when you learn to keep away from buzz-saws. Hazeltine is a hundred times smarter than you are. He's the greatest criminal lawyer in the State, if not in the country. He can make the testimony of honest, innocent witnesses sound like black lies. He can play on the sympathies and prejudices of a dumb-bell jury until they believe that pink is green. You've seen him, time after time, make a fool of you. And yet you wish you could get him into court to defend Flip Wharton!"

But Mr. Yistle was unrepentant and unafraid. It was his day. He was riding a veritable tidal wave of luck.

"Hazeltine wouldn't dare defend Wharton," he declared. "I'm only praying that he will!"

4

A YOUNG MAN with staring black eyes and rumpled black hair walked unaided to the electric chair and was strapped into it. The current was switched on. The young man leaped and strained against the straps, but he did not die. Again and again the current was sent through his body, but it was evident that he had a magical hold upon life. The withering surge of the high voltage left him, each time, as alive as ever.

"You can't kill me!" he cried. "You can't kill an innocent man!"

A clear young voice firmly inquired: "I beg your pardon, but are you Gillian Hazeltine?"

Still in the thrall of that awful nightmare, Gillian opened his eyes. The windows of his bedroom were aglow with the amethyst of dawn.

The voice continued: "I'm sorry to wake you up. But it's terribly important."

Startled, Gillian sprang up to a sitting position. A slim shadow stood beside him in the semi-darkness. Gillian blinked his eyes, reached over and turned on the bedside reading lamp.

The pink glow suffused the face of a slender young man of twenty or twenty-one, who wore overalls and had green eyes and sleek red hair. In the boy's right hand was a blue revolver. It was pointed, not at Gillian, but at the floor.

From the revolver he looked at the boy's face and saw that his small, slightly turned-up nose was powdered with freckles. Gillian's alarm turned to consternation when he suddenly perceived that the boy was not a boy at all, but a girl.

Judged by modern standards, he supposed she was an exceptionally pretty girl. Blinking the sleep out of his eyes, he looked at her again. Yes, she was an exceptionally pretty girl.

Gillian's first lucid thought, as he looked up at the slim, overalled figure, was that this was an elaborate practical joke; his next, that he was the victim of a blackmail plot. At all events, she had no right here; and that revolver was ominous. He coldly inquired:

"What in the devil are you doing here?"

She tried to smile, but it was a ghostly smile. Then Gillian realized that she was scared. She got out, in a faint voice:

"I simply had to see you, Mr. Hazeltine. I'm Polly Wharton."

The famous criminal lawyer fell back on his pillow. In the same faint voice the girl in overalls hurriedly continued.

"I tried all day yesterday to get you on the telephone. Your butler said you weren't home. I—I knew he was lying."

Gillian ran his hand through his rumpled hair.

"Will you kindly tell me," he asked with ironical politeness, "how you got in here?"

Polly Wharton's look of anxiety increased. Her green eyes darted about the room. It was evident that the bravado which had carried her this far was fast ebbing. She was trembling. Small white teeth were fretting a pink underlip.

With all this, she was still trying to smile, as if in a pathetic attempt at reassuring him that her intentions were of the best.

"Where's my houseman?" Gillian suspiciously demanded.

"He—he's downstairs. He was so firm!" The low voice faltered. "He said you weren't home. And he told me to go away. I had to get past him, Mr. Hazeltine! I had to see you. So I just pointed this gun at him."

"Pointing guns at people," said Gillian dryly, "seems to run in the family. What did you do with that Jap?"

"I—I locked him in the closet under the stairs," she confessed. "It's a large closet, and—and I'm sure he'll have loads of air!"

"Give me that gun!" Gillian snapped.

With meekness amazing in one so audacious, Polly Wharton surrendered the weapon. Gillian examined it.

He looked up from the unloaded revolver to the red-haired girl. Her face was now chalk-white to her lips, which were gray. Her chin was trembling.

"Now," he said harshly, "get out of this house!"

Polly Wharton recoiled and looked at him with an air of hurt amazement.

"After all I've been through?" she wailed. "Mr. Hazeltine, you couldn't be so cruel! You've got to help me. I've been up all night, getting absolute proof to bring you that Flip did not kill that man."

"Miss Wharton," said Gillian, "it isn't any use. I saw your brother kill Treidler."

"But you couldn't have!" she cried. "I know what you saw, and I know what Colonel Garth saw. He told me! He told me there wasn't a chance of your defending Flip. But I know how just and fair you've always been. If five thousand dollars is enough, I can raise that much on our farm."

"Miss Wharton, I won't become involved in this case."

"But he's innocent. You know Captain Donovan, the firearms expert, don't you?" Without waiting for Gillian's reply, she hastened on: "I've been with Captain Donovan in his laboratory since midnight, and he's proved beyond the slightest doubt that the bullet that killed Treidler was not fired from Flip's revolver. Captain Donovan got the revolver from the detective bureau and the bullet from the coroner. He made all sorts of photographs and measurements. The two don't match!"

She was holding her hand to her heart as if it were hurting.

"If this is true," said Gillian, "why do you need me? The grand jury will let Flip go on Donovan's testimony."

"But I'm afraid of Donovan. He's been hinting that maybe he'd testify and maybe he wouldn't. I think he's a dangerous man. Mr. Hazeltine, I'm all in. I'll go to pieces if some one I can trust and depend on doesn't take charge of things. I—I tell you—"

"Don't faint!" Gillian shouted. But she did; or rather, she already had. The red-haired girl in the blue overalls sagged, without a sound, to the floor. She lay in a pathetic small heap, with her gray face upward, her slim arms flung out.

GILLIAN SCRAMBLED OUT of bed and into his dressing-gown. He was reputed to be a quick-thinking, quicker-acting man. Now he was in a panic. A fainting woman was a novelty to Gillian. He started for the bathroom for water. He started for his study, where there was a bottle of brandy. He opened his mouth to call for Toro, then recalled that Toro was in durance vile downstairs.

What in Sam Hill did a man do for a woman who had fainted? Her lips were parted, moving slightly as she breathed. Gillian recalled having heard that the proper procedure to take with a girl who had fainted was to place her in such a position that her heels were higher than her head, then throw water into her face.

Sliding one arm under her knees and another under her shoulders, he picked her up and looked anxiously about for some place where her heels might be higher than her head, then decided on the chair which stood beside the opened window. He looked down into her face and noted that her lashes, curving down upon her cheeks, were darker than her hair. Gillian suddenly felt sorry for this unfortunate morsel of humanity. A girl as pretty, as small as Polly Wharton, ought to be protected. What a plucky little thing she was!

Something undoubtedly happened to the heart of this famous hard-boiled criminal lawyer as the small red-haired girl lay for those few seconds unconscious in his arms.

He did not reach the chair beside the window. As he started toward it, Polly Wharton's eyes opened; from the cradle of his arms she looked up at him in wonderment, then consternation, as the pallor of her face gave way to a tide of crimson.

"You—you fainted," Gillian awkwardly explained, and stood her on her feet. "Sit down, Miss Wharton. I'll bring you a drink of water."

Polly Wharton sat down weakly. She said in a faint, husky voice:

"I never did that before in my life. I'm terribly sorry. What a nuisance I'm making of myself!"

"Not at all!" Gillian was astonished to hear himself say. "I don't blame you in the least. Under the circumstances, I'm sure I'd have fainted myself."

She rewarded him with a wan little smile. Gillian hurried into the bathroom for a glass of water. When he returned, she said:

"Will you talk to Donovan? He's waiting outside in my car."

"I certainly will."

Polly Wharton stood up. Her eyes were still overlarge and dark.

"I'll wait for you out there," she said.

"I'll hurry," said Gillian.

From his window, a moment later, he saw her crossing the lawn, to where her car was parked in the driveway. As the girl strode toward that venerable vehicle, the rising sun struck glints of gold from her sleek red hair. She carried herself with a certain audacity. Red hair and green eyes!

As he hurriedly dressed, Gillian devoted a great deal more thought to the red-haired girl than to her brother, perhaps because he had known so many alleged murderers and so few red-haired beautiful girls. How many women, he asked himself, had her courage? How many girls would fight for their brothers as she was fighting for Flip? Here, he decided, was a girl worth while. She was utterly different from any other girl he had ever known.

Gillian's thoughts went on to Captain Donovan. Of the Captain he knew a great deal, not all of which was complimentary. He knew that Donovan was one of the foremost firearms authorities in America. But he also knew Donovan would sell—and had sold—his soul for a mess of pottage.

WHEN GILLIAN, HAVING freed an indignant and sputtering Japanese from the clothes-closet downstairs, went out and crossed the lawn to the flivver, the firearms expert climbed down and greeted him with his sly smile. Donovan was a horse-faced man, with close-set eyes of a baffling color.

In a nasal voice, he began:

"There's no question about it, Mr. Hazeltine. This young lady's brother did not fire the bullet that killed Treidler. I'd stake my professional reputation on it. That bullet was fired from an automatic."

"A rifle?"

"Yes sir."

"That means, the man who killed Treidler might have been in some window across the street."

"Yes, Mr. Hazeltine, he might have. Of course, that remains to be proved. The big point right now is that Miss Wharton's brother didn't do the shooting. But he did shoot his dog, as he claims. I got the bullet out of the dog, and it was certainly fired from Flip's gun. I could take the stand and prove to any jury that Flip Wharton didn't fire the bullet that killed Treidler. It's sort of up to me, isn't it? So far, the police haven't found a single witness who did or didn't see Flip pull the trigger. And it looks as if they won't. It looks as if I'm gonna be the star witness in this case."

"It does look that way," Gillian admitted, and his gray eyes were shrewd.

"I've testified in lots of murder trials," went on Captain

Donovan in his nasal tones, "but this looks like the first time I'll ever take the stand and absolutely decide whether a man goes to the chair or goes free."

"It must give you a feeling of responsibility," said Gillian.

The expert grinned, revealing darkened, scalloped teeth.

"Up to this time," he said, "I've gone into court on a dinky contingent fee. You won't catch me giving my testimony this time for a hundred bucks a day!"

"How much," Gillian inquired, "do you consider your time worth in this case?"

"Ten thousand dollars, Mr. Hazeltine!" Polly cried: "Ten thousand dollars!"

"Yes ma'am. And I won't shave that a dime."

"But how can I pay it?" she wailed. "I can't raise that much money on everything Flip and I own! Mr. Hazeltine, what am I going to do?"

"Nothing," Gillian answered. "We know Flip is innocent. When you are positive of a man's innocence, there's always some way of proving it to a jury. If we can't prove it to a grand jury, we can prove it to a petit jury in general sessions. Donovan, your testimony is worth just two hundred dollars a day to me."

CAPTAIN DONOVAN CHUCKLED. His eyes remained as hard and as opaque as marbles of agate.

"Not a chance, Mr. Hazeltine. You've cleaned up a big fortune out of murder cases. Why don't I have a chance? Look at that swell house! I'll bet it set you back every nickel of sixty thousand. And how much in stocks and bonds have you put away? I'm gonna get ten thousand for my testimony, and I don't care who pays it. I need money—lots of money. Oscar Treidler trimmed me out of pretty close to eight thousand in a real-estate deal a couple of weeks ago, and I'm gonna collect it out of his murder. What's more, if you don't retain me at my figure, I'm goin' on the stand and tell just what I saw yesterday morning, when I was standing across the street from Treidler's office!"

"What," Gillian quietly asked, "did you see?"

"I saw Flip Wharton pull a gun out of his pocket!"

"Did you see anything else?"

"I guess that's enough!"

"Donovan," said Gillian gently, but his gray eyes were dark and smoldering, "I've been wanting to drive you out of this town for a good long while. You're a crook and a double-crosser. If you go down to the district attorney and sell out to him, I'll drive you out! I'll give you just one minute to come to your senses and give me your word you'll tell the honest truth when you go on the stand."

Captain Donovan's upper lip curled backward a little. He made an outward and downward gesture with the flat of his hand.

"Hazeltine, let me tell you something! You can't scare me any more than a canary bird can scare an elephant. You used to be a dangerous proposition, but your teeth have been pulled. You're on the skids and everybody knows it! Yistle and Colonel Garth and their gang drove you out of criminal practice—and they're gonna make a sucker of you in politics! You're a has-been. You're on the soapy chute! A minute, eh? I don't need a tenth of a second to tell you where to head in. Now, if you got anything more to say—"

"Get off this property," said Gillian calmly, "before I kick you off."

THE FIREARMS EXPERT glared, tossed up his horselike

head and strode muttering down the driveway. Gillian and the red-haired girl watched his departure in silence. They watched him until he rounded the old maple tree and was lost behind the lilac bushes which screened the sidewalk.

Then they turned and looked at each other. Polly Wharton's green eyes were blazing. She said slowly:

"That was blackmail, wasn't it?"

Gillian nodded. "Donovan will swear that a revolver-bullet, not a rifle-bullet, killed Treidler—and he'll produce a revolver bullet and swear that it's the one. That kind of evidence is easily faked."

"Mr. Hazeltine, do you think Donovan killed Treidler?"

"I am thinking," was Gillian's answer, "of a synthetic man who might have murdered Treidler. Donovan fits the picture—but he may not be our man. We'll find him, though!"

"First of all," said the slim girl in overalls, "will you please tell me how much you're going to charge me?"

Gillian gave her his flashing smile.

"Who knows? On the Captain's word, I'm not worth much."

"That crook!" The girl snorted. "Mr. Hazeltine, I must have some idea what the cost will be."

"Do you trust me, Miss Wharton?"

Polly Wharton's eyes ran from his black hair, peppered with silver, down his darkly handsome face to his mouth, then back to his gray eyes. On either of her cheekbones there was a bright spot of color.

"Of course I trust you!"

"Then let's not worry about costs. It may not cost you a penny. You may even get a dividend. You have no idea how many factors are involved in the case. I can, if I'm successful, pay off a great many bills with this case. I can pay off my bill to Captain Donovan. I can pay off a tremendous bill to Adelbert Yistle. Perhaps I can even obtain the right kind of publicity for Flip's new air turbine. I have seldom gone into court with a clean-cut case—a great many other factors are always involved. If I can clear your brother of this murder charge, a great many unexpected and exciting results are certain to follow. It will be a tough, uphill battle, Miss Wharton. You must put yourself entirely in my hands. Will you do that?"

"I will do anything you say," the girl answered.

"My first request," said Gillian, "is that you forget, for the time being, all question of retainers and fees. The second is, that you stop worrying. The third is important and extremely delicate. But I must be blunt." His smile was nervous, and it made him look ten years younger. His eyes ran down her faded overalls.

Polly Wharton laughed. Her laughter was that of a girl whose responsibilities have been accepted by powerful shoulders.

"You mean," she said, "overalls aren't being worn this season? I left the farm in such a hurry yesterday I didn't have time to change."

"Have you a dark dress and a black hat?" Gillian wanted to know.

She shook her head.

"You must, from now on, wear black hats and dark dresses," Gillian gravely said. "Murder trials have been lost because some women on the witness-stand failed or refused to dress for her part. We'll go shopping after break-fast."

"Will I have to go on the witness-stand?"

"Perhaps."

"Couldn't I testify to what Captain Donovan said?"

Gillian firmly shook his head. "The jury would never believe that you weren't lying to save your brother."

"But aren't you convinced that Donovan is the actual murderer?"

"I am considering him as a possibility. But there are other possibilities. Before today is over, you will hear the first rumblings of one of the hottest battles ever staged in a Greenboro courtroom. We may have a clearer picture of the murderer. So far, we can only suspect the kind of man that he is."

Polly Wharton looked at him curiously.

"What do you mean by that? How do you know what kind of man he is?"

"By the manner in which he committed the deed," said Gillian. "Unless he is a gunman, he is the *kind* of man who would use a silencer. The man who murdered Treidler would, on this assumption, be a secretive, sly kind of man. He would have other traits in keeping. What man in Greenboro is the kind of man who would use a silencer in killing an enemy? What man in Greenboro *is* a silencer?"

"Captain Donovan!" cried Polly.

"Perhaps," said Gillian.

5

ADELBERT YISTLE, THE district attorney, usually lunched at the Lawyers' Club. So did Gillian Hazeltine. Mr. Yistle was hopeful that Gillian would be lunching there today. There were certain matters he wished to discuss with Gillian; he wanted to bring up certain points bearing upon Gillian's character, and he did not care who heard him bringing them up.

From the doorway of the large dining-room Mr. Yistle looked over the assemblage of lunching lawyers. His mouth presently became hard and slightly twisted; the fires of wrath kindled in his eyes. Seated at a table for two in one of the window nooks was his hated enemy. Across from Gillian sat a beautiful young woman.

The couple at the table did not look up until Mr. Yistle was almost upon them. The girl was the first to acknowledge the district attorney's presence. She did so by glancing up and fixing upon his face a pair of large, lovely green eyes.

"Oh!" she said faintly.

Gillian looked up—and grinned at Mr. Yistle's flushed and angry face.

The district attorney laid his clenched fist on the edge of the table.

"I understand," he said heavily, "that you went into

homicide court this morning with Gale Wharton and entered a plea of not guilty."

"Yes," said Gillian.

"You're going to defend him, after all?"

"Yes," said Gillian.

Mr. Yistle took a deep breath.

"In spite of what you said?" he got out in a strangling voice. "In spite of your promise not to touch the case with a ten-foot pole? In spite of your promise to take the stand as my witness?"

"Yes," said Gillian.

"I don't suppose," said the district attorney with a heroic effort at controlling himself, "that you'd object to telling me why you changed your mind?"

"Not at all," said Gillian in the same cool voice. "I changed my mind when I made the discovery that Gale Wharton is not the man who shot Treidler."

The knuckles of Mr. Yistle's fist had become white and shiny.

"Who," he said with angry scorn, "told you that fish story?"

"I learned it from Captain Donovan."

"You're crazy! Why, Captain Donovan matched the bullet that killed Treidler with Wharton's revolver. He's absolutely proved Wharton's guilt!"

"For a figure," said Gillian, "Donovan would prove that the man in the moon shot Treidler!"

Mr. Yistle banged on the table. Dishes jumped.

"You're doing this to spite me!" he shouted. "You're nothing but a sneak and a liar!"

"Adelbert," said Gillian in a steely voice, "aren't you forgetting that a lady is present?"

"I don't care a damn who's present!" cried the furious Mr. Yistle. "You promised me you'd keep out of this case. You're going to be sorry you broke that promise! I've got you just where I want you now! Wharton is going to—the—chair! He's guilty, and you know it!"

"This large and offensive bag of wind," Gillian said calmly to Polly Wharton, "is our eminent district attorney. He is the gentleman who will move heaven and earth to send the murderer of Oscar Treidler to the electric chair. If he can't find the murderer, he'll accept a substitute. Your brother looks to him like a good substitute. So he'll move heaven and earth to send *him* to the chair."

MR. YISTLE SEIZED the edge of the table. His face was a large red moon. His bloodshot eyes seemed to blaze. He was unconscious of the group of alarmed waiters that had gathered behind him, unaware that many of the men in the dining-room had risen.

"So you're his sister, are you? Well, let me tell you something! If you think this shyster is going to get your brother off, you're mistaken. Your brother is going to the chair!"

"Adelbert—" Gillian began warningly.

"You!" Mr. Yistle shouted. "I know what your game is! It's nothing but a dirty trick to save yourself from going on the witness-stand. You knew I'd make a monkey out of you. You knew I'd have you where I wanted you—at last! Well, I'm going to make you take the stand, anyway! I'm going to make you testify against your own client! When I get through with you, you'll be glad to slink out of this town and never come back! What a joke you are, Hazeltine!"

Gillian suddenly perceived that the boy was a girl.
"What in the devil are you doing here?" he inquired.

Hah! I'm going to make you wish you'd never entered the legal profession! You think you'll find some way of licking me, don't you? Just wait till I get you in that courtroom!"

Mr. Yistle stopped for lack of breath. A strangling sound came from his lips. His bloodshot eyes were glazed.

"You think I can't see right through you? I can read you like a book! You're hoping something will pop up to turn the tables. If you can pull a surprise, you think you'll beat me for the police commissionership! You're a fool, Hazeltine. You're going to be run over by a steam roller." He suddenly lowered his voice. "And don't forget that we've got a five-thousand-dollar bet on that!"

He glared, panting, at Gillian. There was a fire in Gillian's eyes that he had never seen before.

"You got anything to say, Hazeltine?"

"Yes," said Gillian. "Get away from this table. You're annoying Miss Wharton."

Mr. Yistle opened his mouth. But he said no more. He glared at Polly Wharton. With a final withering glance at Gillian, he turned about and stalked away.

The red-haired girl was so pale that Gillian was afraid she was about to faint again. He reached quickly across the table, took one of her hands and pressed it.

"Don't worry," he said.

"But he—he seems so sure!"

Gillian leaned toward her, still retaining her hand.

"Polly, I told you that, before night, you'd hear the rumbling of one of the hottest courtroom battles ever staged in this State. I'm not underestimating Yistle as an opponent. I'm not claiming any magical ability for myself. So far, I haven't the slightest idea who the real murderer is. I want you to pin your faith and your hopes on one thing: In spite of the ruthlessness of district attorneys, in spite of the unfairness of judges, in spite of the stupidity of the average jury, truth has a way of forcing itself through. It's as if Justice were an actual, living person, determined to have her way despite blindness and crookedness and self-seeking. Keep faith in that, Polly."

"I have faith in you," she said simply. "I think you're the most wonderful man I ever knew."

Their eyes met. Gillian started to speak, when another interruption came. A young man with bushy brown hair, dashing down the long room, reached their table.

"Gillian," he burst out breathlessly, "what's this I hear about your taking the Wharton case?"

"It's true."

"Good Lord, Gillian, are you crazy? Don't you realize that it'll kill you for politics?"

"Not if he's innocent."

"But he's guilty! Yistle has an iron-bound case. Have you lost your senses?"

"Polly," said Gillian in his calm, even voice, "may I present Josh Hammersley, the fighting reporter? Josh, this young lady is Gale Wharton's sister."

Josh Hammersley stared wildly at the green-eyed girl. His expression became a little calmer. He breathed deeply and said, "Ah!" meaningly. It was a most eloquent monosyllable. It meant, with the look in his eyes which accompanied it, that Gillian Hazeltine had at last fallen for a beautiful woman—and was making a fool of himself.

"Gillian," he said in a wheedling voice, "let's look at this thing rationally. You don't want to make a false step at this time. You're a man with a great future. Don't throw it away for a—a whim. As sure as God made crabapples, any jury will bring in a verdict against Wharton—and your political career will be over. You'll be absolutely ruined."

"Yes."

"Won't you change your mind?"

"No."

"Then may heaven help you, Gillian! I wash my hands of you! You've gone back on your promises to your party. You're a traitor to the cause. You promised two weeks ago on your word of honor that you'd never enter a courtroom again. I'd have backed you for the governorship! I'd have backed you—yes, even for the Presidency! You've thrown every chance away—for what? I'm asking you—for what?"

"For a principle," said Gillian.

"Bosh! You've let this girl wrap you around her fingers, that's what you've done! You've thrown away a wonderful future. From one of the most popular men in Greenboro, you're going to become, overnight, the most unpopular. You're an utter fool!"

He turned abruptly and walked away, his brown hair bushing out against the breeze of his going.

GILLIAN, WITH A twisted smile, looked at Polly. She had caught her hand to her heart. Her eyes were misty.

"More rumbling," he said.

"No!" she cried. "Everything he said is true! You are throwing away your future when you walk into that court-room!"

Gillian managed a smile. "Polly, we'll find a ray of sunlight somewhere."

"But what have we to fight with?" she demanded. "It isn't enough just to know that Flip is innocent. Justice *is* blind. Everybody is against Flip, and everybody's against you. That man knew what he was talking about. By tomorrow morning you'll be the most unpopular man in Greenboro. How can an impartial jury be selected? You won't be able to find a man in town who hasn't a preconceived opinion."

"Polly, when you hold your chin up like that, I could kiss you. Has anybody ever told you what a wonderful girl you are? I'm going to take advantage of your youth, innocence and helplessness, in a moment—and kiss you before all these envious lawyers!"

There were bright spots of pink on Polly Wharton's cheek-bones. Her freckles had disappeared into a sea of pink.

"Please—" she faltered.

"All right," he said amiably, "I won't. Now, will you be a good girl and stop worrying?"

"But you know very well we—we're lost in the woods."

"We'll find our way out. You're mistaking a lot of thunder for lightning, my dear."

"Look here, Mr. Hazeltine—"

"Polly, two people starving to death on a raft in the middle of the South Atlantic Ocean certainly are entitled to call each other by their first names."

"Very well—Gillian. Then you do admit that we are on a raft in the middle of the ocean! You've just been pretending not to be worried, because you don't want me to worry. If you told the truth, you'd admit that things are utterly hopeless for the three of us. If you don't find the real murderer, Flip goes to the chair, I won't dare look people in the face the rest of my life, your political career will be ruined—"

"And I," Gillian finished for her, "will be denied the right of telling you that I think you're the dearest, bravest girl alive—and what I would like to do about it. Polly, I will admit that black and ugly clouds are lowering. I will admit that the future has looked rosier. But you must admit that I will take your brother into court with the comforting knowledge that he is innocent."

"You must prove to the most skeptical jury ever assembled that some one else is the murderer."

"Yes," said Gillian.

"Without any more proof than we have, do you really think you can?"

"Yes," said Gillian.

"How?" she cried.

"Simply by finding the man who would use a silencer in killing an enemy."

"And you think you can?"

"Yes, Polly."

HIS SMILE WAS reassuring, but he had never been more discouraged in his career. His task was comparable to that of finding a needle lost in a haystack. He must bring the analytical and deductive methods of a detective into the courtroom. He would meet with every kind of opposition.

According to Gillian's reasoning, the kind of man who would employ a silencer in committing a murder would be the kind of man who would cover his crime most cunningly. He would leave no loopholes for discovery. Donovan? Perhaps. He would be faced by that most discouraging of all mysteries—the crime without a clue. He must fall back on human motives; must rely on his skill in worrying the truth from witnesses. Some one must have seen *something*. Some little telltale gesture must, at this moment, be photographed upon the brain of some casual observer. How could he find this person?

There were moments, in the following weeks, when Gillian frankly believed that Gale Wharton was the actual murderer—suffering now from remorse, hoping against hope to be cleared of the ugly charge. In the face of over-whelming public sentiment, it was hard to believe otherwise. Greenboro newspapers, aroused to a high pitch of indignation, demanded that preparations for the trial of Gale Wharton be pushed with all possible expedition. Let this red-handed murderer be brought to the bar of justice without the usual delay! Strike while the iron is hot!

In a session lasting less than an hour, the grand jury

returned against Gale Wharton an indictment of first-de-
gree murder. The trial was calendared for an early hearing
before the Superior Court which was now sitting.

SHORTLY AFTER MIDNIGHT before the day when that
trial, now famous, was to begin, Gillian was the recipient
of a most mysterious telephone call. He was seated at the
desk in his study, in his shirt-sleeves, a thermos bottle of
hot coffee at his elbow, a humidor of fresh cigars ready to
his hand, the stenographic record of the testimony given
before the grand jury in front of him, when the telephone
rang. He picked up the instrument eagerly, hoping the call
was from the Herrendon Arms, where Polly was staying.
He had given her a last message of reassurance only an
hour before, and she had promised to go to bed and sleep.
Perhaps she could not sleep and wanted to talk.

The voice that came over the wire was not Polly's. It was
a man's voice, pitched so low as to be almost inaudible.

"Is this Mr. Hazeltine, the lawyer?"

"It is."

"Well, you don't know me, see, and you ain't gonna know
me," the husky, faint voice said. "Are you listenin'? Can you
hear me?"

"Yes," said Gillian.

"Well, I wanta tell you somethin', see? It's about this trial
that's startin' tomorrow. I happen to know positively that
the guy they're tryin' didn't do the killin', see?"

"Did you see who did?" Gillian snapped.

"I ain't sayin' what I did or didn't see. I'm just tellin' you it
ain't right for that kid to burn for somethin' he didn't have
no hand in. I'm tellin' you, straight, that the guy who did
the killin' is one o' the district attorney's witnesses."

"Which one?" Gillian snapped.

"I got myself to think of, fella," the mystery man growled. "I'm givin' you the tip-off because I don't want it on my mind no longer. I'll just say—"

There was an interruption. Gillian heard a more distant voice saying: "What the hell are you doing with that telephone?"

And the connection was abruptly terminated.

Gillian frantically wiggled the hook. An operator presently said: "Numbah plee-*yuz?*"

"Get me the telephone number of the Station I was just disconnected from."

"One moment. I'll give you supervisor."

It took Gillian ten minutes to find that the mysterious telephone message had originated in a public booth in the lobby of the Hotel Webbington. That *other* voice had sounded vaguely like Donovan's.

Gillian hastened into his coat and out of the house. He drove rapidly through the deserted streets of the city to the Hotel Webbington. The lobby was empty, save for a drowsy night clerk. The telephone operator had gone off duty shortly before midnight, and the only booths were pay stations.

Gillian questioned the night clerk. He sleepily denied having seen anyone in the lobby since he came on, at eleven. He presently admitted that between eleven-fifty-five and twelve-fifteen, he was back in the kitchen "having a little snack." The night bellboy had, at the same time, been similarly engaged. No living soul, it appeared, had seen a man come into the lobby and use a public phone booth at approximately five minutes after midnight.

Disgustedly, Gillian returned home. He was inclined to believe that the mystery man had telephoned him in good faith and was telling the truth. Who had interrupted that precious conversation?

Arriving home, Gillian with painstaking care checked over the list of Mr. Yistle's witnesses. The name Donovan seemed to stand out as if typed in letters of fire.

Pouring himself a fresh cup of coffee and lighting a fresh cigar, Gillian went at the stenographic record of the grand jury with the grim determination to grind the elusive truth out of it with sheer mental power. And at three o'clock, exhausted and hopeless, he fell fully dressed upon his bed.

6

POLLY WHARTON BORE up pluckily through those trying weeks preceding her brother's trial. The spotlight of tabloid notoriety—"Silencer's Sister Keeps Faith"—had been a harrowing experience. Wherever she went she was dogged by relentless reporters and photographers. At first she flew when she saw a camera, but in the end she became reconciled. She would pose as they asked her, always looking the camera squarely and gravely in the lens. She at first indignantly repulsed tabloid representatives who offered her large sums for the story of her life on the farm, her reminiscences of Flip's boyhood; but—in the end, again—she became reconciled.

A week before the trial, acting on Gillian's advice, she surrendered. She accepted the offer of the Greenboro Daily News to write the story of her brother's life for five thousand dollars. Under Gillian's direction, she wrote the story; she told of the hardships her brother had suffered; she fully described his efforts at perfecting an air turbine that might revolutionize airplane travel; and in every paragraph she emphasized her brother's heroism. As Gillian explained it to her, she was being paid five thousand dollars for giving the public a word picture of Flip that would win sympathy for him. And it was vital to his purpose that the public attitude toward Flip be tempered with kindness.

Polly would have written anything he told her. As she came to know him better, her admiration for Gillian grew. She had never known a man with a spirit so armored against the shafts of discouragement. She always felt more confident when he had talked to her. Without the ugly cloud hanging over her, she might have adored him. She was grateful to him, as a wounded animal is grateful when cared for, but her emotions were dulled by despair. When she talked to him, she admired and respected him more than any man she had ever known. But when she was alone, he, like all the other figures in this terrible drama, became a shadowy unreal figure.

Gillian saw to it that she spent a great deal of time with him. Although he did not refer to the subject again, he was tremendously in love with her. He believed it to be his duty, in the protective role he had assumed, to keep her from brooding. Loving her as he did, he wanted to be with her constantly. He took her on long drives into the country, often on the trail of some man or woman, who was said by some one to have been seen at the corner of Walnut and Madison on that fatal morning. Together they combed the neighborhood for possible witnesses.

Polly did not go to court until the jury had been impaneled. She was sure she could not endure the ordeal of the trial without suffering a nervous breakdown. For the week preceding it, she slept hardly at all, and when she did sleep, hideous dreams tortured her.

POLLY HAD NEVER before been in a courtroom. The opening day of the trial was an enlightening and disheartening experience. The pass Gillian had given her admitted her through the milling crowds which packed the courthouse.

"You're doing this to spite me!" Yistle shouted. "You're
going to be sorry you broke that promise!"

The ticket bore a number, as does a theater ticket; it entitled her to a choice seat in the middle of the first row, not
ten feet from the table from which the State's attorneys
would conduct the prosecution. This seat she would occupy
throughout the trial.

The courtroom was almost full when she took her seat.
Indifferent to the buzzing which arose at her appearance,
she looked with tired eyes about her. Within these four
walls would the doom of her brother be sealed? It was
the dreariest room she had ever been in. A cold north
light filtered through dusty windows. Dust seemed to
be everywhere. The golden oak furniture was blackened
and scarred by the passage of how many tragedies! There
was something almost indecent in the atmosphere of the
courtroom, as if it had grown disillusioned to the echoes

of human woe. Old men in rusty blue uniforms moved constantly about. They were all of a type. They had rheumy blue eyes and stooped shoulders; their necks went forward, not upward, and they were all bald. They were, to Polly, so many vultures.

The courtroom buzzed again. Gillian Hazeltine came out of a doorway near the judge's bench, and she found herself looking at him in a new light. He seemed to have grown taller. She had never realized how distinguished he was—this tall, tanned man with the steady gray eyes. His black hair, peppered with silver, was smoothly brushed. His double-breasted blue suit fitted him perfectly. His poise was remarkable. His composure was amazing. He looked slowly over the room, caught Polly's eyes and smiled. She wished he would come over and talk to her, but he busied himself at a long table, unpacking his briefcase.

Some one in the back of the room hissed. Gillian straightened up. The snake-like sound was taken up by others. Polly saw Gillian turn white. He looked about the crowded room with a smile which bared his white teeth. It was like the snarl of a cornered animal, prepared to fight with all its teeth and claws. The district attorney had taken pains to build up public sentiment against the defender of her brother. In newspaper interviews he had hinted that Gillian would stoop to any trickery to get the murderer off.

Bailiffs were trying to restore order, and Polly wondered how Gillian could be so calm. Her heart began to flutter in panic. On this tall, slim man rested her every hope for the future. How could he succeed?

A hush spread over the room as another door opened,

and her brother, between two deputy sheriffs, came to Gillian's table. How thin, how pale, how haggard he looked!

The district attorney was the next to enter the scene of battle. His entrance was attended by a vigorous hand-clapping. Mr. Yistle was popular. He was still riding that tidal wave of luck. The murder of Oscar Treidler had placed Mr. Yistle squarely in the limelight. He was the people's representative; upon him devolved the task of meting out justice to this fiend. Mr. Yistle walked briskly to the table a few feet from Polly, turned about and bowed, as if he were a triumphant actor taking a curtain call. As he turned back to his table he met Gillian's eye, and he grinned scornfully.

Polly heard a man behind her say: "Anybody who thinks this is a murder trial is a sucker. It's a duel between them two guys. Hazeltine will plead insanity, and Yistle will make him look like somethin' run over by a truck. I'll bet yuh they'll be usin' knives before they're through!"

Polly looked at the back of Mr. Yistle's red neck. He was so confident! Suddenly she hated him. He would crush Gillian. He would crush her brother.

Then she heard Mr. Yistle say to one of the attendants: "Tell Judge Manning we are ready."

We are ready! Polly's heart began frantically to hammer.

A door directly behind the bench opened and a man with white hair and a coppery complexion came in. He wore black robes and a genial smile. Polly wondered how he could smile, how he could help but feel the tension between Gillian and the district attorney. Judge Manning looked like a kind, just man. But she recalled what Gillian had said.

"He's close to Yistle, and one of my worst enemies. We

won't find much of the milk of human kindness there. But he isn't crooked."

A bailiff was droning:

"Oyez! Oyez! Oyez! The Superior Court within and for Greenboro County, criminal term, is open and in session at this place. All persons having cause or action who are summoned to appear herein will give attention according to the law."

One of the ancient vultures crept over to Polly and hissed:

"Don't yuh know enough to stand up when the Jedge comes in?"

Pink with embarrassment, she realized that everyone else in the room was standing. She jumped up.

"You may call the jury," said the Judge; and a sheriff hastened out of the room. Twelve good men and true presently filed in and took their seats in the jury-box.

It seemed to Polly that they were a dull and stupid-looking lot of men, but most of them were earnestly frowning, as if fully conscious of their responsibility.

In a sing-song voice, the clerk read the charge. A wave of faintness flowed over Polly, and she caught only disconnected phrases. "To the Superior Court for Greenfield County comes Adelbert Yistle... that the said Oscar Treidler did languish and suffer and did, within a lapse of minutes, die... the said Gale Wharton did then and there commit the crime of homicide against the peace...."

The sing-song voice stopped. Gillian Hazeltine was on his feet pleading not guilty to the charge, and a murmur of excitement ran through the spectators. Mr. Yistle had gripped the edge of his table and was staring. Everyone had presumed that he would plead insanity.

Mr. Yistle walked over to the jury. Lifting a clenched fist above his head, he said:

"Gentlemen, I will undertake to prove to you, step by step and point by point, that Gale Wharton did on the morning of May ninth, with deliberation and premeditation, fire from his revolver the bullet which brought to an untimely end the life of our beloved fellow-citizen Oscar Treidler. In my mind the guilt of Gale Wharton is established beyond all doubt. It will be my task to transplant that conviction to your mind, that you may return a verdict appropriate to the diabolical crime committed by this fiend. I say: Gale Wharton must pay for this monstrous crime by going to his death in the electric chair! Will Dr. Cutler take the stand?"

7

DR. CUTLER WAS the coroner of Greenboro. To Polly it seemed unnecessary to prove that Oscar Treidler was dead, but it apparently had to be done. Dr. Cutler, a square-faced man with gray hair and a gray mustache, took the stand and stated with an air of great caution, in response to Mr. Yistle's rapid questions, that Oscar Treidler had died almost instantly, as the result of his carotid artery being pierced by a .38-caliber bullet.

He stated that he had probed for and found the bullet.

"Was it mushroomed or flattened or twisted or distorted in any way?"

"No sir; it was in perfect condition."

"What did you do with the bullet?"

"At the request of the detective bureau, I turned it over to Captain Donovan, the firearms expert."

Mr. Yistle picked up something from the table.

"Could you identify this as the bullet?"

"No sir; I know nothing about bullets."

"That will be all, Doctor." Mr. Yistle bowed with ironical politeness to Gillian; his smile was contemptuous. "Does my distinguished adversary wish to take the witness for cross-examination?"

There was a titter among the spectators. A bailiff banged on his desk with a gavel.

Gillian did not rise. He glanced gravely at the coroner.

"Doctor, do you know, at sight, the difference between a rifle-bullet and a revolver-bullet?"

"No, I did not know there was any difference."

"How long have you been coroner of Greenboro?"

"Three years." There was defiance in the coroner's attitude.

"How many bullets have you probed for?"

"Five—six, in the course of my entire career as a practicing physician."

"Were they rifle-or revolver-bullets?"

"As I recall it, two were rifle-bullets and three were revolver-bullets—perhaps four."

"At any time during the day of the murder did Miss Wharton, the sister of the accused, call at your office?"

"She did—in company with Captain Donovan."

"Did any officer, any detective, see that bullet before or when you surrendered it to Captain Donovan?"

Mr. Yistle came to his feet with an anxious expression. Polly was leaning forward tensely.

"No," said Dr. Cutler.

Gillian looked thoughtful. He now asked where the Doctor had been when the murder was committed.

"In my office!" the coroner snapped.

"Could you produce witnesses to prove that you were?"

"I object to that question!" Mr. Yistle snapped. "Your Honor, just as I expected, Mr. Hazeltine is not missing the slightest opportunity to discredit a witness of the State's."

"I submit," said Gillian calmly, "that I am entitled to discredit any witness the State offers, if I can do so by honest methods. It is my duty to my client to prove that the chain of evidence being forged by Mr. Yistle has a link so weak, so rotten, that the breath of truth will break it. I will state that the defense will be conducted solely on that basis. I have come into this court knowing only one thing—that my client is innocent."

Mr. Yistle audibly chuckled. Judge Manning leaned forward.

"The witness will answer Mr. Hazeltine's question."

The coroner smiled triumphantly.

"There was a procession of people going in and out of my office at the hour when Mr. Treidler was shot. I can prove that I was not anywhere near the scene of the murder, if that's what's on your mind!"

"You are excused, Doctor," said Gillian calmly.

A SIGH AS of relaxation was given off by the occupants of the courtroom. Polly kept her bright eyes on the district attorney.

The next witness for the State was the traffic officer who had arrested Gale. He testified that on the morning of May 9th, at a little after ten o'clock, he had apprehended the accused in the act of running across the intersection of Madison and Walnut with a wild look in his eyes and a revolver in his hand. He had promptly made the arrest.

A black-haired, blue-eyed young Irishman, he gave the impression of extreme earnestness. His replies were slow, deliberate, careful.

"Yes sir; I jumped on him and took the gun away."

Mr. Yistle questioned him at some length, establishing clearly that Flip Wharton had come running toward him with wild eyes, from the direction of Treidler's plate-glass window.

Gillian took the witness. His first question was:

"Did you hear a shot?"

"No sir."

"Was there a silencer on the gun when you took it away?"

"No sir."

"I want you to think carefully, Officer, before you answer my next question. In your estimation, considering the distance from where you stood, to the window, and the rate at which the accused was running, how many seconds elapsed from the time he started from the window until he reached where you stood?"

The policeman thought. His brows drew together. He bit his lip.

"Four or five seconds."

"Now, please estimate how many seconds elapsed from the time you grabbed the accused until you seized the revolver from his hand."

"Not any—because I seized it as he went past."

"Have you ever fired a .38-caliber revolver?"

"Yes sir—a good many times."

"The barrel gets hot, doesn't it?"

"Yes sir, it does."

"In fact, a single shot warms up the barrel considerably, doesn't it?"

"Yes sir."

"Was the barrel of that revolver hot when you seized it?"

"It was warm."

"Warmer than blood temperature?"

"No sir."

"Then, in your opinion, that revolver had not recently been fired?"

"Objection!" snapped Mr. Yistle. "The witness is not qualified to answer that question."

"The objection is sustained," ruled the Court.

"Exception," said Mr. Hazeltine. "The witness is excused."

"One moment, Officer," said Mr. Yistle briskly. "You just said that that revolver was not warm—not warmer than blood temperature."

"Yes sir."

"Do you mean to tell me that you were thinking of such things as blood temperature when you seized this man and took possession of his revolver?"

"I object," said Gillian. "What the witness was thinking when he made the arrest is not competent testimony."

"Rephrase your question," Judge Manning directed Mr. Yistle.

"Were you excited when you saw that man running toward you—with a wild look in his eyes and a gun in his hand?"

"Yes sir, I was."

Mr. Yistle chuckled softly. "In fact, if you told the honest truth, you'd admit you were just a wee bit scared—so that a few degrees difference in the temperature of a piece of iron wouldn't have been noticed?"

The officer grinned. "I guess that's right. Yes sir."

"That's all, Officer. You may go now."

MR. YISTLE'S MANNER was affable. His air was that of a great kind friend to all the universe. Polly wondered how Gillian could remain so calm. She knew that the district attorney was deliberately trying to irritate him.

The next witness was a tall, red-faced young man with

furtive gray eyes and a loose underlip with which he did strange things. He stuck it out. He twisted it about. He all but wagged it. He gave his name as Thomas Welcher and his address as Cloverdale, which was a town four miles south of Greenboro on the High Rocks Road. Replying to Mr. Yistle's questions, he said that, on the evening of May 8th, he was in the Cloverdale post office when Gale Wharton came in and spoke hotly of his hatred for Oscar Treidler, to a group of men of which he was one. He said that Wharton had made threats.

"Wharton said," testified the witness, "that he'd blow his brains out some day if he didn't stop coming around and bothering him."

Mr. Yistle wanted to know if Wharton had given any reasons for this animosity.

"Yes sir! He said that Treidler had been getting too fresh with his sister. That's her down there in the front row."

"Never mind where she is. What did Wharton say?"

"He said that Treidler had been getting fresh with his sister, and that he'd been too nosey around his plans for that air turbine he was working on, and that he teased his dogs. He said the next time Wharton rubbed him the wrong way, he'd blow his brains out."

"What was his exact language?"

The witness grinned. "I sorta hate to repeat it with all these ladies present."

"You mean he cursed?"

"I'll say he cursed!"

"Well, tell the jury what he said, omitting the profanity."

"He said if Treidler came out once more and tried to get

his goat, he was going to blow his blankety-blank brains out."

"Did you ever hear the accused threaten to shoot or harm Treidler in any way on other occasions?"

"Yes sir, I sure did. He was all the time talking about how he hated Treidler and how he was gonna beat him up or somethin' worse. He used to say, 'I'll carve his blankety-blank heart out!'"

"You heard him make such statements more than once?"

"Sure! I heard him make 'em a dozen times."

Mr. Yistle waved his hand airily, indicating that he was through with the witness.

SLOWLY GILLIAN WALKED over toward the witness-stand.

"Where were you, Mr. Welcher, on the morning of May ninth?"

"In Cloverdale, drivin' my truck for the Cloverdale Express Company."

"Did you ever have a misunderstanding of any kind with the accused?"

Mr. Welcher looked at him resentfully.

"What of it?" he snapped.

"Kindly answer my question."

"Yes, I did."

"Isn't it true that he found you one time, in a drunken condition, tampering with his plane? When you wouldn't leave it alone, he threw you bodily off the premises?"

"I object to that question as immaterial!" snapped Mr. Yistle.

"I wish, Your Honor," said Gillian quickly, "to establish the fact that this witness' testimony is prejudiced."

Mr. Welcher shouted: "No, it ain't true! I was just lookin' at his plane, and he came up and ordered me off, and I said that wasn't no way to speak to a gentleman, and he kicked me off. He was always—"

"Just a minute," Gillian stopped him. "You have sworn to tell the truth, the whole truth and nothing but the truth. If you don't want to stand trial for perjury, you'll stick to facts, Mr. Welcher. Answer my question truthfully!"

"Your Honor," said Mr. Yistle, banging on his desk with indignation, "I request that my distinguished colleague be instructed not to bulldoze my witnesses."

Judge Manning said crisply: "Mr. Hazeltine, you will proceed with your questioning without further attempts at intimidation. Mr. Welcher, you will answer Mr. Hazeltine's question."

"Well, maybe I was touchin' the dog-goned plane, but I wasn't hurtin' it none. He didn't have no right to kick me in the pants and—"

"I'm not asking you for opinions," Gillian checked him. "All we want is facts. Is it or is it not true that on November fifteenth, 1926, you were arrested and sentenced to ninety days on a charge of petty larceny?"

The witness turned pale. "It was a frame-up!" he muttered.

"Answer my question with yes or no!"

"Yes," growled Mr. Welcher.

Gillian turned to Judge Manning. "Your Honor, I respectfully request that the testimony of this witness be stricken from the records on the grounds that he is incompetent to testify, because of a criminal record."

"I respectfully beg the Court to allow Mr. Welcher's testimony to stand!" shouted Mr. Yistle.

"I feel," said Judge Manning gravely, "that the criminal record of the witness is not sufficiently serious to affect the credibility of his testimony."

"Exception," said Gillian.

"Exception is noted. You may proceed with cross-examination."

"I have no further questions to ask Mr. Welcher."

MR. YISTLE AROSE with a wide smile. As far as Polly was concerned, the picture of utter self-assurance he made was hateful. She hated his smug expression.

"My next witness," he said, chuckling, "is none other than that shining light of the legal profession—Mr. Gillian Hazeltine!"

The courtroom burst into laughter. A bailiff banged his gavel. When order was restored, Gillian said:

"Your Honor, I beg to be excused from giving testimony. I have reasons to know that such testimony as I would give is duplicated by another witness who will presumably be called later."

"I submit," chuckled Mr. Yistle, "that my distinguished colleague was legally apprised of the fact that he would be called upon to testify. Will Your Honor rule on this point?"

Judge Manning smiled. "Mr. Hazeltine will take the stand."

Gillian seated himself in the witness chair. In calm, even tones he answered the routine questions. He told clearly and without hesitation what he had seen from his coupé window on that eventful morning.

Mr. Yistle, wearing a catlike smile and spinning a watch-fob around and around, made him repeat his description.

Then he shot the question: "Mr. Hazeltine, based on what you saw that morning, you have come into court with the intention of proving Gale Wharton's innocence?"

"I have!"

Even the jury were frankly and openly smiling now. Mr. Yistle chuckled:

"That will be all. Does Mr. Hazeltine wish to cross-examine Mr. Hazeltine?"

When silence again prevailed, Gillian answered:

"Mr. Hazeltine does. He wishes to ask himself, for the benefit of the jury, if he and they have not observed that the cleanest-cut murder case is often lost by a vigilant and vigorous prosecution? He answers yes. He then asks himself why this is so. It is so, he answers, because people are accustomed to think in grooves. They see a man flash a pistol. They see a man drop dead. Their minds speed down the groove to the conclusion that the man who flashed the gun shot the man who fell dead. Mr. Hazeltine asks Mr. Hazeltine if it is not justifiable to doubt that the accused is the actual murderer of Oscar Treidler. Mr. Hazeltine answers that it certainly is! Mr. Hazeltine believes firmly in the innocence of the accused and will make every effort to prove it! Mr. Hazeltine has finished his cross-examination of Mr. Hazeltine."

8

GILLIAN WAS SMILING. Mr. Yistle was not. He was angry. His eyes were prominent; his face was red. The worm had turned; the bitten had turned biter. In that short, calm speech Gillian had certainly won back a little of his lost popularity.

"Your Honor," said Mr. Yistle, "I respectfully request that the testimony given by Mr. Hazeltine in cross-examination be struck from the record, on the ground that the questions were leading and that the answers were summation."

"The request is granted," said Judge Manning. "Mr. Hazeltine's cross-examination of himself will be struck from the record. Who is the next witness?"

"Miss Myrtle Dibney."

A girl walked to the witness chair. She was pretty, a little too loudly dressed, a little too aware of the fact that her picture would appear in the evening tabloids. She was rouged, mascaraed and lip-sticked to within an inch of her life, Polly thought. Miss Dibney had bold black eyes and an arch smile.

Yes, she said, she had been walking along Madison Street a little after ten o'clock on the morning of May ninth.

"I heard a sorta hissing sound; then I saw a fella ahead of me run away from Treidler's window. There was a hole in the window. He had something in each hand. Both was blue metal. One was a gun and the other was a round steel thing about this long. This fella ran and threw the round thing into a garbage truck that was standin' there."

She said no more. The courtroom was a-buzz with whispers. The silencer at last!

JUDGE MANNING SAID grimly: "If there are any more demonstrations, I will order this courtroom cleared. There is too much whispering and too much laughing and snickering. I want perfect silence. You may proceed, Mr. Yistle."

The district attorney picked up from his table a small cardboard box, about eight inches long. From it he removed a glistening blue steel tube. It was a Maxim silencer. Between thumb and forefinger he held it toward the girl.

"Did it look like this?"

"Yes sir, it looked about like that."

"You had a fair look at it, did you?"

"Yes sir, I did."

"And you distinctly saw him throw it into a garbage truck?"

"Yes sir, I did."

"That will be all."

Gillian came up from his chair and walked toward the girl with the easy grace of a tiger. His eyes were hard. Polly knew that this girl was the first deliberate liar to take the stand so far this morning. And she wondered how Gillian would handle her.

"You say, Miss Dibney, that you were walking down Madison Street and distinctly saw the accused with a revolver in one hand and a Maxim silencer in the other?"

"Yes sir." Her attitude was suddenly stiff and defiant.

"You knew the thing in his hand was a Maxim silencer, did you?"

"Well, I supposed it was."

"After you had seen him run and throw the silencer into the garbage truck, what did you see?"

"A lotta things!"

"Did you look into Treidler's window?"

"Sure! So did everybody else!"

"You saw that Treidler had been shot?"

"Nachally!"

"You knew that a murder had been committed?"

"Certainly! I'm not dumb!"

Mr. Yistle, with mouth open, was anxiously watching his witness, ready to object.

GILLIAN POINTED A long, tanned finger at the defiant girl.

"You saw the accused throw a silencer into a garbage wagon. You saw that Treidler had been murdered. Why didn't you notify the police that you had seen him throw the silencer into the garbage truck?"

"Say, listen! Don't you talk to me like that! I'm a lady. I won't have no—"

"Answer that question!"

"What was the question?"

"I asked you why you didn't notify the police that you had seen the accused throw a silencer into a garbage truck."

"Because I didn't think about it." Miss Dibney was pale. Her eyes were glaring at Gillian.

"How long after this incident did it occur to you that you had seen the accused throw the silencer into that truck?"

Mr. Yistle sprang up. "Stop bulldozing my witness!"

"I'm not bulldozing your witness. She's lying. I'm going to make her tell the truth before she leaves that stand!"

"Your Honor—" Mr. Yistle began.

"Mr. Hazeltine," said the Judge angrily, "you must control your temper. You must not bulldoze these witnesses. I will not warn you again. Proceed with your cross-examination. Stenographer, read Mr. Hazeltine's last question."

The stenographer said: "How long after this incident did it occur to you that you had seen the accused throw the silencer into that truck?"

"I won't be bulldozed," said Miss Dibney firmly.

"I'll rephrase the question," said Gillian. "Did you tell any authority that you had seen the accused throw a silencer into the truck?"

"I did! I told the district attorney."

"Do you realize, Miss Dibney, that at the hour on which Mr. Treidler was shot, there was not a garbage truck on or anywhere near that corner?"

"There was, too!"

"That a careful check-up proved—and can be proved here—that there was no garbage truck there at that time?"

"I don't care! I saw it!"

"Perhaps," said Mr. Yistle quickly, "it was some other kind of truck."

Gillian turned on him. "You will stop prompting this witness."

Judge Manning interposed. "Gentlemen, address your remarks to the jury."

Gillian said: "Will the witness answer my question?"

"Sure, I will! Maybe it was a couple of other trucks!"

THE COURTROOM ECHOED to discreet laughter, quickly

hushed. But the jury remained smiling. Gillian took another tack.

"Did you know the deceased, Miss Dibney?"

The girl's eyes suddenly narrowed.

"What if I did?"

"Answer yes or no."

"Yes."

He came closer to her.

"Isn't it true that between the months February and July in 1925 you were employed by him as a stenographer?"

"Yes."

"Isn't it true that you told a number of people that you were engaged to him?"

"I—I—"

"Yes or no?"

"Yes!" she snapped. "I thought I was engaged to him. He told me so. He said he was going to marry me!"

"Then he fired you?"

"Yes, he did!"

"And didn't you make several attempts at holding him to his promise?"

"I—yes, that's true."

"Did you not, on the evening of January tenth, this year, purchase in Aaron Rubenstein's pawn shop a .38-caliber revolver?"

"I—I—"

"Yes or no?" insisted Gillian.

"Yes!" she cried. Miss Dibney's hands were caught tight in her lap. She was biting her lower lip.

"Isn't it true that you were passing Treidler's window on the morning that he was shot?"

"Certainly. Didn't I say so?"

"Where is that .38-caliber revolver now?"

"I—I threw it away."

"Where?"

"In the river. Say, listen, are you accusing me—"

"You're to answer questions, not to ask them, Miss Dibney. I want you to tell the jury where you obtained your knowledge as to the appearance of a Maxim silencer."

"I—I don't know. Why—why, everybody knows!"

"I beg to differ with you. It is absolutely against the law in every State in the Union to sell, buy or have in one's possession a Maxim silencer. Where did you get the one you used?"

"Objection!" roared Mr. Yistle.

"Sustained," snapped the Court. "Mr. Hazeltine, you are entitled to go to any reasonable length to discredit any witness. I must ask you again to refrain from bullying witnesses into making statements not in accord with their knowledge of the facts. You do not know that this girl ever possessed a silencer, do you?"

Gillian said, calmly: "No, Your Honor, I do not."

"You may proceed with cross-examination."

"I have finished," said Gillian.

MR. YISTLE TOOK the witness again.

"Miss Dibney, will you tell the jury just why you bought that revolver?"

The girl looked frightened. She did not answer.

"Was it because you were afraid—so many thugs and hold-up men on the streets at night?"

"Yes sir!" said the girl eagerly—too eagerly. "That was why!"

A hush spread over the room as a door
opened and the prisoner came in.

"That will be all, Miss Dibney."

Mr. Yistle looked disgusted. For the first time since the trial had started, Polly experienced a thrill of hope. Far from advancing the State's cause, Miss Dibney had somehow created the feeling that she knew more about the murder of Oscar Treidler than she had admitted. And the feeling prevailed that she knew a little too much about Maxim silencers. Pale, obviously frightened, with a guilty look in her eyes, Miss Dibney hastened back to her seat.

The district attorney and his assistants were holding a whispered consultation.

"Captain Donovan will take the stand, please," Mr. Yistle said crisply.

The firearms expert walked to the witness chair with the air of a man accustomed to courtrooms. He was smilingly at ease. His strangely colored eyes roved over the crowd. In his nasal voice he stated that he had obtained Wharton's revolver and the bullet from official sources; that he had, with delicate measuring instruments, established beyond doubt that the bullet which killed Treidler had been fired from Gale Wharton's revolver.

His testimony was unquestionably the most vital that had been given all morning. To Polly, it irrevocably linked her brother with the killing. She wondered how Donovan could lie so brazenly. She saw Gillian watching him with coldly contemptuous eyes. So far, it seemed to her, the battle had been even. She realized now that the district attorney would stoop to anything to secure a conviction. Undoubtedly he knew that Donovan was lying.

ONE OF MR. Yistle's assistants unwrapped a large flat package. It contained enlarged photographs of the rifling of Flip's revolver and of the bullet. They were admitted as material evidence and shown to the jury. In his nasal voice Donovan explained that every pistol and every rifle has a distinct personality; that a bullet fired from a given rifle or revolver could be readily identified by the microscopic irregularities of the rifling, which were clearly shown in greatly enlarged photographs.

Captain Donovan repeated that there was absolutely no question in his mind that Wharton's revolver had fired the bullet that had killed Treidler.

Polly heard the man behind her say: "That guy certainly knows his stuff. This is scientific. You can't get around science."

She wanted to shout: "It's nothing but lies! And that man is the real murderer!" Captain Donovan was still smiling when Mr. Yistle finished with him and Gillian took him for cross-examination. Gillian, with his hands in his coat pockets, walked slowly over to the witness. His gray eyes searched the expert's face. Captain Donovan's smile slowly went away. He looked uneasy.

"Where were you when Treidler was shot?" Gillian snapped.

"I was across the street."

"On Madison—facing Treidler's window?"

"Yes."

"Captain Donovan, you know a great deal about firearms, don't you?"

"Well, I know something about 'em."

"It's your life work, isn't it?"

"I— Yes."

"How well did you know Treidler?"

"Pretty well."

"Isn't it a fact that during the week of April twentieth you had some business deal on with Treidler?"

"Yes."

"What was the nature of the deal?"

"He sold me a piece of land down by the railroad."

"Didn't he tell you that that land would double in value inside of three months?"

"He did."

"And didn't you find out he'd been lying and had deliberately unloaded the land on you, so that you took a loss of approximately eight thousand dollars?"

"That's true."

"And did you not tell Bert Anderson, the clerk in Bellson's cigar-store, that you were going to get even with him?"

"I may have said something to that effect; I was sore."

Gillian leveled his long, tanned forefinger at the expert.

"Didn't you say in so many words that you were going to shoot him?"

"Objection!" shouted Mr. Yistle. "Your Honor, it is a travesty on justice to carry on this trial along these lines. Mr. Hazeltine is making every effort to cast doubt on each witness I present."

Gillian said calmly: "Your Honor, I am entitled by law to cast doubt on any witness who is doubtful. I am dealing only in facts. Mr. Yistle should have selected witnesses who were above reproach. I respectfully request that Your Honor order this witness to answer my question."

Judge Manning was frowning. He hesitated.

"The witness will answer the question." Captain Donovan was pale. "Well, what if I did say that?" he snarled. "I was sore. So would anybody be. I'd been trimmed out of eight thousand—"

Gillian interrupted: "Getting back to your examination of these, the bullet and Wharton's revolver: Did anyone see you make those photographs?"

"No."

"Did anyone from the district attorney's office accompany you when you secured either the bullet or the pistol?"

"No!"

"And you say you were standing across the street when Treidler was shot?"

"I was."

"You're an expert shot, aren't you?"

"I am."

"That's all, thank you," said Gillian.

MR. YISTLE STRODE to the witness.

"What did you see when you were standing across the street from Treidler's office?"

"I saw Wharton pull out his gun."

"Did you see him fire it?"

"I did!"

The courtroom broke into a babble. Mr. Yistle had conserved his most telling shot for reexamination. A bailiff banged futilely with his gavel. Mr. Yistle was grinning at Gillian, and Gillian was glaring at him. Polly heard Gillian say: "You know that's a damned lie!"

The judge sprang up. Everyone in the room arose.

"Court is adjourned until two o'clock," said Judge Manning.

9

A CROSS THE luncheon-table, Gillian said to Polly:

"Don't worry about Donovan. I'm not through with him yet. I'm glad he made that mistake. I can produce ten witnesses who will swear that, in his account of the shooting, he stated definitely that he saw no shot fired. Yistle is plugging every possible loophole. He's beginning to realize that his case isn't as clean-cut as he supposed. If it's necessary, I'll recall every one of his witnesses. The Dibney girl and Donovan have given the most damning testimony so far. Polly, the fight has just started."

"How about Norton Garth?"

Gillian's reassuring smile faded.

"If the Colonel hadn't closed his eyes those ten seconds, Flip would be a free man this minute. I know that he hates to have any hand in this. But he can't get out of testifying— and it will be the most damaging testimony of the trial."

Polly looked at him hopelessly.

"Gillian, do you honestly think we have a chance?"

The lawyer nodded grimly.

"Somehow we'll find the rotten link in the chain. Who was it called me on the phone that night? Who interrupted the call? As far as the Colonel is concerned, I'll do everything under the sun to discredit his testimony. At least, I'll

try. And the Colonel won't lie. But I'll make him wish he
hadn't seen Flip pull out that gun!"

Colonel Garth, as Gillian had anticipated, was Mr.
Yistle's next witness. And likewise his last. Gillian had fore-
seen this, He knew that Mr. Yistle was fond of surprises.

Colonel Garth went to the witness chair with an air of
great reluctance. He seated himself and faced the crowd
with compressed lips and a frown. It was obvious that he
hated giving this testimony which would be helpful in
sending a man to the electric chair. He answered questions
slowly, but in a clear voice which penetrated to the farthest
corner of the room.

"My limousine was, I should say, the third or fourth car
in the traffic line. I saw Wharton pull the gun from his hip
pocket. I knew what was going to happen, because I know
Wharton and his sister quite well, and I was aware of the
bad feeling existing between Flip and Treidler. When I
realized he intended to shoot Treidler, I shut my eyes. I
must have had them shut for ten seconds. I was so upset
that I was afraid I would faint. I waited for the sound of
the shot. It didn't come. When I finally opened my eyes,
Wharton was running diagonally across the street—and
I saw the hole in the window—and I saw that poor devil
die. It was horrible!"

Polly felt sorry for the Colonel. How he had hated to
give that testimony! If he had not closed his eyes those ten
important seconds!

Mr. Yistle was smiling. It was a smile of triumph.

"That will be all, Colonel. Your Honor—the State rests."

Gillian, as he arose to begin the cross-examination,
looked haggard. His face was gray to the lips. His shoul-

ders seemed to sag. To Polly it seemed as if the heart had
suddenly gone out of him. He had come into court to find
the rotten link in Mr. Yistle's chain of evidence. So far, that
link had not manifested itself. What could he do now? She
looked at her brother. Flip was still sagging in his chair,
with his elbows on the table, his chin in his hands.

GILLIAN QUIETLY BEGAN to question the Colonel. Had
he seen a silencer? No. Had he heard a shot, however
muffled? No. Had he not possibly heard a bullet whistle
close past him—a bullet that might have been fired from
across the street? No. Would the Colonel kindly repeat his
description of the occurrence?

The Colonel would gladly. He did so. During the course
of it a change came over Gillian. The color suddenly flowed
back into his cheeks. When he spoke again, his voice had
its old ring. And when Polly saw his eyes, they were flashing as she had not seen them flash since that morning
when he had driven Captain Donovan out of his front yard.

"You say your eyes were closed ten seconds, Colonel?"

"Approximately," was the answer. "Perhaps eight, perhaps
twelve. But I should say that ten would be close."

Mr. Yistle was watching Gillian with growing anxiety.
His lips were parted, as if he was prepared to object.

"And when you opened your eyes, you saw Treidler
dying—or dead?"

"Yes sir."

"And you saw the accused running diagonally across the
street intersection?"

"Yes sir."

"That will be all, Colonel. Thank you."

Gillian then said crisply: "I wish to request an order

from the Court restraining all of the witnesses for the State
from leaving the jurisdiction of this court until the trial is
over. Specifically, I wish Captain Donovan, Miss Myrtle
Dibney and Colonel Garth to remain in case I require
further information from them."

When Judge Manning had given his consent to this
request, Gillian walked slowly over to the jury box.

"Gentlemen," he began, "in the eyes of the law, Gale
Wharton is innocent of the crime of which he is charged
until he has been proved, beyond any reasonable doubt,
guilty. The business of proving him guilty is the responsibility of the district attorney. So long as a reasonable
doubt lingers in your mind, Gale Wharton remains legally
innocent.

"In examining the witnesses put forward by the State,
you have seen me making every effort to establish that
reasonable doubt in your minds. Before I am through, I will
attempt to prove to you that not one of the State's important witnesses is qualified to give testimony in this trial.

"I wish to say to you twelve gentlemen that I have never
come into a courtroom more firmly convinced of a client's
innocence—or more helpless to convey that conviction
to you. I know that Gale Wharton did not murder Oscar
Treidler. I suspect the identity of the actual murderer, but
I cannot yet prove my suspicions.

"You twelve gentlemen will agree with me, I am sure,
that any man will act in any given situation according to
his nature. A man who lies to one man will, we can safely
assume, lie to other men. A man who reveals a trait of
persistence in one action will, we can assume, reveal the
same trait in other actions.

"The presumption of Gale Wharton's innocence devolves upon that human principle. The accused is an impulsive, excitable young man. He is given to talking loudly. There is nothing secretive about his character. My contention is that if Gale Wharton ever killed a man, he would do so openly and violently, because that would be in accordance with his nature. He would not use a Maxim silencer, because that would be contrary to his nature.

"It is conceivable that the man who murdered Treidler might well be the kind of man who would use a silencer. In looking for the murderer, we might well look for a man who is by nature a silencer. Our only other alternative would be to look for a professional killer—a man to whom a silencer would be a business accessory, so to speak. My firm belief is that no professional killer murdered Treidler. I maintain that, in looking for the murderer, it would be intelligent to look for a man who is by nature a silenc-er—a man who, if we could shrewdly examine into his past, would have demonstrated that trait of character in many dealings with his fellow men.

"Who is that man—or woman? It is my intention some-how to find that man—or woman—and lay such evidence before you that my client will be cleared of all stain. I hope to have such evidence to present to you tomorrow. The rest of today I wish to devote to proving to you that Gale Wharton is not and has never been the kind of man who would commit any act stealthily, or with a stealthy instru-ment. Will Major Keel take the stand?"

MAJOR KEEL WAS a tall, slender man of about thirty with pale-brown thinning hair and bright blue eyes. He was earnest, and he looked honest. In answer to Gillian's questions, he stated that he was the commander of the Cloverdale Post of the American Legion. Gale Wharton, he said, was a member of this post.

"I've only known Wharton since the war," the Major testified, "but I know him fairly well. On many occasions I've seen him blow up at Legion meetings. He is a stormy man. He becomes angered easily. When he is strongly for or against a topic that comes up for discussion, he shouts."

The Major went on to tell of specific occasions on which the accused had "blown up." Mr. Yistle listened to his recital as if it bored him. He yawned several times. Now and then he cast a heavy glance at Gillian, and now and then he looked at the Judge. On these occasions he would roll his eyes and shrug his shoulders, and once Polly heard him address an aside to one of his assistants. Boredly he said:

"Stalling—just stalling for time. Hazeltine won't admit he's licked. He's fishing with an empty hook."

And one of his assistants, a tall young man with a prominent jaw, murmured in reply:

"We may not see the bait, but let's keep an eye on that hook."

Gillian devoted the remainder of the afternoon to witnesses who knew Gale Wharton well and who testified that, on this and that occasion, he had been loudly outspoken.

But this testimony seemed to be without value. The courtroom stirred to restless fidgetings. Several of the jurors followed Mr. Yistle's impolite example and yawned. The determined young lawyer for the defense seemed to be getting nowhere. The jury were not interested in fine points in human psychology. They believed Gale Wharton to be guilty. If he wasn't guilty, why didn't Gillian Hazeltine display the brilliance for which he was famous and prove it?

Mr. Yistle, as the afternoon advanced, acquired the smile of the cat that has swallowed the canary. He knew that Gillian did not have a case. He knew that Gillian was sparring for time, hoping against hope for some unexpected development. But what could develop? Gale Wharton had been proved guilty on irrefutable evidence. And Gale Wharton, in the fullness of time, was certain to be electrocuted.

The afternoon session came suddenly to an end when Judge Manning announced:

"Gentlemen of the jury, we are about to take a recess until tomorrow morning at ten o'clock. The Court admonishes you not to speak about this case among yourselves or permit anyone to speak to you about it. You will keep your minds open until the case is finally submitted to you. The defendant will retire."

BETWEEN TWO OFFICERS, Gale Wharton was escorted to his cell. Moving with the chattering crowd, Polly accompanied Gillian to the street. The crowd seemed to be unanimously of the opinion that her brother was guilty—guilty beyond doubt. She heard one man say: "Hazeltine is smart, but they've caught him with all his clothes off this time."

Polly glanced up and saw Gillian smiling grimly. He said nothing until they reached his car. Then he took her hand, squeezed it and said:

"Polly, I'm afraid that our dinner date is off. I expect to be up all night. Be of brave heart—and be on hand tomorrow morning at ten sharp. You may be my first witness.

I'm going to make every effort to destroy Colonel Garth's credibility as a witness. It must be done. For the first time I believe we've got a fighting chance."

The red-haired girl looked gravely up at him. Her eyes were responsively aglow. She had never seen this calm, grave young man so excited. She knew that he was withholding some perhaps startling information from her, and she asked eagerly:

"Is it the Dibney girl?"

"I'm not sure. I mean, Polly, I'm not talking."

"What are you going to do tonight?"

"I'm off on a hot scent—but not a new one."

"Captain Donovan's?"

"It may lead anywhere."

Polly said impulsively: "Gillian, don't run any risks!"

HIS GRAY EYES glowed, and she thought for a moment that he was about to bend down and kiss her. But he didn't. With a vague feeling of disappointment Polly took a taxicab to the Herrendon Arms and went to her rooms. She had dinner served in her living-room, and all evening she sat within reach of the telephone. Gillian generally called at eleven o'clock. But tonight he did not telephone. At eleven-thirty she called his house, and was informed by Toro, in his precise English, that Mr. Hazeltine had not been in all evening.

Polly gave in to her worst forebodings. If anything happened to Gillian, she would simply die. For the first time since Flip's arrest, she unrestrainedly and unashamedly wept. Somehow, by an instinct prompted by terror, she felt that her future, her happiness, the source of all hope depended on Gillian's activity tonight. The outlook had

never been so black. The twelve men on whom hung the
fate of her brother were firmly convinced of his guilt. And
if Flip were convicted—

She took a sleeping-powder but could not sleep. Lying
tense and cold in her bed, she listened to the remote,
ghostly whistles of locomotives. She heard the early stir-
rings of the city. By morning she was limp with the exhaus-
tion of a terrorized "white night." A dozen times she had
seen her brother stumbling to the electric chair, collapsing.
What was to become of her? And her love for Gillian?

So taut of nerves that she could hardly keep back the
scream in her throat, she crept into the courtroom next
morning, one of the first to enter that sordid, dusty scene.
The light from the north windows was colder than ever
before. There was, she felt, something ominous and direful
in the very air. The eyes of the old vultures seemed brighter,
as if they knew that the kill would soon take place and were
inwardly rejoicing.

Her heart began to beat with painful quickness when
Mr. Yistle and his two assistants came in. He looked as if
he had just enjoyed a hearty breakfast, and had just finished
an excellent cigar. His smile was jovial. His face was flushed
with health and good humor.

THE COURTROOM QUICKLY filled. Polly's panic grew.
Where was Gillian? The hands of the clock crawled to ten.
In her distracted state, it was easy to imagine all sorts of
dreadful accidents: He had stumbled upon the trail of the
killer—and had been murdered! He had smashed his car
and was lying somewhere unconscious!

Then—magically—he was standing there at his table.
Her heart rose with tremendous relief, then sank again.

How tired he looked! His face was gray and haggard. There were dark patches under his eyes. His movements were stiff and mechanical, like those of an automaton. Fear, like a black cloud, crept over her. He had failed!

This morning when the Judge came in, she stood up without being prompted. He too looked rosy and well-fed. The jury filed in: twelve men with gray faces and the sad expression of those who confront a painful but unavoidable duty.

"Gale Wharton will take the stand." It was Gillian's voice, yet so husky with weariness that she hardly recognized it.

Her brother arose and moved toward the stand. Something cold raced along Polly's spine. She held her breath until her lungs threatened to explode. There was something ominous in Flip's attitude. His fists were clenched at his side. His walk was a swagger. His eyes, as he seated himself and faced the room, were smoldering with fires of hate and resentment. His face was flushed. His bearing was belligerent.

Mr. Yistle was smiling broadly. He sat tilted back in his chair, his thumbs caught into the armholes of his vest.

POLLY SAT TENSELY forward, gripping the arms of her chair, as Gillian slowly turned and faced the bellicose young man on the witness-stand. She hoped Flip would control himself; yet he never had. Gillian, she feared, was making a great mistake in putting Flip on the stand.

A clerk intoned in a monotonous voice: "Do you swear to tell the truth, the whole truth and nothing but the truth?"

Flip did not content himself with the usual perfunctory "I do." He blazed: "I've been telling nothing but the truth

The coroner smiled. "I can prove that I was not near the
scene of the murder—if that's what's on your mind!"

since this thing started! What good does it do to tell the
truth, when that man over there"—he flung out a fist at
Mr. Yistle— "gets one person after another to lie himself
black in the face?"

Judge Manning bent forward. "Young man, you have
been asked a direct question. You are to answer it directly.
Will you raise your hand and swear to tell the truth, the
whole truth or nothing but the truth, or won't you?"

Flip turned on him with flaming eyes. "Look here,"
he snapped. "You're supposed to give an accused man a
square deal, aren't you? That's your job, isn't it? That's what
we taxpayers are paying you your salary for, isn't it? Well,
am I getting a square deal in this courtroom? I'm not!
You're letting a parade of liars get away with murder! You're
letting this Yistle railroad me to the chair!"

Judge Manning's eyes were sparkling with anger. He
said harshly:

"If you will not answer questions according to the

dictates of this court, you may retire from the witness-stand. You have been asked twice if you will give your oath to tell the truth, the whole truth and nothing but the truth. If you will not answer that question directly, you may leave the stand."

Flip retorted: "I swear to tell the truth, the whole truth and nothing but the truth—which is more than anybody has done so far."

Judge Manning said coldly: "Mr. Hazeltine, you may proceed with your examination of this witness."

Polly felt cold and limp. The slight sympathy she had seen in the jury's faces was entirely gone. Their expressions were hard, their mouths uniformly compressed. By that exhibition of temper Flip had thrown away what little hope remained.

Gillian was saying: "You are a professional aviator, are you not?"

Flip snapped: "I was—before I was arrested for a murder I didn't commit!"

"You were, at the time of your arrest, working on an invention which you believed would revolutionize the mechanics of aviation, were you not?"

"I was—certainly! I'd been working on it for nearly five years. But what—"

Patiently Gillian said: "Will you kindly describe your invention to the jury?"

The prisoner's black eyes flashed as he swung about to face the jury.

"It's an air turbine," he said in a resentful voice. "Its purpose is to do away with airplane propellers. The idea came to me one morning when I was flying at an altitude of about four thousand feet. An eagle swooped down and struck my propeller. It shattered one blade. The plane was crippled, but I was lucky and made a safe landing."

Flip was glaring at the jury as if he was certain that they did not believe a word he was saying. He went on:

"I equipped one of my planes with the air turbine and it works perfectly. I get twenty-five per cent more speed out of that plane, and the gasoline consumption is about fifteen per cent less than when a propeller is used. The air turbine is enclosed in an aluminum shell. I use four of them—two in each wing."

"Is this invention patented?"

"Yes!"

"Who owns the patents?"

"Colonel Garth—one of the men who's trying to send me to the electric chair!"

"I object!" snapped Mr. Yistle.

"Strike that answer from the record," ordered the Judge. "The witness is again instructed to answer all questions simply and directly without opinions or comments. The witness will answer the last question again."

"Colonel Garth," growled Flip.

"Why does he own them?"

"I consigned them to him when he loaned me enough money to carry on my experiments."

JUDGE MANNING INTERRUPTED: "Mr. Hazeltine, I must ask you to state the purpose of this line of question-ing. It does not seem to me to be relevant to the issue."

"I am trying to establish two points, Your Honor. One is that the accused is an industrious young man. The other is that Colonel Garth's testimony against the accused is colored by a wish to have him out of the way, because the air-turbine patents are potentially worth millions of dollars."

Judge Manning said angrily: "The stenographer will strike all of the accused's testimony from the record. Mr. Hazeltine, your tactics in this case have been unpardonable. You are wasting our time with the introduction of irrelevant issues and attempts at blackening the character of an estimable citizen. If you have witnesses to produce who may, in any way, cast light on the presumptive innocence of the accused, produce them immediately."

Gillian replied calmly: "Your Honor, I am working along a clearly defined line—"

"It is the advice of this court to abandon it and pursue some other. Have you any relevant questions you wish to ask of this witness before he is taken for cross-examination?"

"Yes, Your Honor." Gillian turned back to the belligerent young man. "Gale, did you or did you not shoot Oscar Treidler?"

Flip angrily shook his head.

"I certainly did not! I've said that a thousand times. I did not kill Treidler. And it's a rotten injustice—"

"Silence!" snapped the Judge. "Does the State wish to take this witness?"

"Your Honor," purred Mr. Yistle, "the State wishes to ask this witness five simple little questions, all direct, all to the point. Mr. Wharton, I want you to answer these questions carefully. Your counsel has taken pains to show us that time is of no consequence in this trial. Think, Mr. Wharton, and take your time. The first of my five simple little questions is: Did you ever make threats against the life of Oscar Treidler?"

Flip Wharton, gripping the arms of the chair, seemed on the point of springing at the district attorney.

"You bet your life I did!" he cried.

"And did you on the morning of May ninth come to Greenboro?"

"Hasn't it been proved that I did? Certainly, I did! Wasn't I arrested on the morning of May ninth?"

"Evidently you were, Mr. Wharton. Did you have in your right hip pocket the revolver which has been admitted as Material Exhibit A for the State?"

"Certainly, certainly!"

"And did you, at a few minutes before ten o'clock, approach the window of Oscar Treidler and draw that revolver from your pocket?"

"Haven't I admitted that I did?" the witness hotly demanded. "Didn't I say over and over again that I had pulled that gun out of my pocket—but that I didn't shoot Treidler?"

"I did not ask you whether or not you shot Treidler. I asked you whether or not you pulled a gun from your pocket. Did you or didn't you?"

"My God! Haven't I admitted that I did?"

"Yes, you have, Mr. Wharton. And were you, a few seconds later, apprehended by a police officer in the act of running away from that window with a loaded revolver containing one exploded shell?"

"I admitted all that. But—"

"That will be all," said Mr. Yistle, and airily waved his hand.

FLIP WHARTON GLARED at him. He then glared at the jury, and then at the Judge. He lifted his fists and cried:

"But I didn't kill him! I didn't!"

"You are excused," said Judge Manning.

Gale Wharton returned to his chair at Gillian's table. Gillian looked out over the courtroom.

"Is Daniel Plummer here?" There was no answer.

"Is James Osborn here?"

Necks craned, but no one responded.

"Miss Wharton will take the stand."

Polly sharply caught her breath. She wanted to cry out that she could not take the stand, that she would simply break down and disgrace him if she faced all these greedy, eager eyes. She sat as if frozen. Gillian was looking at her anxiously.

"Miss Wharton will take the stand," he repeated.

Polly came falteringly to her feet. She swayed as if she were about to faint. Somehow she found her way to the witness-stand.

She seated herself and looked out with blurred eyes over the crowd. The faces seemed to dance.

Gillian was coming toward her. His eyes were upon her face. They seemed to burn with a queer fire. They reminded her of something—something rather terrible, but she could not recall what. His face was lead-colored. His lips were dry and red, as if with fever. They were moving. They said: "Don't be afraid, Polly."

She had never seen him like this before. It was as if he were no longer a man but some sort of god, and the court-room were in some between-world, swimming with famil-iar faces which had become fantastic. His lips continued to move, his eyes to glow. Polly recalled what he had once said to her:

"It's as if Justice were an actual living person, determined to have her way despite blindness and crookedness and self-seeking. Keep faith in that, Polly."

Polly lifted her chin. The room steadied, and the strange pale mist dissolved. Gillian ceased being a strange god and became again a tired, intensely earnest man. He asked questions. She made faint replies. A man's voice crackled. Judge Manning's face dropped toward her like a swooping inflamed moon. He said sharply:

"Miss Wharton, the stenographer cannot hear you. Please raise your voice."

Gillian added: "Please face the jury. I want you to tell them if you know Colonel Norton Garth."

Polly's head cleared. She recalled that Gillian had spoken of the vital necessity of discrediting the Colonel's testimony. In a husky but full voice she replied:

"I do."

"During the summer of 1926 were you employed as a stenographer in the city engineer's office?"

"I was."

"Late in the fall, were you given a holiday in Miami, Florida, with a girl named Elsie Mannister?"

"Yes."

"Who paid for that trip?"

"Why—why, Colonel Garth!"

POLLY SAW MR. Yistle suddenly rise up like a jack-in-the-box.

"What happened, in connection with your former job, when you returned from Florida?"

"I only held it two days, then Colonel Garth gave me a thousand dollars to help Flip—my brother—pay for the farm."

"Your Honor—" Mr. Yistle began, and stopped.

"You were discharged?" Gillian asked.

"Yes."

"In what department had you been employed?"

"The one that had charge of constructing the new municipal pier."

"You had access to the files pertaining to that construction?"

"Yes."

"When you returned from Miami, did you have cause to believe that those files had been changed or replaced or—"

"I did! They had been changed. New books and certain new card indexes had been substituted."

"Did those new books and card indexes refer to certain concrete work in which it was later brought out that grafting had taken place?"

"They did."

Mr. Yistle was gazing eagerly at Judge Manning. Judge Manning was bending forward with sharp, hostile eyes on Gillian. The attorney for the defense shot his final question:

"You had discovered that new records had been substituted; whereupon Colonel Garth gave you one thousand dollars—and relieved you of your job?"

"That's true," said Polly.

Mr. Yistle angrily objected. "The testimony of this witness is irrelevant."

JUDGE MANNING SUSTAINED his objection. His face

was pink with anger. He struck his desk a soft blow with clenched fist. In a gritty voice he said:

"Mr. Hazeltine, I cannot understand why you are persisting in this line of attack. You are getting nowhere. You are wasting valuable time. I will not permit this trial to drag along in this manner."

"I beg to point out to Your Honor," Gillian replied, "that I am attempting to impeach Colonel Garth's entire testimony, and that I am within my legal rights in so doing. I consider Colonel Garth the State's key witness. I owe it to my client to pursue any course which will shed doubt on Colonel Garth's testimony."

Judge Manning answered: "Mr. Hazeltine, in my frank opinion, the performance you are giving in this courtroom is disgraceful. I can only draw the conclusion that you are attempting to befog the issue."

"I beg to disagree with Your Honor," Gillian said in the same calm tones, but he was paler than before, and the glow in his eyes had become a flame. "I am proceeding along a definite line toward a definite conclusion. My case depends on the testimony of two important witnesses who are not yet in court."

"You mean," said the court, "you are maneuvering for time?"

"No, Your Honor, I am building piece by piece a logical pattern. Does the State wish to cross-examine Miss Wharton?"

Mr. Yistle angrily brandished his hand. "Your Honor, I requested a ruling."

"Your objection to this witness's testimony in entirety was sustained." Judge Manning turned to the stenographer.

"You will strike out all of Miss Wharton's testimony. I hold it irrelevant and immaterial."

"Exception," said Gillian.

"Exception is noted. Have you more witnesses, Mr. Hazeltine?"

Gillian looked over the courtroom. He had the air of a cornered man. His eyes were desperate. His lips were tightly compressed. He said in a voice in which Polly detected a note of desperation: "Isn't Jim Osborn or Daniel Plummer here?"

No one answered. The Judge leaned forward.

"Mr. Hazeltine, if you have no further witnesses, I must order that the State proceed with summation. I am of the opinion that you came into this court without a case but with the hope of stumbling fortuitously upon some line of defense. I do not feel, Mr. Hazeltine, that you have served your client's best interests. Mr. Wharton, if you are dissatisfied with the manner in which your attorney is conducting your defense, you are entitled to request that the court appoint some other."

The prisoner looked at the Judge dully. His reply was hesitant.

"I am satisfied with what Mr. Hazeltine is doing," he mumbled.

GILLIAN GRIPPED HIS fists, as if in an effort to control himself. In a weary voice, he said:

"Thomas Larrigan will take the stand, please."

A broad-shouldered man with closely clipped hair and calf-like brown eyes limped to the witness chair. He looked uneasily about him and bent forward over hands clasped upon his ample stomach. He gave his occupation as farmer.

Gillian asked him if he knew Colonel Garth. The witness said that he did.

"Have you ever received money from him?"

"Yes sir."

"Describe the circumstances."

"I used to be a city milk inspector when Colonel Garth was in the commission business," said Larrigan. "I found out that the milk the Colonel was selling was watered, but before I could make any trouble I was fired—and the Colonel gave me thirty-five hundred dollars to buy a farm."

Judge Manning brought his gavel down with a crash.

"Strike out that testimony!" he snapped.

Gillian said firmly: "I respectfully submit, Your Honor, that this witness is reputable and is prompted by no ulterior motives. I have a legal right to produce witnesses who, by presenting facts, will prove that Colonel Garth's testimony should not be acceptable in a court of law. I have proved that he is a grafter."

Judge Manning half rose from his chair. His face was so red that Polly feared he was on the verge of an apoplectic stroke.

"Mr. Hazeltine, I am instructing you for the last time to produce proper witnesses, if you have them. I will tolerate no more of your water-muddying tactics in this courtroom. Your methods are, I am ashamed to say, contemptible."

Colonel Garth had come forward. His smoothly brushed white hair was disarrayed. He was crimson with anger. With his left hand he grasped the edge of the Judge's desk, and with his right he made a sweeping gesture toward Gillian.

"Your Honor, may I say that I bitterly resent the tactics

that Mr. Hazeltine is employing? He is deliberately attacking my public life. I must ask you to enjoin him from dragging me further into this matter. My acts are open to anyone. I have nothing to conceal. He has placed malicious interpretations upon kindly, generous acts. May I ask who is being tried in this courtroom? Is that unfortunate young man being tried on a charge of murder, or am I being tried on a charge of grafting?"

Judge Manning: "Colonel, I cannot tell you how much I regret the procedure Mr. Hazeltine has adopted. I assure you that any further attempts to discredit you will be properly dealt with. Will you accept my deepest apologies for his unscrupulous methods?"

There was a spattering of applause among the spectators. Bailiffs glared, and the clapping ceased. Polly, clutching the arms of her chair, stared at Gillian. He was glancing at some notes on his table. She saw his hand tremble. But his voice was clear and firm when he spoke.

"Colonel Garth will take the stand again," he said.

Mr. Yistle cried: "I won't stand for it! Colonel Garth has been outrageously insulted by this—this lawyer. I won't have him dragged through mud again!"

"Colonel Garth," said Gillian grimly, "will take the stand again."

The Colonel looked inquiringly at the Judge. Judge Manning glared at Gillian. He had no alternative. He nodded.

The Colonel seated himself. His expression was that of a thoroughly angry man. His eyes were snapping. He held himself tensely upright. And his glare upon Gillian was fiery.

"Colonel," Gillian said quietly, "I want you to describe what you saw from your limousine on the morning of May ninth at ten o'clock."

"I have given that testimony twice," the Colonel snapped.

"I am requesting you to give it once more, Colonel."

Colonel Garth shrugged. "Very well," he said in an irritable voice. "My limousine was, I should say, the third or fourth car in the traffic line. I saw Wharton pull the gun from his hip pocket. I knew what was going to happen, because I knew Wharton and his sister quite well, and I was aware of the bad feeling existing between Flip and Treidler. When I realized he intended to shoot Treidler, I shut my eyes. I must have had them shut for ten seconds. I was so upset that I was afraid I would faint. I waited for the sound of the shot. It didn't come. When I finally opened my eyes, Wharton was running diagonally across the street—and I saw the hole in the window—and I saw that poor devil die."

Mr. Yistle was again smiling. His composure was restored. His star witness was unshakable—absolutely unshakable.

"Well, Gillian," he said, and chuckled, "would you like to hear the Colonel go over it again?"

"I would like, Your Honor," said Gillian, "to have the stenographer make one dozen copies during the noon recess of the testimony just given by Colonel Garth, and one dozen copies each of his two previous descriptions of the incident, the one given in examination to Mr. Yistle and the one given in cross-examination to me. If Your Honor will humor me, I assure you I will bring out a curious and important point having a direct bearing upon the innocence of my client."

Judge Manning hesitated. He glanced at the clock, instructed the stenographer to make the requested copies, and announced that a recess would be taken until two o'clock.

10

POLLY HASTENED AFTER Gillian when he left the court-room, but he vanished into the crowd. She did not see him again until the beginning of the afternoon session. And he looked, she thought, more desperate and discouraged than before.

At Gillian's request Colonel Garth again took the stand. He was no longer angry. But he was frankly resentful, and his replies were rich with hostility.

"Colonel," said Gillian, "you called at my house on the night Treidler was killed, did you not?"

The Colonel snapped: "I did."

"Did you at that time use certain arguments in an attempt at persuading me not to defend Gale Wharton?"

Colonel Garth struck the arm of his chair with a clenched fist.

"How dare you make such an insinuation! I distinctly said I wanted you to defend Gale Wharton. I went so far as to offer to defray expenses of his trial."

"I am not referring to that, Colonel. I am referring to a suggestion you made that, if you and I were on the same side of the political fence, we would go a long way. Do you recall that?"

"I do, distinctly."

"But do you not consider that as an argument against

my defending Gale Wharton, following, as it did, your remark that if I did defend Wharton, my political career would be ruined?"

"Mr. Hazeltine, you are maliciously placing a false interpretation on what I said. I no longer have the slightest wish to have you on the same side of the political fence with me. I no longer wish to have any kind of association with you!"

A juror laughed aloud. Judge Manning stared at him with mild rebuke. The spectators were grinning.

"On the evening of your visit to my house," Gillian imperturbably went on, "you described what you had seen of the murder substantially as you have described it in this courtroom. Your mind is quite clear as to details, is it not?"

"It is, Mr. Hazeltine."

"When you called that night at my house, Colonel, you made a statement—a very trifling statement—that has stayed in my mind. I attached a little significance to it at the time. Not much, but a little. Since then, I have been giving that statement more and more importance. Let us see if we can clear this point up. When your car stopped in the traffic line, just where was it in relation to Treidler's windows?"

"Directly abreast of it, Mr. Hazeltine, as I have said before."

"So that, to see what you did see, it was necessary for you to bend forward and look out of the window above the door? I believe you mentioned that before?"

"I did; yes," the Colonel answered impatiently. "I did lean forward and look out the door window."

MR. YISTLE WAS fretting with his watch-fob. A man in

the back of the room hiccoughed. A motor truck rumbled past under the window.

"On the night of the murder," Gillian went on, "you told me that you were staring straight ahead when you saw Treidler die. Your exact words were: 'When I finally opened my eyes, they were staring straight ahead into the window—and I saw that poor devil die!' What I want to know is: how could you have been staring straight ahead? The phrase 'staring straight ahead' involves the entire body. It means that the body was directly toward the object being stared at. Am I right?"

"Yes. But I don't understand what you're driving at."

"You will presently. Colonel, I have examined your limousine. There is, beside the back seat on each side, a small round window which can be opened. When you are seated, that window is on a level with your shoulder. To have been staring straight ahead, you must have been sitting with your back against the left side of the car, with your feet up on the seat—and staring out of that little round window."

"Perhaps I was! Is it of any real importance which window I looked through?"

"Yes, Colonel. Why did you have your feet up on that seat, so that, in seeing Treidler die, as you did, you were staring straight ahead?"

"What on earth are you driving at?" Colonel Garth snapped. "What would I be doing with my feet up on the seat?"

"That's what I want to know. Why were they on the seat?"

"They weren't on the seat!"

"But how could you have been staring straight ahead if they weren't on the seat?"

"Objection!" cried Mr. Yistle. "Your Honor, I submit that this line of questioning is entirely irrelevant. And I strenuously object to Mr. Hazeltine's bulldozing tactics. Mr. Hazeltine is merely trying to make Colonel Garth appear ludicrous."

Judge Manning answered: "I will withhold a ruling until Mr. Hazeltine has completed his examination."

Mr. Yistle stared at him. There was a strange light in Judge Manning's eyes. Polly, for the first time since the trial began, sensed that his attitude toward Gillian was no longer antagonistic.

Gillian said: "May I have the copies of Colonel Garth's testimony which the stenographer was to have made?"

The stenographer gave Gillian a sheaf of typed pages, and while Gillian sorted them out on his table, the court-room softly buzzed with whispered conjecture. Colonel Garth, in the witness chair, looked annoyed. Gillian made twelve piles of three sheets each. The twelve sets he distributed among the jurors.

"Gentlemen," he said, "I want you to compare the three sheets which I have given each of you. The first is a transcript of Colonel Garth's description of what he saw of the murder as he gave it under examination by Mr. Yistle. The second, as he gave it under cross-examination by me; the third, as he gave it under re-cross-examination this morning."

The sheets rustled as the jurors complied with his request. The foreman was the first to complete the task. When he looked up, Gillian said:

"Do you find any similarity between those three pieces of testimony?"

"I do," replied the foreman. "I find them word for word identical!"

JUDGE MANNING SNAPPED: "Let me see them!"

Gillian carried the foreman's copies to the bench. Judge Manning scrutinized them swiftly. He looked up, glanced sharply at Colonel Garth, and then at Gillian.

"Your Honor," said Gillian, "I request that Colonel Garth's testimony be stricken from the record on the ground that it was memorized. I cite the ruling of Judge Plant in the case of Deering versus Hollingsworth, 1922, Rhode Island, 7309, in which a piece of testimony identically given twice was held to be memorized and was therefore inadmissible as evidence."

"Your Honor," cried Mr. Yistle, "I absolutely insist that you take steps to prevent this scheming lawyer from casting further reflections on the integrity of Colonel Garth. Is it not possible that a happening can be so deeply burned upon the memory that each recital of it will be word for word identical?"

"I will withhold decision on this point also," ruled the court. "Mr. Hazeltine, I want you to continue your examination of this witness."

POLLY WAS BENDING forward with hands clutched together in her lap. Her heart was racing. She knew that at last Gillian had a fighting chance. But Gillian was as calm as ever. He slowly returned to the Colonel, who was not pale but still glaring.

"Colonel," he said, gently, "it hurts me as much as it does

*"Yes sir; I jumped on him and took the
gun away," said the officer.
"Was there a silencer on the gun?" asked Gillian.*

you. But I cannot let an innocent man suffer for the crime of another."

"You are contemptible!" snapped Colonel Garth.

"I told you," murmured one of Mr. Yistle's assistants to the harassed Mr. Yistle, "that that hook might look unbaited, but to watch it just the same!"

"Colonel," said Gillian, "how well did you know Oscar Treidler?"

"Well! Very well, indeed. We were friends from boyhood."

"You grew up on the waterfront together?"

"We did."

"You went through the usual boyhood scrapes together?"

"What do you mean by scrapes?" the Colonel irritably demanded.

"I cannot be specific. But I assume that you went through scrapes. Colonel, will you tell the jury why you gave Oscar Treidler on the first of every month, from the year 1908 to the year 1925, a check for five hundred dollars; and from February, 1925, to the first of August, 1926, a check for one thousand dollars; and from August, 1926, to April, 1928, a check for one thousand five hundred dollars? Will you explain that to the jury, Colonel?"

Colonel Garth was suddenly pale. He gripped the arms of his chair and glared at Gillian.

"I refuse to answer that question!"

"Were you buying something from him?"

"I refuse to answer!"

"Objection!" shouted Mr. Yistle.

"Overruled," snapped Judge Manning. "Mr. Hazeltine, proceed!"

Gillian pointed a finger at the Colonel.

"Was he blackmailing you, Colonel?"

Colonel Garth smacked his left palm with his right fist. The sound, in the silence, was startling.

"Your Honor," he exclaimed, "I refuse to have my private affairs dragged into this court!"

Mr. Yistle quickly added: "Your Honor, the Colonel is not on trial. I object to these questions as immaterial. The Colonel's business affairs have no relation to the issue."

"Again," said the Judge, "I must withhold decision pending the outcome of Mr. Hazeltine's procedure. When he has finished, I will rule on all three points. Proceed, Mr. Hazeltine."

"Thank you, Your Honor. Will the witness answer my last question?"

"Certainly, he was not blackmailing me!" the Colonel indignantly answered. "Why should he or any man be blackmailing me?"

"The only man who could answer that question, if you refuse to do so, Colonel, is the man for whose murder Gale Wharton is standing trial. It is the one missing link in my chain of evidence which proves that Gale Wharton did not murder Oscar Treidler. I am through with you, Colonel—for the moment."

"Colonel," said Judge Manning, "will you kindly seat yourself at Mr. Hazeltine's table? I may wish to question you myself."

Pale and indignant, the Colonel did as he was instructed.

Gillian turned to the crowd.

"Is Daniel Plummer here?"

A VOICE ANSWERED, "Yes sir!" And a tall young man in knee-boots, whipcord breeches and flannel shirt made his way forward. He had the ruddy tan of a man who lives much in the open. Taking the stand, he gave his name as Daniel Plummer, his occupation as surveyor.

Gillian asked him: "Have you completed the measurements which I requested you to make?"

"I have, yes sir," answered the surveyor.

"Kindly read them off to the jury."

"I object to that question as leading," said Mr. Yistle. "What measurements?"

"Objection is overruled," said Judge Manning impatiently. "The time has come to dispense with a few formalities. Mr. Hazeltine, you will proceed with your examination."

The surveyor consulted a slip of paper.

"When seated at his desk, Oscar Treidler's shirt-collar would have been forty-six inches from his office floor," he said. "The hole in the window through which the bullet entered was forty-eight inches from the floor, or two inches higher. The center of the small round side window in Colonel Garth's limousine is, when all allowances are considered, fifty-two inches from the level of the floor of the Treidler office."

The witness hesitated. Gillian said:

"How do those various points align—or do they align?"

"Yes sir, they do! A straight line from the center of the small window in the limousine would pass through the bullet-hole in the plate-glass window—and through the collar of Oscar Treidler!"

MR. YISTLE WAS roaring objections. Judge Manning was banging on his desk with a gavel. Bailiffs were trying to quiet a courtroom suddenly gone wild.

When quiet was obtained, Judge Manning said:

"Mr. Hazeltine, on what grounds are you presenting this evidence?"

"On my former grounds, Your Honor. I am still making every effort to disqualify Colonel Garth as a disinterested witness."

The Colonel had risen. "Your Honor, I am utterly astonished. Do you realize that this crooked lawyer is making an attempt at fastening this crime upon me?"

"You will address the court when you are requested to," said the Judge. "Go on, Mr. Hazeltine."

Gillian faced the crowd again. The tired look was gone from his face. His eyes were sparkling with excitement.

"Is James Osborn here?"

"Yes sir!" replied the high, shrill voice of an old man. He was a sprightly old man with merry blue eyes. Under one arm he carried a bundle.

He trotted up to Gillian, who asked:

"Did you find anything?"

"You bet I did, Gill! I found everything!"

"Take the stand."

The old man seated himself. He smiled amiably at the crowd. He nodded familiarly to the jury. But his very geniality somehow added to the tension in the room. Polly was conscious that her cheeks were burning. She was tremendously excited.

The witness stated that he had, twenty years ago, been retired from the Greenboro detective force on a pension and had since been conducting a private detective agency.

Every spectator was bending forward, as was every juror, in order not to miss a word delivered in that thin old voice. While he talked, he caressed the bundle in his lap with his hands.

Gillian said: "Mr. Osborn, what have you in that bundle?"

The old man quickly ripped off the string which bound it.

"I've got seven pistol-targets, all shot through the bull's-eye. And here, in this rag—"

Mr. Osborn removed the rag and dramatically held high above his head a small blue steel cylinder perhaps six inches in length by two in diameter.

"Tell the jury what that is."

"It's a Maxim silencer for a .38-caliber rifle."

"Where did you find it, Mr. Osborn?"

"In the bottom of a rubbish barrel in Colonel Garth's cellar!"

COLONEL GARTH SPRANG up. He was deathly pale. He leaned upon the table for support.

"Your Honor, this is a cold-blooded frame-up! I've never shot a rifle in my life! I never saw a Maxim silencer before this afternoon! This scoundrel of a lawyer is stooping to the most unspeakable tactics in his attempt to blacken my character. I insist that you prevent him from going farther."

Judge Manning ignored him. He said to Gillian: "If this evidence that you are now presenting is dishonest, you realize, of course that you may be cited for contempt of court and may face an even more serious indictment. Can you prove what your witnesses are saying? I must warn you sternly, Mr. Hazeltine, that it is too late to retract. You must go on to the end."

"With Your Honor's permission, I shall," Gillian replied. "I wish to introduce the seven targets as Exhibit A for the defense, and the silencer as Exhibit B."

"Both are admitted. Proceed."

"I want Bert McAllister to take the stand. Mr. McAllister is, so far, the only eye-witness to the murder I have found. I promised him, for reasons which will shortly be divulged, that I would not call him to the stand unless it was absolutely necessary. Mr. McAllister was, I may say, the last of the backward steps I took from Colonel Garth's statement in my house on the night of the murder. How could the Colonel be staring straight ahead, I was curious to know, unless his body was facing the little porthole in the side of his limousine? That slip of speech of the Colonel's was the only clue I had to work on. With it I coupled the assumption that the murderer of Oscar Treidler was *probably* the kind of man who would, in all his dealings with his fellow men, be a silencer.

"I gave you some indication of that character trait when

I put Miss Wharton and Mr. Larrigan on the stand. In each case he had purchased their silence. I assumed that he must have made some other attempts at silencing Oscar Treidler. And at Treidler's bank I came upon definite clues—records, which I have quoted, extending over a period of twenty years, of checks from Colonel Garth to Treidler. The silencer again! Why was he silencing Treidler with monthly checks? Was it a crooked deal which the Colonel wished to be hushed forever, so that he could climb on and on up the political ladder? I cannot answer that question. But if Mr. McAllister will take the stand, I will satisfy all remaining doubts that Colonel Garth is the man who murdered Treidler!"

TO POLLY, STRAINING forward, the courtroom seemed to resound to the beating of racing hearts. She heard the man beside her expel his breath explosively. She looked at Colonel Garth. He was slumped down in his chair, glaring malignantly along the table at her brother's face. She thought: "The clouds are rolling back." She was limp with excitement.

The man who occupied the witness chair was round of face and ruddy of cheek. He wore the olive-drab uniform of a private chauffeur. As he was being sworn, the Colonel came lurching to his feet and gasped:

"That man is not competent to testify in this court! He has a criminal record!"

Judge Manning gestured to a sheriff. The sheriff walked quickly behind the Colonel's chair and said:

"Sit down. Address the court when you're spoken to."

"But—"

"Sit down!"

"Mr. McAllister," said Gillian, "tell the jury what you told me this morning when I came into court."

The young man twisted his cap. He darted a frightened glance at the Colonel. He took a deep breath.

"I'm Colonel Garth's chauffeur," he said in a tremulous voice. "I was drivin' the Colonel's car the mornin' he shot Treidler. I saw it all in my windshield mirror. When the red light come on, I stopped the car and looked into the mirror like I always do, to see that the fellow behind me don't bump into me. The Colonel was sitting there just the way Mr. Hazeltine guessed he was, but it beats me how he guessed it. His back was against the left side of the car, and his feet were up on the seat. He had a sawed-off rifle in his hand and there was a silencer screwed on the end of it. He was pointing it through the little round window, just like Mr. Hazeltine doped out. I saw a flash come out of it, but all I heard was a sort of *swish*. Then I heard the glass crackle, like, and then I saw Flip Wharton runnin'. It was just pure luck that Wharton was there and caught the blame. I mean, it was pure luck for the Colonel, and—"

"One moment," Judge Manning sternly interrupted. "Why haven't you come forward with this testimony before?"

BERT McALLISTER DROPPED his eyes. He twisted himself in the chair, as if he were suddenly uncomfortable.

"I—I got a prison record, Judge, and I—I didn't want it to get around. I served six years on a twelve-year sentence for manslaughter once. I've been as straight as a string ever since. I've been the Colonel's chauffeur ever since they let me out. He found out about my record, and he's been holdin' it over me. I could tell you a lot of things about that old rat! But I had to keep my mouth shut. I got married and I got a couple of fine kids. I came clean with the wife, but not another soul but the Colonel knew about my record. When I saw him kill Treidler, I didn't dare to tell. It's been on my mind somethin' awful."

Judge Manning silenced him with a curt wave of the hand.

"Don't worry about finding another job. I'll give you one myself. Mr. Yistle," he said harshly, "it gives me some satisfaction to be able to tell you that you will never try another case in this court or any other. I personally intend to bring disbarment proceedings against you. Captain Donovan and Myrtle Dibney will come forward. They have perjury charges to answer to. I will ask the jury to render a verdict of not guilty in the case before us, of People versus Wharton, without retiring. Mr. Hazeltine, permit me to congratulate you on the amazing intelligence with which you have defended your client. I want order in this court! Bailiff—"

POLLY HEARD NO more of that deep voice. She came weakly to her feet. She seemed to float. All about her people were talking excitedly, and a great many of them were laughing. She ran to her brother and hugged him.

Flip threw his arm about her. His eyes blazed; he stuttered when he tried to talk.

They were still chattering and hugging each other in the ecstasy of their relief when a plump middle-aged man with twinkling blue eyes grasped each of them by one arm. He said above the clamor:

"Please pardon my intrusion. My name is Vickner. I represent the United Aerodynamics Foundation. Gillian Hazeltine has been telling me about this amazing air turbine of yours, Mr. Wharton. I think we can obtain those patents of yours from Colonel Garth, if you'd care to let the Foundation underwrite you. We'll certainly be as generous as any of the aircraft corporations. Why not have dinner with me and talk things over?"

"That s-suits me f-fine," stuttered Flip.

A hand was inserted under Polly's elbow. She looked up into Gillian's glowing eyes and wide grin. He looked ten years younger. He guided her out of the courtroom to the sidewalk, and lifted her into his coupé.

HER MIND WAS still whirling as they drove off. It began to clear as they reached the outskirts of the city. With an air of grim determination, Gillian stopped the car on a deserted road high above the river. He switched off the ignition. He turned to her.

"Polly," he said, "I've been a human silencer myself. For weeks and weeks I've worn a muzzle. Now I'm going to take it off and talk."

"Yes," said Polly falteringly.

"In three months, by an overwhelming majority, I'm going to be elected police commissioner of Greenboro. Later on, it is my intention to become governor of this fair State. Perhaps I am talking through my hat. But those are my plans. But that isn't why I drove you way out here."

"No?" said Polly.

"No," said Gillian. "I drove you out here because it is absolutely impossible for me to restrain myself any longer. In less than three seconds you are going to be thoroughly and scientifically kissed!"

"Yes," said Polly.

THE HAUNTED YACHT CLUB

*Murder's shadow hung over Greenfield and the
echoing rooms of its yacht club during the first
of those weird happenings that were to enmesh
the great criminal lawyer, Gillian Hazeltine*

1

A GRISLY SIGHT

PERCHED UPON THE eastern bank of the Sangamo like an evil old bird was the clubhouse of the Greenfield Yacht Club. By day the building was disgracefully shabby and forlorn. On a night when the moon sent down misty light through a layer of bone-white clouds it bore a striking resemblance to a sea gull—a disreputable sea gull, frowzy and gray with age. At night it took on a sinister character, as if it came darkly to life, as if danger stalked there.

The wings, sprawling out on either side of the main body of the structure, were not unlike the wings of an old gull. And as if to make this likeness all the more striking, there was the gull's brood nestling close to her side. They gurgled in the oil-scummed water; they nudged rotting old piles; they clucked in sullen protest in the wash from a trim patrol boat, and seemed to shrink from the blue-white finger it sent poking and prodding along the water front where river pirates might lurk.

What a shabby brood they were! Tipsy houseboats, forlorn launches; schooners, yawls, and sloops, which had once been princesses among their kind. Is anything more pathetic than a gracious yacht, a sailing yacht, foul with neglect? Not if you love small ships.

Twenty years ago this scene would have presented an amazing contrast. The windows, now filmed with age, would have blazed with light. The deep veranda would have been gay and lively with voices, laughter, tinkling glasses. Riding lights would have gleamed where the yachts were moored. Along the paths by the river, sheltered by willows, lovers would have strolled. The scene would have been rich with sentiment, because that was a sentimental age.

Glance at those willows now—gray, dreadful stumps! Twenty years ago all this was meadowland and woodland. To-day—

Immediately north of the forty acres of yacht club property were the great tanks of the City Gas Company—monster steel cylinders which rose and fell as though controlled by some mysterious tide.

To Rufus Lally, caretaker of the Greenfield Yacht Club and a man with a too active imagination, they were the steel lungs of some steel beast; they sucked in gas from hot furnaces and puffed it out through an elaborate bronchial system under the city. In their mighty labors some of their breath escaped, polluting the air about the clubhouse and murdering the grass and trees.

Crowding the yacht club property on the east were the tracks of the Western & Southern. All day and all night locomotives thundered and clanked and clattered over these tracks, filled the river air with soot, and soured it with yet more gas.

Sharp against the southern boundary line of the forty acres was an ugly brick building which housed the most baneful of all industries, a tannery. To the vapors leaking from the steel lungs of the gas monster and the fumes of panting locomotives was thus added the reek of hides in process of becoming leather.

IN THIS DIFFICULT atmosphere Rufus Lally dwelled and ministered to the dying sea gull of a clubhouse. Small wonder that his mind had a somewhat morbid twist. Once a week, after midnight, a black launch with powerful muffled engines slinked in from the bay and left neat burlap bags stacked on the weather-beaten concrete pier. But Rufus Lally was not an ordinary bootlegger. He catered to the wants of only a few men among Greenfield's pillars of society—the few surviving members of the club. The privilege of buying unquestionably good Scotch sustained their interest in the old club.

Rufus Lally was, in spite of appearances, an ambitious young man. It was his ambition to become a doctor—specifically, a toxicologist; he wanted to devote his life to the study of poisons, their effects upon the human anatomy, their detection. He lived as a miser lives. Dimes and quarters squeezed from his wages, and dollars coined easily from his bootlegging, went tinkling into his bank account against the cost of a college education.

He felt that his ambition was worthy of any sacrifice. He was passionately interested in toxicology. It was written in the stars, now reflected on the oil slick on the surface of the river, that his interest in poisons would shortly become even more passionate.

Rufus Lally was seated in an overstuffed chair in the trophy room, reading the greatest work of his favorite author. Subject: Toxicology. Author: Horace G. Cullen, M.D. Dr. Cullen was Rufus Lally's hero. And Dr. Cullen, it chanced, was the president of the Greenfield Yacht Club; one of Greenfield's most prominent citizens.

Rufus Lally's good-looking face, with its cameo profile, was pale. A pair of dark grooves running up and down his high forehead and between his eyes bespoke intense concentration. The fingers of one hand were entwined with curly walnut hair. If fate had cast the dice a little differently, Rufus Lally might have become an idol of motion picture audiences. He was rather too beautiful to be called handsome; rather too sensitive, too reticent, to be called manly.

Over and over Rufus Lally read a sentence, a blunt statement of medical fact: "Among the alkaloids, aconitine is one of the deadliest poisons." He never read beyond that. These words danced and jiggled before his eyes. Curled up in the overstuffed chair, he did not move. He dared not move. He was held rigid by a fear which had dismissed all color from his face and coated it, from forehead to chin, with a clammy wet film. On his forehead and chin were beads of moisture.

He listened, his heart racing at double tempo. Sounds

that should not have been were striking on his ears. Either his extremely sensitive imagination was at last getting the better of him—or the clubhouse was full of ghosts.

Rufus Lally had, or believed fondly that he had, the cold, searching mind of a scientist. A toxicologist must have a cold, scientific mind. A cold, scientific mind does not take stock in ghosts, but it does take stock in hallucinations.

A man, Rufus Lally reasoned, might inhale so much illuminating gas, accumulating its poison in little doses day by day, that his mind eventually became attuned to sounds which did not exist. A man living in the foul air of gas reservoirs, the acrid exhaust of locomotives, the odors from a tannery, might confuse actuality with fancy.

It was as if Rufus Lally were trying to thrust back the groping claws of madness.

HE SHIVERED AS the sound occurred again.

Some one was moving about in the old sail loft!

Yet no one could possibly be in the old sail loft. There was nothing there to attract any one. Every object of value had long ago been looted by the river pirates. No member of the club would dream of visiting the sail loft without first seeing Rufus Lally.

He listened with the intentness which gives to a pinfall the importance of a thunderclap.

The sound became louder. It was as if a length of heavy anchor chain were being dragged slowly back and forth. Clank—rumble—clank!

He was aware that his tongue, the entire inside of his mouth, was dry. He tried to moisten his lips, but his tongue rasped upon them. Rufus Lally argued: "Nobody is up there. It's the wind."

This was a hollow argument; there was no wind. It was a still night, so still that a clammy white mist would form, undisturbed, and lie like thick cream on the river by morning. He wanted to cry out. He was terrified. Queer sounds from the sail loft were occurring every night now. Soft footsteps. Doors softly closing. Whirring sounds, like the wings of great birds taking flight; windows rattling.

"I'm a little overtired. I'll see Dr. Cullen about this first thing in the morning. There's no question—" His racing thoughts ended as a deep groan—a groan as of some being in torture—floated down to him from above.

Resolutely: "I don't believe in ghosts."

But Rufus Lally was shivering uncontrollably now. The tortured groan ceased. Its memory was obliterated by a heavier sound. Some object was being dragged across the sail loft. An anchor? A small windlass? Or were these sounds the products of his imagination?

"I can't stand this any longer. I'll go crazy. I've got to see Dr. Cullen and find if I'm poisoned. I can't stand another night of this."

He was speaking aloud. His voice was as dry as the scraping of a dead leaf in the wind.

This was the tenth night. Usually the ghostly visitations came to an end with the soft banging of a door, a deep sighing, as if some disembodied spirit were soaring back into some other world.

But to-night the sounds persisted. Again came the groan.

"I'm going up there." Hitherto he had not dared. He repeated aloud: "I'm going up there."

He removed his hand from his tousled head and shakily lowered it. Without removing his eyes from the ceiling directly above him, he fumbled for the drawer in the desk beside him. His hand jerked uncontrollably. There was a sharp thud as a plate was dislodged from the desk and fell to the floor. It was—or had been—a plate of chocolate fudge, which his sister Eileen had made for him. Sometimes, when she was off duty or between cases, she came down and tidied up the rooms for him; baked him cakes and pies and made candy for him. On her last visit she had made the fudge.

The crash startled him so that he jumped up. He jerked open the desk drawer and removed from it a blue revolver spotted with rust. And suddenly the hairs on the nape of his neck seemed to bristle. Rufus Lally found himself staring, with eyes of terror, at the window in the eastern wall.

A moment ago that window had been black. It glowed now with a queer light. It was not a light of this world; it was a cold greenish-blue— that dreadful color seen in the faces of men who have met their death by strangulation.

Rufus Lally, horrified, stared and shook as the strange light glowed and waxed brighter.

A shadow fell upon the window. It seemed to be projected from his imagination. A voice, as if from a floating spirit, chanted:

"See Dr. Cullen. See him at once. You're full of poisons."

The shadow upon the window had sharpened. It was a silhouette. High forehead, hooked nose, bearded chin. The profile in caricature of Dr. Horace Cullen!

The young man raised the revolver and fired at the silhouette. His aim was excellent. The profile vanished. The green light went. Splinters of glass fell tinkling to the floor, and there was a hole in the upper left-hand pane as big as a silver dollar.

The student of poisons rushed to the window. He peered out through the hole that the bullet had made. He saw nothing—nothing but the familiar litter in the yard, etched faintly by moonlight.

He drew back sharply as a sound filled his ears. It resembled the sound of a fire siren heard on a still night at a great distance—a rising wail. Rufus Lally's teeth were audibly chattering. He did not stop for hat or coat.

2

MURDER!

DAN WHARTON, THE keeper of the newspaper "morgue," was alone. Except for the slow, measured ticking of a wall clock, the city room of the Greenfield *Morning Times* was silent. The last news item had gone down to the composing room some few minutes before. It had been a dull night for news. Every one had gone home promptly.

In every important newspaper office is a department known as the morgue. It is a repository of newspaper clippings, thoroughly indexed and cross-indexed, pertaining to events and persons, but particularly to persons, since behind nearly every event is at least one person.

The keeper of the morgue is generally a man who has grown old and practically useless in newspaper harness. Dan Wharton was no exception. Once, in the halcyon days of journalism, he had been a star reporter. Later he had outlived his usefulness on the copy desk. Palsied and bent with age, he was clinging to the last job he would ever hold on any newspaper.

Dan Wharton should have been retired on a pension, turned out to pasture, so to speak; but newspapers do not retire men on pensions. So Dan Wharton clung to his job and took pride in two things: the fact that his morgue was the most complete, the best indexed in Greenfield, and the fact that he was always the last man to leave the office.

He lingered hours after other men had left—and who could guess what thoughts, what dreams of a golden, vigorous past filled his mind in those hours!

Presently he would turn out all the lights and drop in at his favorite speakeasy for a nightcap and a sandwich.

One of the group of telephones on the city desk began to ring. Dan Wharton tottered out of the morgue to answer it. He knew what it was. Some wife of some reporter wanted to know where her husband was. Dan Wharton smiled. He would lie glibly; he was good at lying. To-morrow the reporter would take him out and buy him a drink or give him a good cigar. Dan picked up several receivers before he found the right one. A voice barked at him:

"City room?"

"Yes," quavered the old man, and his smile vanished.

"Anybody there? This is Josh Hammersley."

If there were star reporters any more, Josh Hammersley would have been known as a star reporter. He was probably the best reporter in Greenfield.

"Only me—Dan Wharton," quaked the keeper of the morgue.

"Oh, my Gawd," said Hammersley. Then: "Dan, listen. Can you take a story? It's hot. It's red hot. Take it. I'll give you the head and the drops. It's to be a seven-column streamer. Grab a pencil. Ready?"

"Y-yes," croaked the man who had once been a better reporter than Josh Hammersley would ever be. "Ready. Shoot it."

"Here's your head: 'Dr. Cullen Killed By Madman.' Got it?"

"Yes!"

" 'Caretaker of Greenfield Yacht Club enters study of eminent scientist and shoots him through brain. Killer a medical student and protégé of Dr. Cullen's.' That's the first drop. Got it?"

"Yes!"

" 'Police quiz murderer, who denies killing. Is in state of collapse.' That's the second drop. Got it?"

"Yes!"

" 'Dr. Cullen was in sixty-eighth year and world renowned as toxicologist. Got that?"

"Yes!"

"HERE'S YOUR STORY: 'Dr. Horace G. Cullen, one of Greenfield's leading citizens and a scientist of world fame, was shot and instantly killed this morning in his study at about 1:15 A.M. by Rufus Lally, the caretaker of the Greenfield Yacht Club, who is described by the police as being mentally unbalanced. The shot was heard by Dr. Cullen's butler, Benjamin Ashe, who rushed into the doctor's study to find his employer lying upon the floor with a bullet between his eyes, dead, and Rufus Lally standing over him with a Colt .38 revolver in his hand.

" 'No motive for the crime is known. Lally, since his employment as caretaker of the Greenfield Yacht Club, an institution practically defunct, has been a protege of Dr. Cullen's. Lally, evidently a great admirer of the scientist, was studying toxicology with the intention of following in Dr. Cullen's footsteps. Lally put up no resistance when Ashe, the butler, grappled with him, but submitted and waited until the police came. When he was arrested and charged with the murder, Lally hysterically denied the act.

" 'Little is known about Lally, except that he graduated from Central High School four years ago and worked at odd jobs until Dr. Cullen obtained for him his present employment at the old yacht club. He is about twenty-four years old. The police say they have suspected for some time that Lally has been carrying on a small bootlegging business among members of the old yacht club. Lally has a sister, Eileen, who is a trained nurse.' That 'll do, Dan. Rush it down to the composing room. Tell the foreman to kill anything he wants on the front page to get it in. Even if the presses have started, it must get in."

Old man Wharton did as he was instructed. He tottered down to the composing room; he tottered back. His old eyes were gleaming and bright pink spots glowed on either cheek bone. He was too excited now for a nightcap and a sandwich.

He returned to the morgue. For some minutes he was too excited to do anything but stand and stare at the filing cases which lined the walls of the little room to the ceiling.

Dan Wharton seated himself with a tremulous sigh in a worn old chair. He pressed his bony hands against his temples.

Something was stirring at the back of his brain; some groping, elusive memory.

He lowered his hands to his knees. The memory began to take shape, to assume clear outlines. He stood up and began opening filing cases, removing clippings. His hands shook. His eyes took on a brighter gleam as he arranged clippings on the battered old table against the back wall.

Even Dan's teeth were clicking with excitement. He arranged the clippings in a geometrical pattern. It was shaped like a star with six points. It was part of Dan's complex system of cross indexing, this star arrangement. And putting down the clippings in this pattern was very much like arranging the parts of a picture puzzle.

He read each one through as he laid it down. He was presently asking himself if his old brain was tricking him, as it was doing so often lately. Or was he groping along the trail of the biggest piece of news that had burst on Greenfield in years?

If his fumbling old mind was on the right trail, his discovery, coupled with the Cullen murder, would shake Greenfield to its civic roots!

Dan Wharton placed the clippings in an envelope. He put the envelope in his pocket. He would go to the speakeasy now. He must have a drink to help him think. Then he would see Gillian Hazeltine.

3

BAD OMENS

THE TELEPHONE ON the desk in Gillian Hazeltine's study rang for fully twenty seconds before he became aware of it. And when he sat up in his chair and reached for the instrument, his actions were as clumsy and slow as those of a man in a stupor.

It was unlike Gillian Hazeltine to be clumsy, as it was unlike him to take cat-naps over his work. He was a man of tremendous vitality, never requiring more than five or six hours of sleep. Frequently he worked from twenty-four to thirty-six hours on end, sustained by hot black coffee, strong cigars and his indomitable energy. But within the past few weeks a change had stolen over him. He felt stupid and sleepy.

There was a dull ache in his head and a stifled sensation in his chest. It was as if the very spark of his existence were threatened. Dying men trying to fight back from the pit of eternal nothingness must have that sensation.

The struggle was so real that cold drops of sweat formed on Gillian's forehead. Something dreadful must be wrong to cause that horrible, clawing feeling inside his chest. It was like a nightmare, and the voice that came pouncing at him down the wire was like a voice in a nightmare—harsh, rasping, somehow ominous.

"Gillian Hazeltine?"

Even in his drowsy condition Gillian recognized in that voice the accents, the intonation of a thug.

Thickly he said "Yes."

"You don't know who I am, and you don't need to know. See?"

"Who is this?" Gillian demanded.

"Never mind. Listen! I'm tellin' you somethin' fer your own good. Get me? I'm tellin' you to clear out of town as fast as you can clear. Hop a rattler somewhere—and stay there."

"What," Gillian said coldly, "is this all about?"

"I'm tellin' you nothin'," said the harsh voice. "If you don't want a knife or a bullet in the back, hit the cinders! I want you out of town, and I'm givin' you fair warnin'."

Gillian jiggled the hook. When an operator answered he snapped:

"What number was calling me? Quick!"

The unknown's voice snarled:

" 'Twon't do you no damned good."

The line clicked again. A girl's clear voice said in Gillian's receiver:

"Number, please?"

"Get me that number!" Gillian barked.

"I'm sorry, sir; your party has disconnected."

Gillian hung up the receiver and placed the phone on his desk. Not only his face but his entire body was wet, dripping, with perspiration. He ran his hand through his thick, curly black hair, which was peppered with gray—a minor reason for his enemies' calling him the Silver Fox.

It was not the first time he had been threatened in this way. Nor had those threats always been empty ones. The bullet-proof windows of his coupé had saved him once from a fusillade of bullets. On another occasion a man—a maniac—had attempted to stab him in the back.

Trouble of some sort, he reasoned, was afoot. A new war in Greenfield's underworld? Or was that Chicago gang back again, thirsting for more blood, more hi-jacking money?

Gillian stared at the telephone suspiciously. Had that conversation actually taken place—or had he imagined it? Everything seemed so unreal!

A SMALL MAN with black beads for eyes in a face the shape and color of a roasted almond came floating into the room like a ghost—a yellow-faced ghost in a white robe and straw sandals with crimson cross-ties. The sandals on the carpet made a sound like wind in dry branches.

No one but an Oriental could possibly look so dignified in a cotton nightshirt. In his almost painfully precise English, Gillian's houseman, Toro, said:

"I heard your voice, sir."

Gillian stared at him from heavy-lidded eyes.

"What else did you hear?"

"Nothing, sir."

"The telephone bell?"

"No, Mr. Hazeltine, I did not hear any bell."

Gillian swung his chair about. The expression on the criminal lawyer's face was one of kindly interest. With such an expression did he gaze at key witnesses, at lying witnesses, in the court room dramas in which he had often figured.

"You did not hear this telephone bell?"

The black eyes were as expressionless as black glass marbles.

"No, Mr. Hazeltine."

"But you heard my voice."

"Yes, Mr. Hazeltine."

Gillian's eyes narrowed still more. He wondered why he should suddenly be so distrustful of this Japanese. He had thought that there was a great deal of fine sentiment in Toro's attitude toward him. Certainly there should have been. Gillian had reached out and plucked Toro from the shadow of the penitentiary at a time when Toro was so involved in a certain transaction in drugs that the steel gate had all but clanged upon him. Gillian had seen in Toro a relatively innocent goat; had spared him that clang of doom.

Toro, within the limits of his cold nature, had always seemed grateful; but there were times when Gillian was skeptical. He knew that Toro occasionally fell into old ways and smoked opium. It was curious, Gillian reflected, that he should somehow associate Toro with that recent telephone conversation.

"Is there anything I can do, Mr. Hazeltine?"

The telephone began ringing again before Gillian could answer. He picked up the instrument with more vigor than he had shown in many days, but before lifting the receiver he shot a tight smile at the Japanese.

"Did you hear it ring that time?"

"Yes, Mr. Hazeltine." The black beads remained fixed on his face, as if watchful, waiting.

"Gillian?" a voice shrilly inquired.

"Yes."

"This is Van."

"Who?"

"Dennis Van Zant. Did I get you out of bed? I want to see you about something that's important—damned important!"

Gillian involuntarily sighed. Dennis Van Zant was, in Gillian's estimation, one of Greenfield's greatest nuisances; a busybody; a man who was always butting into other people's business. Van Zant was the type of man who is always forcing his way into committees. He bored Gillian. Recently he had married Cornelia Goodwin, who bored Gillian even more. Gillian had no patience for social climbers. He asked wearily:

"What can I do for you, Van?"

THE AGITATED VOICE of Dennis Van Zant blurted: "You're still a member of the Greenfield Yacht Club, aren't you, Gill?"

"I am," said Gillian after a moment. He had kept up his membership for years, because of a sentimental debt he felt that he owed the past. He had met his first wife there; had courted and won her there, back in the days before the gas tanks, the railroad and the tannery had moved in. When the dues had been raised rather exorbitantly he maintained his membership because of the opportunity it gave him to secure excellent whisky at fair prices.

"Gill, have you been buying your liquor from that youngster who's the caretaker there?"

"Some of it."

"Your Scotch?"

"Yes."

"When did you get your last lot of it?"

"I don't remember. Possibly a month ago."

"Any lately?"

"Wait a minute." Gillian looked at the Japanese, who was still standing in the middle of the room, his yellow face absolutely devoid of expression. "Toro, when did that fellow at the yacht club deliver the last lot of whisky?"

"He delivered a case about two weeks ago, sir."

"Two weeks ago," said Gillian into the telephone. "Anything the matter with it?"

"I can't discuss it over the phone. I'm down at the city chemist's laboratory. It will be worth your while to wait up until I can get there. I can make it in about an hour."

"I'll wait," said Gillian. He hung up and looked at the little silver clock at the back of his desk. It was one thirty-five.

"Is there anything else, sir?" Toro asked.

"Are you in a hurry to go anywhere?" Gillian answered.

"No, sir."

Gillian turned back to his desk. His brain was too dull for thinking. He wished he could think clearly. Somewhere trouble was brewing. Its presence had always been indicated by late telephone calls.

The back doorbell would presently ring, and some white-faced devil would come trembling in and want advice, help, counsel.

Another gang war? He hoped not. But bad booze frequently meant gang trouble. Gang trouble meant deaths.

And death, in the old days, would have meant hard work for Gillian, the shrewdest, smartest criminal lawyer in the State.

He was no longer practicing criminal law. After serving one term as police commissioner of Greenfield he had hung out his shingle as a corporation counsel.

And how his old enemies had cheered!

Gillian wondered what was taking place behind that inscrutable yellow mask, those beadlike black eyes. Was Toro, once a crook, returning to old ways? What was Toro up to?

"You can go back to bed."

"Very well, Mr. Hazeltine. Good night."

WHEN HE HAD gone, Gillian reached into a humidor of solid gold—a gift from a grateful client named Nicky Beamer, whom Gillian had saved from the electric chair—and brought out a beautifully fashioned blond cigar. These cigars, the gift of another grateful client, had cost that client just one hundred dollars for a box of one hundred. Gillian was the recipient of many such gifts.

He bit off the end of the dollar perfecto, lighted it, and puffed at it with the expression of a man who has unexpectedly bitten into a bad apple. The smoke tasted as burning rubbish smells.

The disgusted man reached across the desk and pulled toward him a plain white cardboard box about six inches square by three in depth. He removed the cover and picked out a dusty brown cube an inch thick each way. He tucked the brown cube into his mouth. It fairly melted on his tongue. This, at least, tasted as it should taste.

It was Gillian's favorite confection—chocolate fudge.

He loved chocolate fudge, often consuming as much as half a pound of it in a day. Homemade fudge; not the store kind. Grateful clients among the gentler sex kept him supplied.

A far-away tinkle sent a shiver down his spine and caused his jaws to cease working. In the still house the silvery tinkle had had a ghostly sound. Perhaps it was his imagination; perhaps it was the back door.

The tinkle occurred again. Other sounds followed it— the scraping of Toro's sandals on a carpet or rug.

Gillian turned his chair about and faced the doorway into the hall. The darkness of the hall gave way to a soft flood of amber light.

Electric switches clicked downstairs. Gillian held his breath. Perspiration was oozing out on his face again. Mechanically he reached for another cube of fudge.

The murmur of voices floated up the stairwell to him. He did not move. It was as if he were riveted to the chair.

He clutched the arms of the chair and waited. The murmurs grew louder. Evidently Toro was protesting. Then silence fell. Gillian listened intently. The murmuring had ceased. It was followed by a sound that puzzled him; brought a sour grimace to his mouth, a squint to his steel-gray eyes. *Tap-tap—tap-tap-tap!* Like a woman's high heels on a hardwood floor.

Some one, gasping for breath, was racing up the stairs.

Gillian, gripping the arms of his chair, bent forward. His eyes ached with the strain of staring at the doorway.

A girl in white seemed to be catapulted into the room. It was as if some one had pushed her in. She caught at the door jamb with one hand, clung to it, and swayed.

She was in the uniform, he dazedly saw, of a trained

nurse. The starched white dress; the little white cap. At her throat was the blue-and-gold pin of the Greenfield Hospital.

Gillian slumped forward and stared at her. He did not believe, at first, that she existed. She was as unreal as that threatening telephone conversation had been. Not until somewhat later did he recall how pale she was; how big and dark with excitement her eyes were.

All he took in, as he dully stared, was her white uniform and her hair under the black hat. It was red—the red of glowing coals in a furnace.

Red-headed women topped the list of Gillian's superstitions. He disliked black cats, he abhorred starting an important task or leaving on a long trip on a Friday, he was not at all partial to the number 13, but of red-headed women he was actually in fear. They always brought him intensely bad or good luck—and the only one who had ever brought him good luck was the girl he had married, Violet, now far away in California convalescing from an operation. All his other experiences at the hands of red-headed women had been uniformly disastrous. Red-headed women had spoiled case after case for him, or had caused him untold difficulties up to a hazardous victory.

The ghost's left shoulder had sagged against the door jamb. She was trying to catch her breath. Her lips were parted. Her breast rose and fell with rapid panting. Her eyes, looking at him from the corners, glittered with emotion. They were brown. He had known green-eyed, blue-eyed and golden-eyed red heads, but never a brown-eyed one. There was a light on the wall near her. Its rays caused her pupils to glow redly.

"Are you Mr. Hazeltine?"—a husky whisper of a voice.

"I am."

"Will you come down to the Fourth Precinct jail with me right away? They've arrested my brother for murdering Dr. Horace G. Cullen!"

4

STRONG EVIDENCE

GILLIAN STOOD UP. He thought of that threatening telephone call, of his unexplainable doubts concerning Toro. Smoldering trouble was bursting into flames.

He indicated a chair beside his desk and said calmly: "Sit down, please."

Gillian gave the red hair another glance filled with misgivings, as the girl obeyed, crossing the room, and settling down on the edge of the chair with her hands tightly clasped on her knees.

He seated himself in the swivel chair, facing her. Her brown eyes were enormous. Her face was as white as death. Even her lips were colorless. Either she was a terribly frightened girl—or a terribly clever actress. He had seen lying women on the witness stand deliberately work themselves into this state. Her arms were trembling.

Gillian said: "They've arrested your brother for killing Dr. Cullen, have they?"

"Yes. But he didn't do it!"

"What is his name?"

"Rufus Lally."

Gillian's steel-gray eyes narrowed slightly. The red-headed girl was shaking all over now.

"Try to pull yourself together."

"I feel faint. May I have a drink of water?"

Gillian responded quickly: "How about a little whisky?"

He saw her stiffen. Then: "No—no, thank you."

"Just water?"

"If you please."

Gillian knew that the vacuum carafe at the back of his desk was filled with fresh ice water. But he did not reach for it. Instead, he arose and walked into his bedroom, which adjoined his study. He started across the bedroom toward the bathroom. In bedroom slippers, he walked silently. Halfway across the bedroom he stopped and looked back.

The red-headed nurse had risen, was peering at the objects on his desk. She looked furtively toward the darkened bedroom, where he stood, picked up the cigar he had been smoking, laid it down, then lifted in both hands the white cardboard box of fudge.

Gillian waited. She replaced the box of fudge and seated herself. It seemed to him that she was faintly smiling, but he could not be sure. He hastened into the bathroom and returned immediately with a glass of water.

She sipped only a little of it. The color, in his absence, had returned to her face. Bright pink spots glowed on either cheek. She was strikingly pretty. He judged that she was about twenty-five.

"Feel stronger now?"

"Yes, Mr. Hazeltine."

"Tell me just what happened."

She obliged: "I have been night nursing. Some one at the Fourth Precinct jail, a keeper or a porter, telephoned me and said that my brother had been arrested on a murder charge. I was only a few blocks from the jail. I hurried over, but they would not let me see Rufe."

Her voice was low but firm. She spoke in the mechanical way of one who has memorized his lines.

"**WHAT TIME DID** the murder take place?"

"A few minutes after one."

"Any witnesses?"

"I don't believe so."

"How was Dr. Cullen killed?"

"He was shot through the brain. He died instantly."

"But not by your brother?"

"No, Mr. Hazeltine. I'm positive my brother had nothing to do with it. He wouldn't harm a—a mouse."

"Where was your brother when the murder happened?"

"They say he was in the doctor's study and that he had a revolver in his hand when the butler went in."

"The police say that?"

"Yes. That's what the butler told them. He held Rufus until the police arrived."

"Know any other details?"

The girl shook her head. "The sergeant at the desk told me that much. And so I came right here. I knew you'd help me, because I've always heard how you take the part of any one who is persecuted or oppressed. Rufe adored Dr. Cullen. He—he worshiped him! Some one else killed him—and Rufe is being blamed for it."

Gillian nodded understandingly. He was thinking rapidly, trying to piece together the parts of this puzzle. Somehow, he was certain, they would eventually form a comprehensive picture. They generally did. Trouble was flaming in Greenfield. Who was at the source of it? Who had been his mysterious telephone caller? Where did Toro fit into the picture?

"Who do you think did the killing?"

"I don't know."

Gillian picked up the telephone and presently said into the mouthpiece: "Spruce 4000." He watched Miss Lally's face. Spruce 4000 was police headquarters. A few seconds later, he said: "Connect me with the homicide bureau." Then: "Let me talk to Bill Murdock."

"This is Bill Murdock," said the gruff voice.

"Gillian Hazeltine, Bill. What's the lowdown on the Cullen murder?"

"We've booked a guy named Lally—Rufus Lally. He's it, all right."

"Make a confession?" Gillian asked.

"Nope. He's claiming his mind was a blank when it all happened. Says he heard a lot o' ghosts walking around down at the old yacht club—he's the caretaker there—and ran up to tell Doc Cullen about it. He says he don't remember nothing from the time he left the clubhouse until the doc's butler grabbed him."

"Any witnesses?"

"Nope."

"Just what happened?"

"Well, it looks to me, Mr. Hazeltine, like this bird had it all figured out. He had access to the doctor any time o' day or night by just walking in a side door. He was a sort of a pet of the old man's, so the butler says. He went in the side door to-night as usual, pulled out his gun and plugged the old gent. Shot him between the eyes and killed him that quick. When the butler ran in—which he did right after hearing the shot—Lally was standin' there with the gun in his hand and Doc Cullen lyin' face down on the rug."

"Lally was standing over him?"

"Yes—with the rod in his hand, still hot. The butler grabbed the gun, and he says the barrel was hot and there was a smell o' gunsmoke in the room."

"DID LALLY SAY anything?"

"Sure! When Ashe, the butler, grabbed him, Lally says: 'God, what have I done?' And Ashe says: 'You've done plenty. You've killed the doctor.' Then Ashe called headquarters and I went right up. Lally's rod is a .38 caliber Colt. I measured the hole in the doc's head. It was a .38 caliber hole all right."

"Find the bullet?"

"Nope. I left that for the coroner."

"What did Lally say to you?"

"Plenty! He talked a blue streak. He said the old clubhouse was haunted. For a couple of weeks, he said, there've been spooky sounds. To-night, he said, they was worse than ever. And to cap the climax, he said, to-night there was a green light at a window, and he says he saw a face, or a shadow thrown by a face, on the window. It was Doc Cullen's face, so he says. He says he was scairt pink. He took a shot at the window, he was so rattled, he says."

"Have you sent anybody down to the yacht club to check that?" Gillian asked.

"Why bother?" grunted Bill Murdock. "There were two empty shells in the gun. He used one on Doc Cullen. I don't care how he used the other one, as long as he didn't bump off somebody else."

"What else does Lally say?"

"He just sticks to his story. Mind a blank from the time he plugged the face in the window until Ashe grabbed him. Spooks in the yacht club. He broke down and cried all over me. If you ask me, he's a slick actor. He's taken a lot of trouble to plant an insanity plea. He's crazy, all right— like a fox!"

"How about a motive?"

"That," answered Bill Murdock, "is up to the district attorney. I got enough evidence to fry this baby a dozen times. Why bother with motives? Probably the doc had somethin' on him. Don't ask me. I'm nothin' but a dumb detective."

Gillian thanked him, hung up the receiver and called another number. A sleepy voice presently answered. It was the voice of Judge Carson Woolwich.

Gillian said: "Hate to disturb you, judge; but it's pretty important. Dr. Cullen was murdered this morning at about one o'clock."

He heard Judge Woolwich gasp. "Murdered!"

"Shot in his study. The police have arrested the caretaker of the old yacht club—Rufus Lally."

"How was this murder committed?"

"Shot through the brain."

"How horrible! What was the motive?"

"That's what I'm curious to know."

Judge Woolwich asked quickly: "Are you defending Lally?"

"No, judge. I'm merely an interested bystander. I understand that you drew the doctor's will. I know it isn't ethical to divulge any of the contents of it, but it would be useful if you could tell me whether or not Lally was named as a beneficiary."

There was a long pause. Then:

"Lally and his sister Eileen were both named as beneficiaries. Each was to receive twenty-five thousand dollars in cash."

"Thank you, judge."

GILLIAN HUNG UP the receiver and turned to Eileen Lally. Her face was again white, and her eyes were enormous. At that moment, they seemed to Gillian larger than any human eyes he had ever seen. Alarmingly large and beautiful. The lawyer in Gillian made him exclaim to himself: "What a witness she would make!"

He said to her: "I'm afraid that the case against your brother is pretty tight."

Her voice, a hard whisper, came from parted gray lips which seemed hardly to move.

"My brother did not kill Dr. Cullen."

"Who did?"

"Some one with a grudge against Rufe."

"Why do you think that some one had a grudge against him? Did he have any enemies?"

"So far as I know, none. But strange things have been happening at the clubhouse lately. As if there were ghosts. As if it were haunted."

"Did he say it was haunted?"

"He has too much sense for that."

"Do you know if any one else heard these sounds?"

"I don't know."

"Did you go down yourself to investigate them?"

"No. I could not leave this case. I intended going down

to-morrow night, because my patient no longer needs a night nurse."

"You have only your brother's word that these sounds took place, haven't you?"

"I would take his word."

"Perhaps those sounds were only in his imagination."

She nodded. "Perhaps they were. But he did not kill Dr. Cullen. He told me that these ghostly sounds had been disturbing him. He was afraid that he had been poisoned little by little by inhaling the gas that leaks from the City Gas tanks."

Gillian bent toward her. "Miss Lally, it is my very painful duty to tell you that many women have come to me, just as you have come to-night, firmly believing in the innocence of some man of whom they are fond—some man accused of this crime or that. They will continue believing in his innocence until the bitter end."

"I know my brother is innocent."

"Why did he take that revolver along?"

"Perhaps he was too terrified to know what he was doing. Perhaps his mind was a blank."

"Did any one tell you so?"

"No—but isn't it possible?"

Gillian shrugged. He was more than ever convinced that this startlingly pretty, red-headed girl knew more about the circumstances of Dr. Cullen's death than she was admitting. What, he wondered, did she know about that mysterious telephone call?

He called sharply: "Toro!"

There was a faint scuffling sound in the hall just outside the door. Toro appeared, calm, inscrutable, his black eyes without expression. Why had he been eavesdropping outside that door?

"You may go to bed, Toro. I won't need you again to-night."

"Very well, Mr. Hazeltine."

5

AN INSIDIOUS DANGER

HE SAW THAT the red-headed girl's face was once again suffused with pink, and again he wondered just what her game was. He reached into the white cardboard box, selected a cube of fudge and placed it in his mouth.

The red-headed girl watched him. She had slumped down in her chair. She sat up erectly.

"Mr. Hazeltine, I believe that some one came to the yacht club and made those sounds for a purpose."

"What purpose?"

"I don't know. I came to you because I don't know. It is a mystery. You are the one man in this whole State clever enough to clear up that mystery. Will you do it?"

"I am no longer practicing criminal law, Miss Lally."

"But you'll make an exception in this case! Please say you'll help me!" Miss Lally's eyes were large and bright. Here, Gillian realized, was a woman on the verge of tears. Tears without the aid of glycerin!

He said: "It was more than a simple decision to stop handling criminal cases. I made a promise."

"To whom?" she snapped. The words came out of her small red mouth like bullets. Gillian was startled. Before he could answer, Eileen Lally said swiftly: "Your wife?"

A wave of red crept up Gillian's neck. His face became brick-red. He said stiffly: "We won't go into that."

The amazing young woman was instantly sorry. She bent toward him and held out her hand in a placating gesture.

"I didn't mean to be personal."

"As for defending your brother," Gillian said, "you would be foolish to retain me even if I were available. I am in no physical condition to take a case as difficult as your brother's obviously is."

"You think my brother is guilty!"

"I don't say that. I do not believe in circumstantial evidence. The circumstantial evidence is against your brother. He had an excellent motive for killing Dr. Cullen. And the police are convinced that he did kill him. I would not form an opinion so early."

He paused. The girl parted her lips as if to speak, but evidently changed her mind. She compressed her lips and narrowed her eyes. They seemed to bore into Gillian. She opened her mouth again.

"In all murder trials," she said, speaking slowly, "the accused is nothing more than a pawn in a big chess game. Or, better still, a piece of scenery against which is fought a battle of wits between the counsel for the defense and the State's attorney."

"Cynical," Gillian admitted, "but reasonably true."

"Justice, the merits of the case," the girl warmly went on, "have nothing to do with the verdict. The cleverest lawyer—the smartest of the two legal fighters—triumphs over the other."

"That," Gillian disagreed, "is not always so. Truth has a way of speaking through the mouths of the smartest liars."

"But, generally," she argued, "the cleverest lawyer wins. The present district attorney is a very stupid man."

"Many people," said Gillian, "have made the mistake of thinking that. It is his public pose. It is a deliberate and very disarming and deceiving pose. The district attorney is a dangerous foe. I know."

"You have whipped him in any number of court room battles!"

"Yes," Gillian agreed, "and he would love nothing more than to see me go into court to defend your brother—in my present state of health."

THE RED-HAIRED GIRL continued to stare at him from narrowed eyes. The intensity of her stare made him uneasy. He knew now that she had a clever brain—too clever. Her lips were pursed. Her eyes reminded him of bees. They were running over his face, pausing here, going on, stopping there. From his lips they leaped to his eyes.

She said briskly: "What's wrong with your health?"

"I don't know."

"Haven't you seen a doctor?"

"I haven't a doctor. I've never needed a doctor. I've never been sick a day in my life."

"What are your symptoms?"

Gillian lifted his hands in a weary gesture.

"I've lost my pep. I want to sleep all the time. My thoughts are pretty morbid."

"When did this start?"

"It's come on gradually. Three or four weeks ago. It may be mental."

"It sounds like liver. Your eyes look a little jaundiced. Will you put that light on them?"

Gillian twisted the shade of his desk light until the light was shining on his eyes.

With red lips still pursed, she nodded.

"It may be old age," said Gillian.

And for the first time since she entered the room, a flicker of humor crossed her face, twinkled a moment in her eyes—was gone.

"You don't look older than twenty-nine or thirty, but you must be—with all the water you've sent under the bridge."

"I'm thirty-eight."

Like a breeze returning to ruffle the calm of a lake, humor returned to her face. A dimple magically appeared beside her mouth.

"You call that old?"

Gillian grinned wryly. "I don't know much about it. I didn't call it old until I began having these symptoms."

"Have you had much sickness?"

"I've never been sick a day in my life," Gillian boasted. "Until lately, I've never needed more than five hours' sleep. I've had the energy of a truck-horse. I never grew tired. Look at me now!"

She was looking at him; hadn't withdrawn her eyes for a second from his face.

"How much do you drink?"

"Not much."

"How much is 'not much'?"

"Four or five highballs a week."

"You may," said the red-haired girl, "have a slight cirrhosis of the liver. It may be something else. It certainly isn't age. Do you know what age really is?"

"Yes," said Gillian promptly. "It's growing old."

"Age," the beautiful redhead corrected him, "is the new measuring stick we use for determining how much sickness a man has had. So far we haven't been able to use it very practically. But we do know that sickness, not years, causes old age. You've never been sick in your life, you say. Therefore, according to the new medical standards, you're very young. I know men of thirty who are twice your age."

"That's comforting," said Gillian. He reached for a cube of fudge and slowly masticated it. He smiled. "You're a smart girl."

"I DON'T DENY it," said Miss Lally. "I showed how smart I was by coming straight to you—about my brother. What are you eating—fudge?" She shook her head as he reached for the box. "No, thanks; I don't eat sweets. How much of this stuff do you eat?"

"Sometimes a half pound a day."

"Never disagrees with you?"

"Hasn't so far."

"It's home-made, isn't it?"

Gillian nodded. "Clients sometimes play the Oriental trick of showing their gratitude with gifts. That humidor was one. I saved one of the worst crooks in the country from the electric chair. It happened that he did not commit the murder with which he was charged. I don't know who sends this fudge."

Miss Lally leaned forward and selected a cube.

"A woman, of course."

"Why a woman? My houseman makes fudge for me when I run out of it. Good fudge."

"As good as this?"

There was an expression in her eyes that baffled him.

"Yes."

"This fudge," said the girl, mysteriously, "was made by an expert."

"How can you tell?"

"Its creaminess. Anybody can make fudge. Only an expert can make it creamy."

Miss Lally held the lump of fudge between her thumb and forefinger and turned it this way and that as if it were a gem. But she did not taste it.

She presently returned it to the box and said in a slow deliberate voice: "May I smoke?"

"Certainly." He opened and extended toward her a silver box containing monogrammed cigarettes.

She waved it aside decisively. "No, thank you. I prefer my own." Why, he wondered, had she been so abrupt? Why had she picked up his cigar when he had gone to fetch her a drink of water? Why was she so interested in the fudge?

Her red hair glinted like new copper wire. Her pupils glowed redly before he took the match away. Her cheeks were a warm rose. She was a beauty. The line of her cheek from ear to chin made an alluring curve. She was beautiful. She knew that she was beautiful. She was, he was certain, acting. What scheme did she and that brother of hers have afoot? Merely the deliberate murder of Dr. Cullen?

The red-haired girl seemed to be lost in thought. She held her cigarette gracefully, with an air of experience. She inhaled slowly, sometimes expelling the smoke in faint blue jets from her nose. He had guessed that she was a clever little adventuress. Yet she had provided him with nothing but vague suspicions to work on. What was her racket?

SO IMMERSED WAS Gillian in the task of speculating about her that he was startled when she said casually:

"You have also the symptoms of chronic arsenic poisoning."

Gillian all but leaped out of his chair. He repeated the one alarming word hoarsely: "Arsenic!"

Her bemused eyes remained upon his face. She made a disparaging gesture with her cigarette hand.

"Only a possibility. It's hard to understand how a man with your vigor who does not eat or drink to excess would develop an ordinary cirrhosis. You don't vomit, do you?"

"No!" Gillian gasped.

"You wouldn't. Not in chronic arsenic poisoning. If it were acute, you would."

In spite of his agitation, it occurred to Gillian that all of this talk about arsenic might well be so much red herring drawn across the trail of her real intentions—whatever they were.

"It seems to me," she went on, "that a man in your position must have a great many enemies. Haven't attempts ever been made on your life?"

"Not two hours ago," Gillian answered, "some man told me I would be liable to be killed if I did not leave town."

Her eyes sparkled with innocent astonishment.

"You should be very careful."

"I cannot avoid shots in the dark or knives in the back."

"No," she said.

Gillian was growing angry. He had found, in the past, that it is difficult to detect the difference between innocence and a clever imitation of innocence. This girl baffled him.

A faint silvery tinkle downstairs caused her eyes to shine. She whispered: "Front door?"

"I think so."

"I'll answer it."

Before he could protest she was out of the room. He heard her high heels tapping on the landing; tapping again in the hall below. The sound awakened an assortment of memories, some pleasant, some painful. On the whole, it was not unpleasant to hear a woman's heels *tap-tap-tapping* in his house again.

He could not get Eileen Lally's shining brown eyes out of his mind. Did they stand for shining innocence or were they deceiving? He was certain on one point: he must watch his step.

Beautiful women had led him into mazes of trouble before. He must not permit this one to arouse his sympathies or even his interest.

He heard murmurs. A moment later: "This way, please. Yes, Mr. Hazeltine is ill." Then the sound of heavy feet ascending the stairs.

Dennis Van Zant walked into the room, his round face pink with exertion or excitement, his blue eyes more prominent than usual. They reminded Gillian of the eyes of a puppy that has gorged itself.

Van Zant radiated an air of self-conscious importance. He generally did. He had evidently stumbled upon something this time to feel very important about.

Gillian permitted his hand to be shaken by the pudgy hand of the plump little busybody.

Van Zant made clucking sounds of sympathy which, to

Gillian, were reminiscent of the cluckings of a fussy old hen.

"Gill," he gushed, "I never dreamed you were laid up!"

"Oh, it isn't serious, Van."

"But it's serious enough for you to have a trained nurse! What's the matter?"

"Nothing but a little touch of liver." Gillian did not take the trouble to set him straight on Miss Lally's status. Why bother?

"Gillian, I wouldn't have come if it hadn't been so important. But it's damned important."

"Yes?" Gillian recalled that Van had said the same thing over the telephone. How damned important it was.

Van was removing a long square bottle from his overcoat pocket. On the face of it was a black label lettered with gold. It was almost full of a clear reddish-brown liquid.

"You see this?" he demanded.

Gillian looked from the flushed, excited face of Van to the bottle of Black Label Johnny Walker.

Van said excitedly: "It's out of a case that Lally delivered to me last week!"

Gillian heard the red-haired nurse gasp.

With the bottle clutched dramatically in his hand, with his head thrown back, Van made his important disclosure.

"This stuff is poisoned!" he cried. "It's full of arsenic!"

6

CHALLENGE

GILLIAN LOOKED FROM the bottle to Dennis Van Zant, and from Van to Eileen Lally. She had stopped just inside the door, as if fearing to intrude. Van seated himself in the chair which she had been occupying. There was no longer any doubt about it: Van had finally stumbled upon something that made him as important as he had always wished to be.

The red-headed girl had caught one hand to her cheek. Her eyes were fixed on the back of Van's pink neck. They were large and, to Gillian, they looked dangerous.

Perhaps the mystery of this girl was about to be explained now. But she said nothing.

"That's serious," said Gillian to Van.

"You're darned tootin' it's serious, Gill! I'll tell you how it came about. I got suspicious of the stuff because of the way I've been feeling lately. Sleepy all the time. No ambish. No pep. I don't seem to think straight any more. Funny little sounds in my head. Queer little sensations in—"

Gillian interrupted:

"And you bought this liquor from Rufus Lally?"

"I did!"

"And you're positive there's poison in it—arsenic?"

"I'll tell the cock-eyed world I'm positive! Didn't I take this bottle down to Harry Zarrow, the city chemist, tonight? Didn't he test it before my very eyes? Will you kindly tell me why Rufus Lally should put arsenic in my Scotch? What did I ever do to him? I hardly knew the guy. I've paid him cash on the nose. When he delivers a case to me, he gets the money at once!"

Gillian glanced over Van's shoulder at Eileen Lally. She had not moved. She was still staring at the back of Van's neck.

"How," asked Gillian, "do you know that it was Lally who put arsenic in your liquor?"

"Good night, Gill! Didn't I tell you I had it tested? Didn't Zarrow tell me there's just enough arsenic in the stuff to give a man chronic arsenic poisoning if he drank a highball or two every night?"

"All very well. Van. But why pin it on Lally?"

"Jiminy, didn't I buy it from him? I'm not pinning it on anybody." Van seemed hurt.

"But you're not certain that Lally put it in."

"Of course not."

"Then take my advice as a lawyer and don't tell anybody else that Lally put arsenic in your or anybody else's booze. You can be sued for defamation of character if you perpetrate a rumor like that."

"All right, all right, all right. Only I'm going to check up on that bird. I'm going to get samples of liquor from every man he's been selling to. My personal opinion is that Lally is cracked. He has a case of hero worship on old Doc Cullen, and spends all his time reading up on poisons."

The red-haired girl broke in: "Why not? He's studying

to be a toxicologist. Isn't a man entitled to follow any career that appeals to him?"

Dennis Van Zant turned about in his chair. His prominent blue eyes ran slowly from the small black hat on her gleaming copper hair to her small feet.

"It's wrong," the girl asserted, "to accuse anybody of such a thing unless you're absolutely certain."

Gillian was tired of this argument and he was tired of Van's self importance. He went to a corner cabinet and opened a deep drawer at the bottom. From this he removed four full bottles of Black Label Johnny Walker and a fifth which was only partly full.

"TAKE THESE DOWN to Harry Zarrow's," he said, "and leave them to be analyzed. As long as you've started this, Van, why not make a night of it? Pick up samples of whisky from other members of the club. Take them to Zarrow for analysis. Arguments won't get us anywhere. We want material evidence." Van arose. He sent another glance at the pretty redhead. His air was that of a judge about to hand down a decision.

"Might I ask why you are so interested in Rufus Lally?"

"Lally," Gillian answered the question, "is this young lady's brother."

Van looked at her with round, astonished eyes.

"Her brother," Gillian continued, "was arrested an hour or so ago on the charge of murdering Dr. Cullen."

"He did not murder Dr. Cullen!" the girl cried.

Van's puppylike eyes bulged again.

"Whew!" he said. "When'd it happen? How'd it happen?"

"And my brother did not put arsenic in your whisky or anybody else's whisky!"

Van was staring vacuously at Gillian.

"Dr. Cullen," Gillian explained, "was found dead in his study this morning shortly after one o'clock. He was shot through the brain. Miss Lally's brother was captured in the study a moment after the shot was heard by the doctor's butler. Lally had a gun in his hand, still warm, with two exploded shells."

"Good night!" breathed Van.

Gillian was looking past him, and past Miss Lally. On tiptoe he ran to the doorway. Flattened against the wall was Toro. Gillian said angrily:

"What are you doing here?"

"Awaiting your commands, Mr. Hazeltine."

"I told you, a half hour ago, to go to bed."

"But I thought my services might be required, sir."

"When I require them," Gillian snapped, "I'll let you know about it."

He wanted to ask Toro what in the devil he was up to. But he knew that the Japanese would reply with a flowery evasion. With the dignity of a Buddhist monk, Toro strode down the hallway toward his room. Gillian returned to his study.

Van was gathering up the bottles of Johnny Walker. His eyes, it seemed to Gillian, were all but popping out of his pink, round head. He stuttered:

"Wh-who are the other mum-members, Gill?"

"Who has the membership list?" Gillian asked. "Who's the secretary?"

"Isn't Bruce Pennyfeather?"

"I'll call him." Gillian did so. The voice of Bruce Pennyfeather, a wholesale druggist, was presently coming sleep-

ily over the wire. But it became wakeful when Gillian had
related, briefly, a few of the night's activities.

Yes; he was the secretary of the club, and he had a list of
the members. Gillian held the phone while Pennyfeather
went for the list. His voice, on his return to the phone, was
agitated.

"Gill, there are only four of us left. Dr. Cullen was the
fifth. There's yourself, me, Van Zant and Jeffery Whitaker.
I'm coming right up to your house."

"Do so," Gillian urged him, "and bring Jeff along. Van is
here now. He'll stop at your house and Jeff's for the whisky.
Good-by!"

Gillian swung around to Van.

"Run along. Stop at Pennyfeather's and Whitaker's.
Drop the stuff at Zarrow's and come back here."

"All right, all right, all right!" In his agitation, Van let
one of the bottles fall. It smashed on the floor. He bleated,
and Gillian said: "Clear out of here. Pull yourself together."

Van almost ran out of the room, the bottles clicking in
his arms.

EILEEN LALLY WAS leaning heavily on Gillian's desk. Her
face was so white that Gillian was afraid she was about
to faint. She was blinking tears out of her eyes. A woman
crying modestly into a handkerchief was trying enough; a
woman crying shamelessly was devastating.

"You're wrong," she declared in a husky voice. "My
brother did not kill Dr. Cullen. My brother did not poison
this whisky!"

Gillian took her by the elbows and lowered her into the
chair which Van had just left.

"My dear girl, I'm not accusing your brother of killing Dr. Cullen or poisoning the whisky. I have never yet accused any man of committing any crime unless I had overwhelming proof that he was guilty. If you're going to be hysterical, lock yourself in my bedroom until you're yourself again. I haven't time for hysterics."

The telephone bell began to ring again. Gillian with a groan of impatience picked up the receiver. A woman— another hysterical woman—was at the other end.

"Gillian—Gillian! Where is Van?"

Gillian groaned anew. "Cornelia?"

"Yes! Where is Van? He left here hours ago to take some whisky to the city chemist's to be analyzed. I'm afraid something's happened to him."

"Nothing's happened to him," Gillian soothed her.

"But the whisky was poisoned! Harry Zarrow told me so! He said it was full of arsenic."

"Cornelia," Gillian said sternly, "will you calm yourself? Van didn't drink the whisky."

"But he *has* been drinking it!"

"Van is perfectly all right. He was in this room less than ten minutes ago."

"Gillian, I'm frantic with worry. I simply won't stay in this house alone a moment longer. I'm coming over."

"Cornelia, I'm going to be very busy. I'm sorry."

"I don't care. I'm coming over. I won't stay in this house alone. The cook is away for the night and I'm all alone. I'm coming right over!"

Gillian started to protest, then realized that his protestations were being uttered to an empty line. Angrily, he jammed the receiver on the hook. He turned to the red-haired girl and growled:

"Another hysterical woman!"

"I am not hysterical. Do you blame me for being so worried?"

Gillian wanted to shout: "I blame you for being a foxy little redhead with a knife up your sleeve!" But he said, soothingly:

"No, my dear. If I were you. I'm certain I would have gone to pieces long before this."

"Because you think my brother is guilty!"

"There is a dim possibility," said Gillian, "that this fighting loyalty of yours is misplaced. But I repeat that I do not consider your brother guilty. I am merely trying to piece together a few scattered shreds of evidence which may mean one thing or another."

"You've said in so many words that you think my brother is sufficiently deranged to poison the whisky he has been selling to his friends and—and benefactors. Putting arsenic in his friends' whisky!"

Gillian stared at her. Her lips were gray. Her face was as pale as death. In that tragic mask only her eyes were alive—hot, warlike brown eyes. Her lips were clamped tight. If she were acting, this was her masterpiece of the evening. Her voice, when she spoke again, was lifeless, too—dull, dreary and, to Gillian, shocking.

"YOU'VE GOT TO help me. You can't turn me away. He's innocent."

One hand was limp in her lap. The other was clenched into a small white fist with which she was softly, slowly beating on the arm of the chair.

"He did not poison that whisky! It's a frame-up—a cold-blooded frame-up!"

"Ah!" Gillian breathed. "By whom?"

"That's for your brain to find out. I told you it's a mystery—a black, horrible mystery. Some fiend had done all this and is pushing off the blame on my brother!"

Now she was beating on the arms of her chair with both fists. Hard, timed thumps.

"You've got to help! You're the only man in this State who can help!"

Gillian said firmly: "Miss Lally, I don't want to be rude. But I've got a big night's work ahead of me. I can't stand any more of this. I'm going to ask you to excuse me. In the morning, perhaps, I'll help you select an attorney."

"But you won't take charge of the defense?"

"I'm sorry."

The red-haired girl compressed her gray lips.

"I'm not going."

Gillian said nothing. He watched her. His brain said: "Acting! Acting! What in the devil has she up her sleeve? What does she know about this murder?" He smelled a rat. He suspected the existence of niggers in the woodpile.

"I'm going to stay," she insisted. "You need a nurse. I'm a good one. You won't find a better nurse in Greenfield. I'm a graduate of the Greenfield Hospital."

"This," Gillian argued, "is absurd. I don't need a nurse and I don't want a nurse. Most of all, I don't want you for a nurse."

The girl waved his protest aside with both agitated hands.

"In the morning," she rapidly went on, "we'll find whether you're an ordinary cirrhosis case or a chronic arsenic case. If it's arsenic, I want to be on hand. Whatever happens, I am going to be here. You'll find me an excellent nurse, Mr. Hazeltine."

"I won't have you. I don't want you."

"I'm going to stay. I'm going to do detective work."

Gillian reached for the telephone.

Eileen Lally demanded: "What are you going to do?"

"Phone the police. I'm going to have you locked up."

"Oh, no," said the red-haired girl.

Something in her tone arrested his hand. Gillian looked at her quizzically.

"Why not?"

"Because you aren't a coward. Because you always give the underdog a chance. And because you do need a detective in this house—perhaps to protect your own life!"

"I'll give you thirty seconds to explain that," Gillian snapped.

The red-headed girl jumped up. She hastened to the door. She cried: "Come in here, you sneak!" And stood back.

Gillian watched the doorway with breathless interest.

Toro walked in, an enigma in a cotton nightshirt.

7

AN ASTOUNDING PLOT

TORO'S HANDS WERE crossed on his chest. He might have been an Oriental priest about to perform some mystic ritual. His eyes were glimmering slits. He looked from his master to the red-haired girl, but not inquiringly. His manner was bland. His face was devoid of all expression. "You called, sir?" he asked.

The impudence of it caused Gillian to utter a short laugh. It sounded like a bark. Eileen Lally looked at Gillian and said: "Well, Mr. Hazeltine?"

Gillian snapped: "What were you doing in that hall?"

"Awaiting your commands, sir."

This time the girl laughed, shortly, and without mirth.

"I told you to go to bed."

"I retired, Mr. Hazeltine, but I returned."

"Why?" asked Gillian.

"I thought my services might be required."

"Why?" This was uttered by Gillian and the girl in the same breath.

Toro's yellow eyelids fluttered up. There was now a mysterious gleam in those black beads.

"Because, Mr. Hazeltine, I thought you might require my protection."

"From whom?"

"This young lady, sir."

"Why!" cried Miss Lally. "How preposterous!"

Gillian said grimly: "Elaborate on that, Toro."

The Japanese shrugged. His face twisted into an expression, half smile, half grimace, of humility.

"It was enough for me to know that she is the sister of the man who murdered Dr. Cullen, sir."

"That hasn't been proved," said the girl.

"The riddles of this life," was Toro's comment, "are penetrated by the powerful sunbeams of the alert intellect."

Which was the kind of reply that Gillian had expected. Toro might be guilty of any crime, but the confession of it would never issue from his lips. The girl was evidently as foxy, in her feminine fashion, as was Toro in his Oriental way. Here was a deadlock; and here were the ingredients of no end of clashes.

Gillian was a man who habitually accepted a challenge, because he liked a good fight. He did not know just what designs the Lally girl had upon him; but he was certain that, with her in the house—that flaming red hair!—he would have all the fighting he wished.

So he said, as if nothing had gone before: "Toro, this is Miss Lally. She has come to nurse me through my illness. Miss Lally, this is Toro, my houseman."

The red-haired girl said nothing. Her brown eyes were taking an inventory of the Japanese, as if she were measuring his agility, his resources, as an antagonist. Color had sprung back into her cheeks. Her lips were cherry-red again. There was a vigilant air about her. Her lifted chin, her tip-tilted nose, gave her piquancy.

An inward voice warned Gillian:

"Watch your step. This red-head is more dangerous than any you've ever met."

He said aloud: "Miss Lally is to be in absolute charge of this house."

Toro bowed graciously. His breath hissed softly through his amazingly white teeth. He murmured:

"Words would fail to convey my delight at her advent."

Eileen Lally's eyes hardened. She said crisply:

"People will be coming and going the rest of the night. It might be a good idea for you to get into some more appropriate clothes."

Gillian saw Toro's eyes flash. But the flash was instantly gone. The Japanese bowed ceremoniously. The bow was accompanied by the ceremonious hiss of his breath through his teeth.

"Miss Lally's slightest whim," he murmured, "shall be acted upon as an imperial edict from heaven."

He withdrew. Gillian watched the red-haired girl. He thought he detected a glimmer of triumph in her eyes. She had certainly scored an important point—thanks to his leniency. She had acquired power. What was she going to do with it? Not until later did she satisfy his curiosity.

THE FRONT DOORBELL was ringing again. She left the room to answer it. What, Gillian wondered, was her mystery? And what was the mystery of Toro? With two schemers who hated each other in his house, interesting developments were apt to be forthcoming. Or did they really hate each other? Gillian gave it up.

A frowzy old man came up the stairs behind Miss Lally and into Gillian's study. He must have been seventy-five years old. His face was incredibly wrinkled; his back was bent. It took Gillian perhaps five seconds to realize that the frowzy old man was quite drunk. His nose at the tip was pink. His eyes were glassy. His progress across the room was none too certain. In a quavery voice the tipsy old man said:

"You're the renowned lawyer, Gillian Hazeltine, aren't you?"

"I am," said Gillian.

"I came up here to see you," the old fellow declared, "because I've got a secret."

"That's interesting," Gillian said politely.

He looked inquiringly at Eileen Lally and wondered why she had permitted this tipsy old man to enter the house. But she was looking eagerly at the old man.

"It's a s'prise," the old man elaborated. "It's the biggest s'prise that's ever been sprung on Greenfield."

"Let's have it," said Gillian urgently.

"Yes, sir." The old man began fumbling about in his pockets.

The front doorbell was ringing again. Reluctantly Miss Lally went to answer it. But she reentered the room as Toro, dressed for his duties, hastened down the hall and downstairs.

"It's about this Lally case," the old man went on. "You knew that Dr. Cullen had been murdered?"

"I knew."

"By the caretaker of the Greenfield Yacht Club. Yes, sir. I took that story over the phone myself from Josh Hammersley. I'm the keeper of the Greenfield *Times* morgue. You know what a morgue is in a newspaper office?"

"Yes."

"Well, sir—" He paused. Toro had ushered two men into the study, Bruce Pennyfeather and Jeffery Whitaker. Pennyfeather was a tall, lean, horse-faced man with iron-gray hair and intense gray eyes. Whitaker was a few inches shorter, a square-built man, with square shoulders, a square face, a squarish head. His hair, what there was of it, was white, his face red. He was almost completely bald.

Both men were agitated. Their eyes were nervous. Both shook Gillian's hand in the solemn manner of men about to depart on long journeys on desperate causes, or of men greeting one another at funerals.

Toro magically appeared with chairs for them, and retired from the scene. The two newcomers glanced at the frowzy old man and evidently dismissed him as unimportant to the occasion.

"DR. CULLEN'S DEATH," Bruce Pennyfeather expressed himself in gloomy tones, "is a horrible shock, Gillian. I can't realize it. I had lunch with him only yesterday." The wholesale druggist wagged his head.

"And this whisky business," put in Jeffrey Whitaker. "I tell you, Gillian, it makes me sick to think about it."

"Gentlemen," broke in the tipsy old man, "I have a message for you. But first, tell me, are all of you members of the Greenfield Yacht Club?"

The three men looked at him. He had seated himself on a chair against the wall. His sunken eyes glittered at them. The heat of the room had turned the tip of his nose to the arresting color of a maraschino cherry.

"We are," said Gillian. He looked around as Dennis Van Zant entered the room, rubbing his hands.

"Well, Van, what news?"

"It's true!" panted Van. "Harry Zarrow ran a quick test on all those lots of whisky. Arsenic in 'em all, by heck!"

Gillian said: "Your wife called up a while ago, Van. She's on the way over. Hysterical."

Van groaned. "Oh, Lord! I forgot to give her a ring. She'll make a scene."

"Perhaps," Gillian said, "Miss Lally can handle her."

"I'll try," answered the red-haired girl. "There goes the doorbell again."

"Run down and tell Toro," said Gillian, "that I am home to no reporters. They'll be popping in next. If it's Mrs. Van Zant, try to quiet her. Tell her Van is here and in the pink of health. Van, will you shut that door? Gentlemen, please sit down. Here are cigars, cigarettes and matches. I'm sorry I can offer you nothing to drink."

Pennyfeather smiled grimly. Whitaker's eyes narrowed. The frowzy old man looked from one face to another and said:

"Gentlemen, have I the honor to address members of the Greenfield Yacht Club?"

"You have," said Gillian.

"My name," said the old man, "is Dan Wharton. As I was telling Mr. Hazeltine when you came in, I am the keeper of the morgue at the Greenfield *Times*. I have a sup—I have a s'prise for you."

He grinned at them. He was answered with grim stares.

"You know that Dr. Horace G. Cullen was murdered to-night by the caretaker of the Greenfield Yacht Club."

The door clicked and swung open as Gillian said: "Yes, we knew that Dr. Cullen was murdered."

A woman screamed. The five men turned and saw a slender woman clutching the doorknob, her eyes staring.

"Van!" she wailed. "Van, darling!"

Van arose with a look of disgust. Gillian sank his teeth into his cigar and silently swore. Van bored him, but Van's wife irritated him. Like Van, she was an opportunist and a busybody. She was a social climber. She had been a school-teacher until her late thirties, when she married Van. The opinion was prevalent that she had roped Van into it.

Gillian shared that opinion. He chewed his cigar to shreds as he watched her performing now. She was cling-ing to Van, patting his face. She had been so worried. Why hadn't her dear baby telephoned her as he had promised?

Gillian said, "Oh, hell," under his breath, and, aloud: "Cornelia, we're really pretty busy. Won't you wait down-stairs until this confab is over? It won't be long." Rude, but necessary.

IT WAS SELDOM that she had the chance to hold the center of any stage. He should have known better than to expect her to relinquish that glorious opportunity to dramatize her anxiety before so many men.

"Gillian, if you knew how I've suffered to-night! Please—please don't ask me that. I'll be good. Really, I will."

Gillian groaned. "Somebody bring Mrs. Van Zant a chair."

Toro did so. Cornelia seated herself beside her husband and clasped his hand. She feasted adoring eyes upon his pink, embarrassed face. Gillian almost swallowed the butt of his cigar when she said: "Sure my baby boy see's all right?"

"Sure," said Van gruffly.

Gillian took pity on him and gave him a cigar and held the light for him. Thank God he wasn't married to a Cornelia Van Zant!

He said briskly: "Toro, no one else is to be admitted to this house to-night. If any reporters come, hit them on the head with some heavy blunt object."

"Yes, Mr. Hazeltine."

Gillian finished applying a fresh light to his dead cigar and said:

"Now, gentlemen, let's get one tantalizing mystery over with. Mr. Wharton, finish your story, and kindly be concise."

Old Dan Wharton blinked at him. He looked dazed. Every one was gazing at him expectantly.

"Well, gentlemen," quavered the old man, "as I was saying: right after I took the story over the phone about Dr. Cullen's murder, I went into my morgue—"

"Your what?" wailed Cornelia.

"The morgue in a newspaper office," Gillian patiently explained, "is a room where newspaper clippings are filed for reference."

Dan Wharton's head was shaking with palsy or excitement or both. He proceeded:

"I went into my morgue, and I got an idea. I began thinking about all the people in Greenfield who've been dying off lately. And I began taking out clippings. I found that in the past eight months about forty well-known people in Greenfield have died. Most of them were of the generation that came right after mine—people ten or fifteen years younger than I am. I'm seventy-six."

He paused and looked about as if for comment, but nothing was said.

"Out of those forty people, gentlemen, nine were members of the old Greenfield Yacht Club. Here are the nine clippings referring to their deaths."

He paused again and held toward Gillian a soiled manila envelope, a fat envelope. Gillian accepted it and spilled out its contents upon his desk. Old man Wharton went on eagerly in a steadier voice:

"You will notice a curious thing when you read those clippings. Of those nine men, four died by their own hands—they shot themselves or leaped from windows. The remaining five died of the same disease—cirrhosis of the liver!"

There was a silence. Then Cornelia Van Zant exclaimed: "What does it mean?"

GILLIAN PUFFED AT his cigar and looked steadily at the old newspaper man.

"Just what conclusions," he asked, "do you draw from that?"

"I hate," the old man quaked, "to answer that. Maybe I'm just a dotty old man. But it struck me that if Rufus Lally murdered Dr. Cullen, he might have murdered these other gentlemen."

This time the silence was longer. The four surviving members of the old yacht club looked at each other. Gillian looked longest at Bruce Pennyfeather, who had gone ash-gray, as if he were about to topple over.

Gillian uttered the thought that was in the mind of each: "Who was to be the next on that list?"

He had forgotten Cornelia. With a low moan, she toppled out of her chair.

Van and Gillian lifted her from the floor; carried her into Gillian's bedroom and placed her on the bed.

Miss Lally's cool voice behind them said:

"I'll take care of her."

"You'll find spirits of ammonia in the bathroom," said Gillian. And, to Van: "You've got to take her home. We're facing a mighty grim situation."

"I don't see that," put in Jeffery Whitaker, from the study. "You've got the man locked up who's been killing our friends off."

Eileen Lally turned from the bed where lay the gasping Cornelia, and rushed into the study.

"That isn't true!" she cried. "The man who killed Dr. Cullen is in this very room! And the man who killed all these other men is here! Who else but a vile Jap would work out such a scheme—and carry it through?"

"Toro!" Gillian gasped.

8

TORO EXPLAINS—SOME THINGS

TORO DID NOT move. He stood a few feet inside the study door, his arms folded on his breast in his characteristic attitude, his beady black eyes glinting, his face a study in expressionlessness. He said nothing.

Gillian went behind him and shut the door; placed his back against it.

"Miss Lally, you will have solved a tremendously important problem if you're talking rationally."

"Don't worry about my being rational. Any poisoning that's been done, he has done."

"Just a moment," Gillian stopped her. "Dr. Cullen was killed this morning at about one o'clock."

"One fifteen," old man Wharton corrected him.

"Toro," Gillian asked, "what time was it when you came into my study—heard me talking on the phone?"

"One forty, sir."

"You were in your nightshirt, if I'm not mistaken."

"Yes, Mr, Hazeltine."

"I'm afraid, Miss Lally, that Toro has a perfect alibi."

"I beg to contradict," said Toro, "but Toro has not a perfect alibi, much as he wishes he had. At one thirty I

*The man's feet were
inches above the floor*

entered this house, after having gone out to walk and to breathe in the purity of the night air."

"He is being so frank," said Miss Lally promptly, "because some one probably saw him."

"The intuition of a woman," Toro returned, "may penetrate the basest of a man's intentions. It is true. At one thirty, when I turned off the street, I encountered Mike Callahan, the policeman on this beat. We exchanged greetings."

"Dr. Cullen's house is less than a ten minutes' walk from here," Bruce Pennyfeather put in.

"But," said Toro, "I did not pause when I passed Dr. Cullen's house."

Miss Lally lifted her hands and let them fall. Regardless of what Toro said, she had shifted a burden of suspicion to him. But Gillian was not so easily swayed.

"Did you know that Toro had taken that walk, Miss Lally?"

"No, Mr. Hazeltine; but I suspected it."

"Why?" asked Jeffery Whitaker.

"When?" asked Gillian.

She answered them slowly as follows:

"Toro has carefully avoided saying so, but he is a frequent visitor to the old yacht club. I have encountered him there, talking to my brother. When I appeared, he always slunk away."

"I did not mean to seem to slink," said Toro.

"What were you doing there?" Gillian snapped.

Toro replied: "Mr. Hazeltine, there is a species of shell-fish indigenous to the river mud of my native land which I find duplicated in the tidewater mud of the Sangamo River. I sometimes visit the Greenfield Yacht Club in search of specimens of that shellfish. It is one ingredient of a dish that I particularly fancy."

The red-haired girl snorted her incredulity. Even Gillian smiled grimly.

CORNELIA VAN ZANT came tottering out of the bedroom. She was a little less charming than Gillian had ever found her—and he had never found her charming. Her face was pale and moist. Her dark, straight hair hung down in straggling wisps about it.

"Van, darling," she got out in a frail whisper; "I've heard all that has been said. It means that we are not yet safe. Who knows but what this scheming Oriental may not murder all of us?"

"You'd better," said Gillian coldly, "take your wife home, Van."

"Come, darling," said Van wearily.

She came. She linked her arm through his; rested her weight heavily upon his shoulder. He reminded Gillian more than ever of a gorged puppy.

Toro gazed at Gillian. "Shall I accompany them to the door, sir?"

"Not a chance!" snorted Van. "I guess we can find our way home!"

When they were gone, Gillian said: "Toro, I don't know what to do with you. As an old law-breaker, you realize as well as I that I can't have you locked up, not even on suspicion."

"I am grateful for that, sir," said his houseman. "I feel that I am needed here." He looked point-blank at Miss Lally when he said this, and she glared at him.

"Both of you are needed here," said Gillian. "You both interest me."

Bruce Pennyfeather sprang up. His horselike face looked longer than ever.

"As far as I'm concerned," he said irritably, "this discussion is getting us nowhere. Words—words—words! In my opinion, the man who murdered Dr. Cullen is safely locked up. If it is true that nine other members of the club were murdered, he must have been their murderer, too. I am inclined to take a skeptical view of that theory. It is too far-fetched."

Jeffery Whitaker said explosively: "Don't be too damned sure, Bruce! Remember that Gill is an older hand at this business than either you or I. He wouldn't be wasting his time if he thought that the case was closed. My opinion is that some murderous fiend has been committing these murders; and that he still may be at large."

He looked about him with an air of defiance.

"You may call that theory far-fetched, too; but I have the feeling that the lives of the four surviving members are still in danger. Frankly, I am frightened, and I am not a physical coward. How can I sleep now, with the feeling that some one may be plotting to take my life—to steal in on me while I sleep, to poison me in some way, to stab me in the back?" He stopped and said, irritably: "Well?"

EVERY ONE LOOKED at Gillian. Only Bruce Pennyfeather wore a faint, twisted smile. The others were grim.

Gillian said slowly: "I am inclined to side with Jeff."

"Then," cried Miss Lally, "you can't believe that my brother is guilty!"

"I did not say that," responded Gillian. "No one so far has advanced the theory that your brother may have had an accomplice—or accomplices. I advance it only as a theory."

"It's an absurd theory!" the redheaded girl cried.

"Which," said Gillian, "remains to be proved—or disproved. Mr. Wharton, will you accept my thanks for paying us this invaluable visit?"

"I would lose my job," said the old man, "if the managing editor ever found I had made it. What I did tonight— bringing those clippings to you—was unethical. I should have consulted him first, but I knew they would be important to you. Maybe I can make up for it by scooping the rest of the papers with this story."

Gillian said: "Gentlemen, I must ask you to excuse me now. I have an errand to perform."

There was a concerted movement toward the door.

The red-headed girl waited until they had gone. She waited until the house was silent. She heard Toro creep down the back stairs. She walked through Gillian's bedroom and into the bathroom. A window at the far end of it overlooked the back yard. She went to this window and looked down.

The moon had set some hours before. For some moments she saw nothing but blackness. Then a white beam of light stabbed the blackness. It moved slowly off toward a thicket at the eastern end of Gillian's property. It flashed on and off.

Miss Lally hastened back into Gillian's study. Every one, it seemed, had some important errand to perform. So had she. She began opening desk drawers and shutting them. Finally she found that for which she was searching—a pearl-handled revolver. She broke it open dexterously and lifted out one of the shells. She dropped the shell back into the chamber, snapped the gun shut and hastened downstairs.

9

AT THE DISTRICT ATTORNEY'S

MR. ADELBERT YISTLE was enacting his favorite role—that of a boob. Mr. Yistle was not a boob. But he preferred having the public believe that he was one. As a young lawyer—early in his career—the first time he was called upon to address a jury, he had been so awkward, so tongue-tied, so completely the boob, that the jury, without any regard for the merits of the case, but out of sheer sympathy for Mr. Yistle, had given his client the verdict. And Mr. Yistle, being a smart young man, had had sense enough to realize why the jury had brought in that verdict. The lesson was a valuable one. Thenceforward, he was, before juries, a boob. When he tried cases before judges, he was not a boob. In short: Mr. Adelbert Yistle knew how to play his game as district attorney.

Mr. Yistle was playing the boob now for the benefit of the smallest possible audience—one. He was pounding softly on his desk with a mighty fist. A square-built man, with a judicial forehead surmounted by a mop of iron-gray hair, and a pair of massive jaws surmounted by an iron-gray mustache, Mr. Yistle was a commanding figure.

"Fear your enemy most when he appears to be softest," said Mr. Yistle to his assistant, Mr. Bullock. He repeated the words as if he relished them. "Fear your enemy most when he appears to be softest. When he is at the end of his rope, when he is flat on his back, when his resources appear to be exhausted—fear your enemy, Mr. Bullock!"

Mr. Bullock, who was a pale, thin young man with kind blue eyes, a disappearing chin and a prominent Adam's apple, said: "Yes, sir!" effusively and clinched his remark with: "You're absolutely right, Mr. Yistle!"

The district attorney looked at Mr. Bullock indulgently. He enjoyed kidding Mr. Bullock. He enjoyed saying meaningless things in a ponderous way—as he often said them to juries—and he enjoyed Mr. Bullock's responses. Mr. Bullock had more synonyms for the word "Yes" than any five men Mr. Yistle knew. Mr. Bullock was the champion long-distance yes-man.

Mr. Bullock acted like a boob because he could not help himself. But he was not a boob. He was a clever young lawyer who chanced to have a case of terrific hero worship. He thought that Mr. Yistle was the greatest lawyer in the world. Mr. Yistle did not repay that admiration with the kindliness which it perhaps deserved. We may as well admit that Mr. Yistle had a streak, a wide streak, of cruelty in his make-up.

Now he became serious. He paced the great Bokhara rug on his living room floor and eased his mind. He said:

"There is no question but that the grand jury will return an indictment against this Rufus Lally for the murder. And there is no question that Lally's case, when it comes to trial, will be one of the most sensational we will be called upon to prosecute this term."

"Indubitably," assented Mr. Bullock.

Mr. Yistle looked at him with a faint smile. "Indubitably" was Mr. Bullock's latest addition to his long list of words meaning "Yes."

THE DISTRICT ATTORNEY forcefully went on:

"I am curious to know if Gillian Hazeltine will put his oar in. This is precisely the kind of case in which, in the old days, he would have been most interested. Spectacular! Sensational! Sordid! Shameful! It is a tainted case, Bullock. It is the kind of case which might turn unexpectedly against the smartest prosecution. Alienists might easily befog the issue to such an extent that the murderer, at the hands of a bewildered, chicken-hearted jury, would be given a verdict. I hope you realize that, Bullock."

"Emphatically, Mr. Yistle!"

"From what the chief of the homicide squad just said on the phone," continued the district attorney, "the mind of this Lally is unbalanced. He will naturally enter an insanity plea—throw himself on the jury's mercy. We must prevent that."

"Yes, *sir!*"

"We must therefore prepare our prosecution with more than usual pains. We must leave no stone unturned."

Mr. Yistle brought his great fist smashing down to the library table. The lamp jumped. Books jumped.

He roared: "We must send that scoundrel to the electric chair if it is the last act of our lives! You are to devote yourself exclusively to this case. Hire all the expert witnesses you wish. Sending that rascal to the chair, letting him writhe in agony for this crime that he has committed, it is our public duty, Mr. Bullock!"

Mr. Yistle's eloquence suddenly ebbed. Mr. Yistle looked a little ashamed. He cleared his throat and said:

"Yes, Jarves?"

His butler had entered the room; was standing just inside the doorway: an Englishman whom Mrs. Yistle had hired and of whom Mr. Yistle stood in awe.

"Yes, Jarves?"

"Two gentlemen are here to see you, sir: Mr. Whitaker and Mr. Zarrow."

"Send them right in."

Jeffery Whitaker, looking more grim than ever, came into the library, followed by Harry Zarrow, the city chemist. Zarrow was a sallow-faced young man, prematurely bald. He wore thick, gold-rimmed spectacles which gave him a scientific look. His demeanor was exceedingly calm. He even looked a little bored.

"I suppose," said Jeff Whitaker, "that you have heard of Dr. Cullen's murder, Mr. Yistle."

"We were discussing it," admitted the district attorney.

"And I presume that you know Mr. Zarrow."

"I know Harry well," said Mr. Yistle. He knew Harry Zarrow so well that he did not like him in the least. Harry had often figured as an expert witness, both for and against Mr. Yistle and the People. Harry was an honest man; he never told lies on the witness stand or committed them in his laboratory, but his fees, as a witness, were exorbitant.

"Have you heard," Mr. Whitaker asked, "about the poisoned whisky?"

The district attorney blinked at him.

"What poisoned whisky?"

"The whisky that Rufus Lally was selling to members of the Greenfield Yacht Club."

Mr. Yistle stared at him.

"This is news," he said. "Be seated, Mr. Whitaker."

"To make a long story short," Mr. Whitaker began, "Rufus Lally was a bootlegger. Every week a rum runner delivered to him a consignment of whisky which Lally then distributed among the various members of the club. Being a member of the club, I chanced to be one of Lally's steady customers.

"We have discovered, thanks to Dennis Van Zant and Mr. Zarrow here, that Lally has been putting arsenic in that whisky!"

"Amazing!" breathed Mr. Yistle. "How did you discover it?"

"A month or so ago," Mr. Whitaker answered, "I noticed that I was feeling groggy, dull, pepless. On comparing notes, I find that Gillian Hazeltine, Dennis Van Zant, and Bruce Pennyfeather have observed the same symptoms in themselves. Our suspicions aroused, we sent samples of the stuff to Harry Zarrow. He confirmed our worst suspicions. Mr. Zarrow, will you kindly tell the district attorney what you found in that whisky—what poison?"

MR. YISTLE, MR. Bullock and Mr. Whitaker looked at Harry Zarrow. The chemist looked bored. He always looked bored when people became dramatic over chemicals. To him they were mathematical symbols. He answered in a laconic voice:

"Arsenic."

"Arsenic!" exclaimed Mr. Yistle.

"Arsenic!" bleated Mr. Bullock.

"Arsenic," reiterated Mr. Whitaker.

"How much arsenic, Harry?" asked the district attorney.

"Well," said the chemist with a sigh, "I didn't make a thorough quantitative analysis—nothing but a simple arsenious trisulfide precipitate test. And by the way, Adelbert—with a cold look at Mr. Yistle—"we might as well have it understood that I am not going to testify in this case for a lousy twenty-five dollars a day."

"We will discuss that later," said Mr. Yistle stiffly.

"I don't care how much later we discuss it," drawled the chemist, "but it has got to be OK with me or I'll get sick and not testify at all. Just paste that in your hat!"

"In other words," Mr. Whitaker, impatient at this quibbling, went on; "the symptoms that Gillian Hazeltine, Dennis Van Zant, Bruce Pennyfeather and I have been suffering are the symptoms of chronic arsenic poisoning!"

"Good Lord!" murmured Mr. Yistle. "I knew, of course, that Lally had been interested in poisons, preparing himself to become a toxicologist, but I never dreamed—"

"And that is not all, Mr. Yistle," Mr. Whitaker interrupted. "We four men who are the surviving members of the old yacht club feel that the finger of doom is pointed at us. Why? The fifth to go was Dr. Cullen. In the past eight months, so we have discovered, nine other members died, and of those, five died of cirrhosis of the liver—which is a disease closely resembling, in its symptoms, chronic arsenic poisoning!"

Mr. Yistle stared at him with every evidence of horror. But Mr. Yistle was not in the least horrified. His mind did not run in such obvious channels. He was thinking of the importance of this case. If these amazing suspicions were founded in fact and could be proved—if it were verified that Rufus Lally was the murderer not only of Dr. Cullen, but of from five to nine other prominent citizens—it would become the most sensational case that he had ever handled.

While he fixed eyes glittering and dark with horror upon Mr. Whitaker, Mr. Yistle thought on: The Lally case would excite the national imagination. It would draw special correspondents from the New York and Chicago papers. It would attract armies of motion picture photographers. Mr. Yistle, glimpsing himself thus in the dazzle and glare of limelight, was not displeased. He had one eye fixed unwaveringly upon the governor's mansion. This case would give him much worthwhile publicity.

And the only obstacle which might have stood in the way of his triumph was removed. Gillian Hazeltine, with his brain dopey from arsenic, would be in no condition to touch this case. Mr. Yistle was glad that Gillian Hazeltine had chronic arsenic poisoning. Mr. Yistle was not a hypocrite. He frankly and cordially hated Gillian—hated him because Gillian was so much foxier than he; hated him because Gillian had once made of him a laughing-stock. But Gillian had given up criminal law. And Gillian was a sick man.

Mr. Yistle rubbed his hands together, but with no appearance of glee. His eyes remained horrified.

"You can rest assured, Mr. Whitaker," he said vigorously, "that I will send that scoundrel to the chair."

"**BUT THAT IS** not the point," argued Mr. Whitaker, his face seeming redder and his jaw squarer than before. "I am not a coward, Mr. Yistle, but I am frankly afraid. We are certain—Gillian Hazeltine is certain—that Lally must have had an accomplice or accomplices."

"Utter nonsense!" snapped Mr. Yistle.

"It seems," went on Whitaker, "that Hazeltine's house-man, a Japanese, has been, secretly, on intimate terms with Lally. He may even have committed the murder. Another very likely suspect, in connection with these poison cases, is Lally's sister. She and Lally are both beneficiaries under Dr. Cullen's will."

"I refuse to accept that theory," stated Mr. Yistle. "It is just like Hazeltine to befog the issue. Thank God he is not going to take this case—or another red-handed murderer might go free! There is no question in my mind that Lally deliberately planned these murders—including yours, Mr. Whitaker—not because he is insane—oh, no, he is not insane!—but because, in his zest as a toxicologist, he wished to watch the effect of arsenic on his victims. I would say, offhand, that he murdered Dr. Cullen because the doctor was getting wise to him."

"The thing that puzzles me most," said Jeff Whitaker, "is the fact that Gillian Hazeltine has hired Lally's sister as his trained nurse."

Mr. Yistle stared at him. "Is that true?"

"Yes, Mr. Yistle."

The district attorney strode across the room to a telephone which sat on a table. He picked it up and called Gillian's number. There was no response. He restored the receiver to the hook after a long wait, and said:

"Gentlemen, you will have to excuse me. I have important business to do. Mr. Bullock, if I don't see you before morning, be sure to be at the homicide court when Lally is brought up for hearing. If he is not represented by counsel, I want to know whom the court appoints."

Mr. Yistle, while startled eyes followed him, hastened to a handsome mahogany desk of the colonial period. From the bottom drawer he removed a .45 caliber army automatic pistol. This he thrust into his hip pocket.

"Mr. Bullock, I'd like a word with you alone."

His assistant trotted after him into the hall. In a low voice, the district attorney said:

"Keep Whitaker talking—about anything, until you have a chance to slip out of the room and call police headquarters. I want him followed from now on, day and night. He's one of the worst crooks in Greenfield. He may even be involved in this case. He's much too eager. When you've attended to that, begin checking up on this Lally girl.

"You can also check up on Hazeltine's houseman. I know there's a suspended sentence hanging over him—something to do with drugs. Why is Lally's sister nursing Hazeltine? What is back of it? Bullock, so help me, if Hazeltine butts into this case, I'll smash him! I'll make him wish he'd never entered a court room!"

10

A MYSTERIOUS ATTACK

GILLIAN HAZELTINE HAD, upon leaving his house, entered his coupé, driven it halfway down the block, switched off the ignition and lights and parked. He waited until all of his callers had departed. He waited until the red-haired girl came down the steps and started toward Riverside Boulevard. Then he started the car and gave chase. She wore a small black hat and a blue raincoat.

At the corner of Riverside and Maplewood the girl boarded a Summit Avenue street car—an owl. Gillian pursued the street car through the residential district, through the business district and beyond. At the corner of Summit Avenue and Dover Street, the girl in the blue raincoat alighted. She drew the raincoat tightly about her as she started down Dover toward the river.

Gillian parked his car and followed. The secrecy of his pursuit was abetted by a cold, dense fog which had rolled in from the Atlantic within the past half hour. It placed fantastic halos about the street lights. It deadened sound. A whistle on the river sounded eerie, remote.

Great sprawling shadows in the fog became mysterious and threatening monsters. With the steady, cold breeze came the acrid odor of illuminating gas.

It was, for a girl, a dangerous neighborhood. Raucous voices, a woman's drunken shriek burst from a frowning building with light streaming from the edges of shades.

A door opened. A man came lurching out. Light fell in a flood on the white face of the girl in the blue raincoat.

Gillian paused. The man shouted at her and beckoned. She ran into the enveloping fog. The man cursed. Miss Lally ran on.

Gillian did not see her again until he reached the railroad crossing—the bottle neck into the storage yards of the Western & Southern. Here, the red-haired girl paused while a switch engine clanked by. Gray smoke Swirled about her, smarted her eyes, made her cough.

She hastened across the tracks toward the misted skeletons within which the tanks of the City Gas Company mysteriously rose and fell. Reaching River Street, she turned south, hugging a tall steel fence, bending her head against the fog. She was walking more slowly now and looking alertly from side to side. Gillian kept a hundred feet behind her.

An automobile slithered past. It was a closed car, long and gray. Not until it was well past did it occur to Gillian that the car had been without lights—a gray ghost of a car slinking through the fog.

The girl ahead of him began to run. By the time the car had vanished, the girl had reached the opening in the shabby wooden fence which inclosed the yacht club property.

Gillian waited at the opening in the fence until he saw a light in her hand flash on. It played along the eastern side of the clubhouse.

She stood perfectly still, as if listening. She waited for perhaps twenty seconds. Gillian heard nothing save a persistent dripping sound—drops of water, freeing themselves from the withered skeletons of willow trees and spattering in the mud.

Extinguishing the light, the girl encircled the northern wing of the building. Gillian, careful to make no sound, followed. Again the flash light in her hand flicked on. This time its beam was directed against the kitchen door.

Black water gurgled. The wind was growing stronger. The timbers of some invisible boat groaned as a wave washed it against a pile.

THE RED-HAIRED GIRL removed a key from her purse and inserted it in the lock. But the door was unlocked. She replaced the key in her purse and entered the kitchen. She closed the door silently. Gillian listened intently, hoping that she would not lock it from the inside.

Gillian moved cautiously to a window beside the door. The girl was standing in the middle of the kitchen looking at the drainboard. A skillet, a saucepan, a plate, a cup, a saucer and silverware were on the drainboard.

The window was filmed with greasy soot. Gillian rubbed a spot clean with the tip of a gloved finger. He saw the girl reach down and pick up a pair of shoes which stood under the sink. They were black shoes and covered with mud. The girl dropped them as if she had been shocked, and the light in her other hand wavered.

She then walked across the kitchen and entered the service pantry. Gillian encircled the building, this time on the west side, and saw the red-haired girl walk through the dining room and into the trophy room. He took his position at another window and was deeply interested in the expression on her face when a large river rat scampered across the floor, close to her feet. She was not, apparently, startled or frightened, although the light from the flash light, diffused against her face by the light walls, was poor. She did not move, but watched the rat until it disappeared in the direction of the kitchen.

The red-haired girl sprayed the light about the room. Several objects evidently aroused her interest. One was a book, lying face down on the floor, a book with a dark-blue binding. Near by was a small red dish, and scattered about near this were a dozen or more dusty and broken brown lumps. Fudge! Gillian watched her with growing interest.

She picked up the book and glanced at its title page. She closed it and placed it on the desk. She then knelt down and scooped up the fragments of fudge into her hands. These she carried to the fireplace and tossed them into the thick bed of ashes. Returning, she picked up the red dish, wiped it clean with a rag she found on the desk, and placed the dish in her purse.

The red-haired girl was very pale. The light went off. Gillian anxiously waited, listening. He wondered who had been in that gray sedan. He was certain he heard footsteps on the other side of the clubhouse, then all sounds were banished by the near-by chugging of a locomotive.

The flash light went on again. Gillian went to the hall door and looked through the window. The girl was slowly climbing the steps which led into the sail loft. He waited until she reached the top, then tried the door. It was locked. He hastened to the kitchen and let himself in; fumbled through the service pantry and dining room and so into the hall.

He stopped at the foot of the stairs and listened. Two sounds occurred simultaneously. One was from the girl in the sail loft—a faint cry, as of alarm; the other was the soft clicking of the latch in the kitchen door. The pursuer was evidently being pursued!

There were further sounds from the sail loft, a heavy dragging sound, then a scuffling. Firm footsteps sounded in the kitchen.

Gillian went up the stairs. The sail loft was in total darkness. He said tensely: "Miss Lally!"

She cried: "Help me! Quick!"

Then powerful hands closed upon Gillian's throat. He spun about, trying to free himself. He struck out with both fists, one of which engaged his unknown assailant on the chin. The other went wild. He heard a grunt, as of pain, and struck again. This time both fists struck the unknown's face.

A third time Gillian struck out. His mysterious antagonist uttered a curse. This was followed by a heavy thud. Evidently the man was knocked out—or, at least, down.

He called: "Miss Lally, where's your light! Turn it on, please!"

SHE ANSWERED, CLOSE at hand, in a gasping voice: "Strike a match! Come here and help me!"

A hand reached out and closed firmly on Gillian's ankle. Gillian kicked it with his other foot. The man on the floor cursed.

Gillian started toward where the red-haired girl's voice had originated. He stumbled over something, and fell to his hands and knees. Dust rose into his nostrils. He coughed. His groping hand encountered a smooth metal cylinder. It was a pocket flash light. He found the slide and depressed it.

The beam shot out and played upon a strange panto-mime. A few feet beyond him a tall dark figure was stand-ing, moving slightly, almost imperceptibly, from side to side. All Gillian saw at first were the man's shoes and the lower legs of his trousers. Beside the legs stood a box. On this box stood Miss Lally.

Gillian, dazed by his fall, looked at the man's feet with growing incredulity. Defying the law of gravity, the man was standing four inches above the floor.

Gillian sent the beam of light traveling upward. It came to rest on the face of Bruce Pennyfeather. The face was purple. Bulging glazed eyes stared at him. From his neck a rope ran upward to a block and tackle attached to a peg.

Miss Lally was trying to untie a knot in the rope. She exclaimed:

"This man is alive. Hurry!"

She jumped down from the box and Gillian climbed up. The knot was too tight for him to loosen. He opened his penknife and hacked away at the rope until Bruce Penny-feather fell. Gillian removed the noose from his neck and said to the girl:

"Do what you can for him. He looks dead to me. I'll go down and phone for a doctor."

"No, you won't!" growled the man whom Gillian had knocked down. He was lying face down. Now he rolled over and sat up.

Gillian stared at him and exclaimed: "Good Lord, Bert! So it was you!"

The district attorney groaned. One eye was closed and already beginning to discolor. Blood was running in a threadlike stream from one corner of his mouth.

Mr. Yistle fumbled in his right hand coat pocket and brought forth a small metallic object which glittered as he placed it to his mouth. He blew, but so feeble was the blast that the police whistle gave but a weak trill.

"I'll do it," said Gillian. He took the whistle and blew upon it vigorously.

Bruce Pennyfeather groaned. His chest began to heave. Miss Lally said: "He'll be around in a minute."

"All right," said Gillian. "Now tell me what you know about this. Talk fast, because the police will be here in a moment. It's surrounded. The district attorney was taking no chances. He never does."

"That," muttered Mr. Yistle, "is a lie. And I'm going to have you locked up on a charge of felonious assault."

"And be laughed out of town," said Gillian with grim humor. "Talk up, Miss Lally."

She whimpered: "Please take me out of this horrible place before I go to pieces. How can I think."

"You'd better try."

"I came here to see if I could find some proof that my brother did not kill Dr. Cullen."

"Does this prove it?"

"I'm certain that something could be found that would prove that his story is true—that some one came here and made sounds to frighten him, to make him believe this place is haunted."

"You're sticking to that story, are you?"

"Yes."

"What have you found?"

"Only a pair of warm shoes."

"Warm?"

"In the kitchen—"

DOWNSTAIRS A DOOR slammed. There was a murmur of voices, then a shrill squeal, as of protest. Heavy feet trampled on the stairs. Miss Lally said breathlessly:

"Whoever wore those shoes—"

The room seemed suddenly to blaze with flash lights. Behind them were broad shoulders. Brass buttons glittered. A deep voice growled: "Git in there, yuh rat!" And a small man with a yellow face was pushed in.

Miss Lally's eyes narrowed. She said excitedly:

"There's your man!"

Gillian seized his houseman by the elbow and snapped: "Toro, what are you doing here?"

"Seeking evidence, Mr, Hazeltine."

The district attorney was swaying on his feet, holding a handkerchief to his injured eye. He was the focal point of a half dozen police flash lights. A sergeant murmured:

"Faith! Who did that to your face, Mr. Yistle?"

"Never mind! I ran into a door! Take those damned lights away."

The lights were withdrawn from Mr. Yistle's face and distributed elsewhere. Some of them beamed on Gillian, others on the red-haired girl. Then the gasping man on the floor was discovered. Bruce Pennyfeather's hands were moving now. His mouth was open and he was breathing noisily.

Two policemen sat him up. One of them thumped him on the back. Mr. Pennyfeather coughed. The focal point of all the lights, he blinked his eyes and coughed again—a faint, strangling cough.

"We found him up here," said Gillian, "hanging by a rope to a peg in the ceiling. What happened, Bruce—trying to commit suicide again?"

Mr. Penny feather would not or could not answer. His head was bent forward. His chin rested on his chest. His fingers were groping at his neck.

"I'm sick," he moaned.

The sergeant knelt beside him, placed a comradely arm about his shoulder.

"What happened, Mr. Pennyfeather?"

"I—I was assaulted," said the wholesale druggist in a husky whisper. "I was assaulted and carried up here and hung up by that rope—to die."

"Who did it?"

"I—don't know."

"Where did all this happen?" Gillian prompted him.

"Here—out on the road. I came down here to—have a look at the place. Some one must have climbed into my car. Whoever it was, he reached from behind and fastened his hands about my throat. He carried me into the club-house. He struck me a terrific blow on the back of my head. I remember nothing more."

The sergeant investigated the back of the wholesale druggist's head with his fingers.

"I don't feel no bumps," he announced.

"You didn't see your assailant?" Gillian questioned.

"N-no."

"It sounds fishy to me," said the sergeant. "Things like that don't happen."

"If you're holding back any truth," Gillian said sternly, "you'd better think fast and talk. This wouldn't be the first time you tried to take your life, Bruce. Any attempt at suicide on this particular night might have a particularly significant meaning. Where were you when Dr. Cullen was murdered?"

Bruce Pennyfeather considered. He groaned again.

"I was out driving."

"With whom?"

"Alone." He raised his head and blinked into the lights. "Gillian, you can believe me or not. I don't care a damn what you believe. I was attacked and strangled by some one—some powerful man. I didn't try to commit suicide."

"WELL," GROWLED THE sergeant, "maybe this guy knows something about it. Bring that Chink over here."

"I am not a Chink," Toro stated calmly. "I am a Japanese."

"This girl," put in Mr. Yistle, "may know more about this than she pretends."

"I do," said the red-haired girl in a hard little voice. "I know who did it. That Jap did it!"

The flash lights were now focused on her white, strained face.

Gillian asked: "What makes you so sure, Miss Lally?"

"I am sure enough. Before you men trample them all away, look at the footprints, the heel marks, in the dust on this floor. Then compare them with the shoes you'll find under the sink in the kitchen."

"Sergeant," said the district attorney, "send a man down to the kitchen for those shoes."

A man was dispatched for the shoes. Gillian asked: "Where did you pick up Toro, sergeant?"

"He was in this building, Mr. Hazeltine. He was climbin' out of a window when we saw him and grabbed him."

The man returned with the shoes. The sergeant examined them. He placed one of them on a footprint in the dust. It appeared to match the footprint perfectly. He shook the shoes at Toro.

"These yours?"

"Yes!" cried Miss Lally.

"Yes," admitted Toro.

"He wears them," the red-haired girl insisted, "when he comes down here. He is all the time coming down here. He wears these to walk around in the river mud, so that he won't spoil his other shoes. My brother lets him keep them in the kitchen."

"This is gettin' complicated," said the sergeant. "So you're the sister of the guy we pinched for killin' Dr. Cullen!"

"My brother did not kill Dr. Cullen! That Jap did! Where was he when Dr. Cullen was murdered? Ask him!"

"Where," growled the sergeant, "were you—you yeller rat?"

"I was taking a walk," said Toro.

"Alone?"

"Quite—alas—alone!"

"What," Gillian broke in, "were you doing down here to-night?"

"I was seeking evidence, Mr. Hazeltine, to confirm a theory I had formed earlier in the evening."

"Never mind your theories," the sergeant growled.

"This," said Toro imperturbably, "is a theory rich in

merit. To-night when I saw this young lady, I was suspicious of her."

"Why?" Gillian snapped.

"Because she is the sister of the man accused of murdering poor Dr. Cullen. You wondered, Mr. Hazeltine, when I hovered about in the doorway. It was to watch her. I wished to enlighten myself upon a mystery. Why was she so deeply interested in a box of fudge upon your desk? When I learned that you are suffering from chronic arsenic poisoning, my interest in that fudge became even keener. You do not drink enough whisky to have been poisoned by the arsenic it contained. That fudge has been coming anonymously to you, Mr. Hazeltine. In light of the sinister circumstances, I merely wish that you would have that fudge analyzed."

"He's talking," the red-haired girl cried, "to cover his own crookedness. Why was he here to-night?"

"Because," answered Toro, "I presumed that you would be here. I wished to observe you. I did. I saw you gather up spilled fudge from the floor. I saw you dispose of it in the fireplace and hide the dish."

"That dish," said the red-haired girl, "is an heirloom."

Mr. Yistle snorted. "What, I'd like to know, has fudge got to do with the murder of Dr. Cullen and the attempted murder of Mr. Pennyfeather?"

"It might," Gillian reasoned, "have a great deal to do with it."

"I'm convinced," argued Mr. Yistle, "that this girl is, in some way, connected with the attempt at killing Mr. Pennyfeather."

"I CAN GIVE her a clean bill of health—on that point," said Gillian. "I followed her here from my house.

I followed her into this building. She was alone."

The district attorney uttered a sharp, short laugh. There was no mirth in it.

"Give me credit for some intelligence, Gillian. God knows what you have got up your sleeve, but you aren't going to put anything over on me. You're up to something foxy. I'm certain that this girl knows more about Dr. Cullen's murder than she's admitting."

"I repeat," put in Toro, "that I would be relieved if you had that fudge on your study desk analyzed for arsenic. A grain of sand can obscure the view of an ocean."

The red-haired girl glared at the Japanese. And Toro, lifting the curtain of inscrutability from his eyes for the first time to-night, glared at her.

The district attorney snorted. "I think they're both lying. I think they're both acting. My opinion is that they're both in on this. It lays a nasty mess at your doorstep, Gillian: Your trained nurse and your houseman accomplices to a murder! Sergeant, you'd better lock them both up."

"On what charge?" Gillian demanded.

"As accomplices."

"Prove it!"

The sergeant interrupted: "Gents, I ought to have somethin' to say about this. Ain't you both workin' a little bit ahead of the grand jury?"

"Don't worry about this case getting to the grand jury!" Mr. Yistle cried. "Lock them both up, sergeant!"

"You can't do it," Gillian protested. "If you lock either

of them up you're going to have the fight of your life on your hands."

The district attorney laughed again. "You mean," he said with heavy irony, "your sense of justice is outraged and you're going into court to defend them."

"I am," snapped Gillian.

"Supposing," said Mr. Yistle humorously, "we strike a bargain. I'll admit I haven't much evidence against the girl, although I may have later. But I'm going to hold this Jap."

"If you hold him," Gillian responded, "I'll go into court and—"

"Defend Lally?"

"Yes."

"Sergeant," said Mr. Yistle, "that Jap is under arrest. Take him along. Book him for felonious assault."

He turned to Gillian. "You jury fixer! You judge briber! I'm warning you! If you pull any of your crooked tricks I'll have you disbarred!"

11

PREPARING FOR BATTLE

THE SUN WAS breaking through the fog when Gillian turned his car into his driveway. He parked it at the side door and wearily climbed out.

The paper boy had left the Greenfield *Times* between two of the porch palings. Gillian plucked it out, leaned, heavily against the roofpost and read the screaming headline:

DR. CULLEN KILLED BY MADMAN

He glanced through the account of the murder, and went into the house. It would be a big day for the newspapers. The afternoon papers, the tabloids, would pick up the story; ensuing editions would screech with developments." The city would buzz with it. Business men over luncheon tables would discuss it heatedly. Clerks would steal time from their work to argue about it with stenographers. Day laborers would lean on their picks and shovels and exchange weighty opinions.

Before nightfall a terrific force of public sentiment would be in motion. This force would be directed, a rising tide, against Rufus Lally.

There had been a time when Gillian would have welcomed this overwhelming public sentiment against a client. He loved a good battle. But now he did not feel equal to it. He was not, mentally or physically, prepared for battle. His brain was dull, sluggish.

Gillian wearily climbed the stairs to his study, certain that he had undertaken the most difficult case of his entire career. The light was still burning on his desk. The drawer from which Miss Lally had removed his revolver was still open. He reached into the golden humidor for a cigar, bit off the end and lighted it.

Gillian picked up the box of fudge. He placed the cover upon it and dropped it into his coat pocket. He went downstairs and reentered the car.

Gillian drove rapidly down town. He stopped his car beside the small, dingy brick building which housed, with other industries, the laboratory of the city chemist. Harry Zarrow, with a stained white rubber apron over his clothes, met him inside the door. Harry had worked most of the night analyzing whisky. He needed a shave. His face was gaunt and dirty and his eyes were bloodshot and sunken.

"How much of a job is it," Gillian asked, "to run off an arsenic test?"

"Are you kidding me?" Harry asked. "Or have you another batch of bum booze to be analyzed?"

"All I want to know," Gillian answered, removing the box of fudge from his pocket, "is whether or not this candy contains arsenic."

"Gillian, in the course of the next day or two, as soon as this news comes out, everybody in this neck of the woods is going to want whisky, candy, jelly and everything else analyzed for arsenic. Is it important?"

Gillian said: "The outcome of this test may give me a close guess as to who murdered Dr. Cullen."

"I thought they had the murderer locked up."

"They've got the wrong man locked up."

"That means you're going to defend him. But can you get him off?"

"He has a fighting chance."

"And if you do the fighting, he'll get off—maybe! I understand Yistle is after you, tooth, nail and claw."

"He always was."

"Well, he'll know he's been in a fight. Come with me and I'll analyze your damned candy."

GILLIAN FOLLOWED HIM into a small, sour-smelling room which was full of the strange paraphernalia peculiar to the science of chemistry—retorts, flasks, condensers, long glass tubes, Bunsen burners, bottles of chemicals.

The chemist began setting up an apparatus on a table. Gillian watched with intense interest. Harry Zarrow had, with his strange apparatus, been instrumental in saving so many men from the electric chair—and sending so many others to the same unpopular piece of furniture—that the effect of test tubes upon the majestic course of the law no longer excited him.

He laconically explained:

"We make hydrogen in this bottle, Gillian. The hydrogen—a gas—passes through this U-tube, which is filled with calcium chloride to remove all moisture. The dried gas then passes through this long, hard-glass tube under which this burner is placed. Presto!"

He struck a match and held it to the tapering tip of the tube. A flame sprang to life and hovered there.

"That, Gillian, is burning hydrogen. You'd better become familiar with this procedure, as you're apt to have to know about it for your big trial scene. Now, through this funnel and into the flask, I put a few drops of a solution containing a sample of your fudge. By the way, who made the fudge?"

Gillian did not answer. His eyes were fixed upon the dish in Harry's hand, from which a brown liquid was dripping into the funnel. The funnel was attached to a long glass tube running through a rubber stopper into the flask.

"What happens?" Gillian nervously asked.

"If there is arsenic present," the chemist answered, "the gas now coming through and burning is one of the deadliest of known poisons—quite as deadly as the poison gases our highly civilized armies used for killing each other in the war. If this flame should go out and if the gas contained arsenic, a few whiffs would kill us both. Now! Get that smell, Gill?"

Gillian sniffed. He detected an offensive odor.

"What does it mean?"

"Watch!" Harry picked up a white porcelain disk. He held it over the flame. Where the flame played upon the glossy white surface a bright yellow spot was forming.

"Notice the metallic luster?" the chemist demanded. "That is arsenious trisulfide!"

"Meaning that there is arsenic in the fudge?"

"Yep. There's arsenic in your fudge. And I suppose you'll thunder it forth in a hushed court room and send some poor rat to the chair."

"It won't be Lally."

"Who will it be?"

"I haven't decided. In the meanwhile, you'll do me a big favor by forgetting my arsenical fudge."

"Consider it forgotten. I hope you win your case. It's going to cost you a hundred dollars a day for my testimony. As I told Bert Yistle, I'm through being the key witness in these murder trials that are making you fellows rich and famous unless I get mine."

"You'll get yours. Thanks, Harry."

"So long," said the weary chemist. The revelation in the sordid little laboratory had cleared the cobwebs from Gillian's brain. He had, in a twinkling, penetrated to the motive behind those other successful and unsuccessful attempts at murder with arsenic. To uncover the identity of the real murderer was now largely a matter of eliminating the innocents.

A newsboy was shouting as Gillian approached his car. Gillian whistled, bought an extra and frowned at the screaming headline:

LALLY CONFESSES CULLEN MURDER

Gillian glanced down the lines of black type. The caretaker of the old Greenfield Yacht Club, he read, had signed a statement; had made a clean breast of the murder; had admitted that he had committed it deliberately, in cold blood.

HE TOSSED THE paper into the gutter and drove to the Fourth Precinct jail. A tall, square-jawed man of thirty-five, with prominent black eyes, was coming down the steps as

Gillian started up. He wore a double-breasted blue serge suit and a black derby, which was cocked over one eye.

He paused and said cheerily: "Hello there, Mr. Hazeltine! I hear you're going back to criminal practice. You're getting to be as bad as Sarah Bernhardt."

Gillian smiled. Tom Murphy, of the homicide squad, was an old friend.

"I'm afraid the kid is going to fry, Mr. Hazeltine."

"Think so, Tom?"

"Well, he admits it. He signed a Statement awhile ago."

"How many burning cigars did you stick in his face to pry that out of him, Tom?"

"Don't look at me. Mr. Hazeltine. The district attorney is the boy who did the work."

"Were you there?"

"In the background—scenery."

"See it all?"

"I didn't miss a trick."

"It was rough, eh?"

"It had to be."

"How," Gillian inquired, "would you like to be on the right side of this fight?"

"You mean, you're going to make a jury believe that that kid is innocent?"

"He is innocent."

"Can you prove it?"

"I'm going to try."

Tom Murphy tilted back his derby and scratched an area midway down the part in his oiled black hair.

"I guess you know, Mr. Hazeltine, there isn't much this side of murder I wouldn't do for you, after the way you stood by me in that liquor scandal when you were police commissioner. Hell, I'll take the stand and lie myself black and blue if you say so."

"I don't want you to. I don't want you to tell anything but the truth. It may mean your job, but don't let that worry you."

The detective was gazing at him admiringly.

"I'll tell the truth, all right, Mr. Hazeltine. But I want to know what makes you so sure that kid in there didn't bump off the old doctor. I'll bet you're the only man in this city who thinks he's innocent."

"I know he's innocent."

Tom Murphy grinned. "All right, who did it?"

"One of five or six people, all of whom I know—all of whom will testify in the course of the trial."

"Is it that Jap?"

He looked at Gillian eagerly, but Gillian had assumed a poker expression.

"Did you know," Murphy asked, "that Yistle was letting the Jap go, because of insufficient evidence? I hear he's going to pinch the Lally girl—the good-looking redhead."

"Mr. Yistle has even less evidence against her," said Gillian.

"Do you think she's mixed up in this?"

Before Gillian could answer with an evasion, three eager young men had come sprinting up the steps and closed in upon him. Gillian recognized one as a reporter from the *Evening Bulletin*. They began firing questions at him.

"Is it true that you're taking the Lally case. Mr. Hazeltine?"

Gillian said that it was.

"But do you think for a minute that Lally is innocent?"

"I know he's innocent."

"Who committed the murder?"

"I'm not certain enough to tell you."

"Who do you think did it?"

"I can't answer that."

"The Jap Yistle arrested last night?" one reporter asked.

"Lally's sister?" another demanded.

"I don't know. I'm not talking."

"Do you think that whoever it was murdered Dr. Cullen and tried to poison you, Dennis Van Zant, Pennyfeather and Jeff Whitaker is the same one who poisoned the five others?"

"MAYBE THERE WAS more than one," said Gillian.

"And you have your suspicions, Mr. Hazeltine?"

"I have."

"Then you aren't going to try to get Lally off with an insanity defense?"

"Did I say that?"

"Well, will you?"

"The fight's too young."

"But you'll let us quote you, won't you, Mr. Hazeltine, that you're certain that there was a diabolical, fiendish mystery behind the deeds, and that the blame has been foisted upon Lally?"

Gillian laughed. "That sounds like a tabloid."

"It is, sir. The Greenfield *Graphic*. I can go that far, can't I?"

"Yes," said Gillian.

The three eager young men bombarded him with further

questions, but Gillian remained noncommittal. When the reporters had gone, Tom Murphy said:

"Mr. Hazeltine, I'd like to work with you on this case. Will you speak to the chief?"

"I will, Tom, thank you," said Gillian. "I'll need plenty of expert help."

Gillian went into the jail. His mind, as he entered the dark corridor within the entrance, was like a blackboard upon which a fresh white piece of chalk was writing names. These were the suspects from whom Gillian must sift the murderer or murderers of Dr. Cullen:

Eileen Lally, the sister of the accused man.

Toro, Gillian's houseman.

Bruce Pennyfeather.

Jeffrey Whitaker.

Dennis Van Zant.

Benjamin Ashe, Dr. Cullen's butler.

Another name or two might be added to that list of suspects. But of one thing Gillian was certain: the murderer of Dr. Cullen would, some time during the trial, take the witness stand.

12

THE TRIAL OPENS

IT CHANCED, IN the days preceding the Cullen-Lally murder trial, that the newspapers were hungry for news. No wars bulked on any horizon. No enterprising aviators were planning, in one staggering hop, to span any ocean. Political news was dull. The Hoover administration appeared to be running smoothly. The Cullen murder case found its way to the front pages of the nation's newspapers—and stayed there.

The Cullen murder case was a mystery—and the public loves a mystery. Mr. Yistle, the State's attorney, through the veins which collect and disseminate news, was daily pumping startling disclosures. He and his large staff were taking pains that the public become fully acquainted with the vicious character of Rufe Lally.

Where material evidence, eyewitnesses, are lacking, a trial may be won in this manner before it begins. As the days passed, Rufus Lally was caricatured in the press of the nation as a ruthless fiend.

The public loves a mystery, and it loves a fight. The Cullen case might not have stayed so long on the front pages if Gillian Hazeltine had not provided the mystery and the fight. He insisted that there was a mystery, that Lally was being blamed for another's crime.

Hazeltine's decision to defend Rufe Lally was, of itself, news of national importance. It had been news of national importance when he announced his retirement, two years previously, from criminal practice. He was an idol of the public because he was a fearless, ruthless fighter—and because he invariably took the side of the under dog.

He stated in an interview which appeared not only in every newspaper of consequence in the country, but which was broadcast over a radio hook-up of forty stations, that he had returned to criminal practice solely "because I believe the accused to be an innocent man—the victim of a foul plot against his name and his life. I'll fight to prove his innocence as I've never fought in a court room before."

Days before the trial newspaper correspondents and special writers came flocking into Greenfield. An elaborate telegraph office was established in the basement of the courthouse. The Lally trial promised to be another "trial of the century."

On the eve of the trial a newspaper announced that, in the Greenfield Board of Trade, betting on the outcome was being conducted on a basis of five to one against an acquittal verdict.

Gillian had secured numerous postponements on the grounds that he required time for collecting evidence, and the district attorney had fought each attempt. Mr. Yistle wanted an early trial.

Hours before the court room was thrown open to the public the streets about the courthouse were black with the morbidly curious. There would be room for but a handful of them.

The courthouse was ringed about by police. In the corridors a riot squad was on hand to enforce order. But even they were helpless against the human millrace which flooded into the dingy, dusty old room when the doors were thrown open. An hour was required to seat those for whom there were chairs and to eject those for whom there were not.

A bailiff banged continually on a desk with a gavel and shouted: "Order in the court! Order in the court!"

Mr. Adelbert Yistle was the first of the participants in this exciting drama to enter the scene. His appearance was greeted by a storm of whispers and some handclapping, which was promptly subdued by the bailiffs.

He looked stern and businesslike. He looked as if the duty of sending a fiendish murderer to the electric chair rested lightly upon his fine broad shoulders. His jaw looked squarer than usual. His eyes had a determined light in them. He would remain, unless the tide unexpectedly turned against him, the champion of the people, of right, of retribution.

The district attorney was followed by his assistant, Mr. Bullock. They proceeded to one of the tables in front of the bench and began to open brief cases and to arrange their contents in little piles. Near by, at the reporters' table, pencils were scribbling.

The bailiff banged with his gavel. Some one shouted: "Stand up!" There was a flutter of excitement as Judge Simpson, an elderly man with white hair and a golfer's tan, walked in behind the bench and seated himself.

A bailiff chanted: "Oyez! Oyez! Oyez! The Superior Court within and for Greenfield County, criminal term, is open and in session at this place. All persons having cause or action who are summoned to appear herein will give attention according to the law."

HIS LAST WORDS were lost in another murmur of excitement. Gillian Hazeltine, gray with weariness, came down one of the aisles and took his place at a table near the one which had been taken by the district attorney. He looked gaunt. His clothes looked as if they needed pressing. They did. He hadn't been out of them for three days.

Mr. Yistle saluted him with an affable wave of the hand and a patronizing smile. The contrast between the two enemies was striking: Mr. Yistle, so fresh, so rosy, so confident; Gillian, so gray and weary and worn.

Gillian acknowledged the district attorney's greeting with a slow nod and the briefest of smiles. And Mr. Yistle whispered to Mr. Bullock:

"That man is still sick. Doesn't he look awful?"

"Yes, sir!" chirped Mr. Bullock.

"You can tell by looking at him that he hasn't any surprises up his sleeve. He's licked." The two men chuckled.

"But we've got to watch out for his tricks!" Mr. Yistle murmured. "Do you remember the time he pretended he was drunk, and the jury was so sorry for his client that they gave him a verdict, because they thought Gillian wasn't giving him a fair deal?"

"I remember," said Mr. Bullock. "Yes, sir; I certainly remember *that* case!"

"And do you remember the trial of Jacob Schwartz, when

Gillian slipped in a juryman, whose name was also Jacob Schwartz, knowing damned well that one Jacob Schwartz would never let another Jacob Schwartz be convicted if he could help it?"

"We had used up our last peremptory challenge at the time," recalled Mr. Bullock.

"We must guard against his tricks this time," said Mr. Yistle.

A louder murmur arose in the court room. A door at the rear had opened. The prisoner was coming in. Necks craned. Some one hissed. Another spectator booed. The bailiff played a tattoo with his hammer.

Rufus Lally came in, handcuffed between two sheriffs. His face was white, his cheeks were sunken, his eyes "were dazed. His gray lips were moving slightly, as if he were mumbling a hopeless prayer. The cameo beauty of his profile made a number of the spectators gasp. Rufus Lally did not look like the kind of man the newspapers represented him to be—a cold-blooded fiend. He looked like a saint.

For a moment he faced the crowd, with his chin up, his head back. Then he all but collapsed into a chair beside Gillian. The handcuffs were removed from his wrists, and he fell to rubbing them with his long white fingers.

The process of impaneling a jury was begun at once. Never, perhaps, in the history of important murder trials was a jury impaneled so quickly. Mr. Yistle used but two of his peremptory challenges, because he did not really care who served on the jury, so sure was he of winning his case. His only question was:

"Are you opposed to capital punishment?"

If the jury candidate said "No" or "I am not," Mr. Yistle accepted him.

Gillian was even easier to please. For the first time in his long career as a trial lawyer, he had entered a court room almost unprepared. He was fully convinced that his client was innocent; that he was the victim of a diabolically clever plot, yet he had only a guess as to whom the real murderer might be. So ingeniously had the murderer executed his plans, so cunningly had he destroyed all evidence, that Gillian entered court with nothing but suspicions. The outcome of this trial rested wholly upon his quickness of mind, his ability—for which he was famous—of ferreting the truth out of witnesses.

BY NOON, THE process of impaneling the jury had been completed. Twelve men and women stood up and swore to hearken closely to all testimony, and to render a fair and honest verdict.

The clerk now read the charge.

"Number 5773!" he cried in a ringing voice. "To the Superior Court for Greenfield County comes Adelbert Yistle, attorney for the State in said county, and on his oath of office complaint and information does make that on the 12th day of October, Rufus Lally, of the town of Greenfield, in said county, with calculation and deliberation, did slay by means of a lethal weapon one Dr. Horace Gerald Cullen, in the said town and county; did shoot him so that the said Dr. Horace Gerald Cullen did languish and suffer and did, within the lapse of a few minutes, die, so that the said Rufus Lally did then and there commit the crime of murder against the peace of the people of the State and their dignity and contrary to the form of the statute in such case made and provided."

The ringing voice stopped. Gillian Hazeltine was on his feet pleading not guilty to the charge and the pale, handsome young man at his side was the focal point of every eye in the court room.

Mr. Yistle began his opening address with the easy confidence of a man who is certain of victory. It was not necessary for him to act the boob. He was crisp, vigorous—as confident, as positive, as Mussolini in his most dictatorial moments.

"Gentlemen and ladies of the jury, that man—that Rufus Lally—has entered this court room presumably innocent and presumably sane. That is the law. It is my duty to prove to you beyond a reasonable doubt that that man, that fiend, is guilty of the crime with which he is charged and that he committed it while in full possession of his mental faculties.

"It has been advanced that Rufus Lally is insane. Believe me, ladies and gentlemen of the jury, I have gone over the evidence in this case with the most microscopic care. Over and over I am convinced that Rufus Lally is guilty—and sane. I will prove to you not only that Rufus Lally committed this hideous crime, but that he is not insane; that he is a cold, calculating intellect—a man who loved to murder, a man who went about murdering with a clear mind and a deliberate intention. I will prove to you that he killed not only Dr. Cullen—one of the finest, grandest men that this great city has ever boasted—but that he killed him for the deliberate reason of preventing the discovery of his previous murders! I will prove that he cunningly brought to their death five of Greenfield's most upright citizens—"

"Objection!" Gillian interrupted. "I beg to point out, your honor, that the defendant is being tried in this court for the murder of but one man."

Judge Simpson looked at Mr. Yistle. Mr. Yistle and Mr. Bullock exchanged smiles. They had expected this. They were prepared.

"Your honor," said the district attorney, "the State wishes to establish, with credible witnesses, that Rufus Lally killed Dr. Cullen in an attempt to conceal a plot. The State wishes to prove that Rufus Lally conceived and attempted to execute a diabolical plot."

"Objection overruled," said Judge Simpson. "The State may proceed."

It was first necessary for Mr. Yistle to prove that Dr. Cullen was dead. He did so by calling, as his first witness, Dr. Bartrom, the coroner.

13

FIGHTING HARD

DR. BARTROM, A sad-looking man with long drooping black mustache and a deep, hollow voice, took the witness stand.

Dr. Bartrom was sworn, and Mr. Yistle began to question him.

"Are you the coroner of Greenfield?"

"I am."

"On the night of October 11—or, to be precise, early in the morning of October 12—were you called to examine the body of a man found dead at 1212 Riverside Boulevard?"

"I was."

"Did you recognize the man?"

"I did."

"Kindly tell the jury who he was."

"He was Dr. Horace G. Cullen."

"He was dead?"

"He was; yes, sir."

"Kindly describe to the jury how, in your professional opinion, his death was caused."

"His death was caused," responded the witness, "by the entrance into his brain of a bullet. It entered the brain at a point midway between the two eyes, precisely between the right and left cerebral hemispheres."

"How long after his death occurred," asked Mr. Yistle, "did you make this examination?"

"I should say, about an hour," answered the coroner. "I was at home when the call came. I entered my sedan and drove at once to Dr. Cullen's."

"Did you probe at once for the bullet. Dr. Bartrom?"

"I did."

"You found it?"

"I did."

"Kindly tell the jury where you found this bullet."

"It was lodged against the back of the skull. It was badly flattened, or mushroomed."

"Was it a mushroom bullet?"

"No, sir; it was a common lead bullet."

"A revolver or an automatic pistol bullet?"

"A revolver bullet."

"What caliber?"

"Thirty-eight."

"Kindly tell the jury what you did with this bullet."

"I gave it to your assistant, Mr. Bullock."

"That will be all. Counsel for the defense may take the witness for cross-examination."

Gillian walked toward the coroner and looked at him gravely.

"Doctor, would you say that that bullet had caused Dr. Cullen's instantaneous death?"

"I would; yes, sir."

"Would you say that there was any evidence of a struggle in the doctor's study?"

"No, sir; there was no evidence of a struggle."

"No desk drawers pulled open or anything of that sort?"

"No, sir; nothing of that sort."

"You and Dr. Cullen were great friends, were you not?"

"We were the closest friends—lifelong friends."

"Then," Gillian shot at him, "will you kindly tell me why you did not have finger-print experts immediately at the scene of the crime to go over that room inch by inch?"

Dr. Bartrom flushed.

"I DID NOT consider it necessary." His tone was resentful.

"But as a close friend, a lifelong friend of Dr. Cullen's, you wished to see the real murderer brought to justice, did you not?"

"Indeed I did. And still do! As far as I am concerned, the real murderer has been brought—"

"I request," snapped Gillian, "that that answer be stricken from the record, your honor."

"It is so ordered," complied the judge.

Gillian went closer to the puzzled, angry coroner.

"Do you realize, Dr. Bartrom, that there is no direct evidence, no material evidence to prove that the accused shot Dr. Cullen? Do you realize that he was arrested and held and is being tried merely on circumstantial evidence?"

"Objection!" roared Mr. Yistle. "My eminent colleague is resorting to supposition, as usual."

"Sustained," ruled the bench. "I will ask you to refrain, Mr. Yistle, from personal comments."

"Exception," requested Gillian.

"Exception is noted. You may proceed."

Gillian turned his back and walked away. He was through with Dr. Bartrom. He had merely established an important point—the key point, in fact, on which his defense rested.

Mr. Yistle's next witness was Professor Whitby, a stooped old man with a white Vandyke, who wore gold-rimmed spectacles.

Having been duly sworn, he answered the first of Mr. Yistle's questions in a voice surprisingly robust for a man of his aged appearance.

"Yes, sir; I am known as an authority on firearms."

"Will you kindly examine this revolver, and these two bullets, which I hereby beg your honor to permit me to introduce as material evidence, exhibits A and B for the State, and tell the jury whether or not you have seen them before."

The revolver and bullet were tagged by the stenographer and passed on to the professor.

"I have seen these before, yes."

"Describe the circumstances, please."

"Both were brought to my laboratory by a Mr. Bullock, who is seated over there at that table and who is, I believe, the assistant State's attorney. He wanted me to determine, by scientific methods, whether or not this bullet had been fired from this revolver."

Mr. Yistle: "Will you tell the jury of the results of your investigation?"

Professor Whitby: "I ascertained that this bullet might have been fired from this revolver."

Gillian slowly arose. His bearing was that of a watchful dog.

"Both are the same caliber, are they?" asked Mr. Yistle.

"Yes. Both are the same."

"And your scientific examination led you to the firm belief that this revolver fired this bullet?"

"Yes."

"I merely wished to know," said Mr. Yistle gently, "that you were certain in that belief—that this revolver fired this bullet. That will be all, professor."

Gillian said to the witness: "Professor, you say you are certain that this bullet was fired from this revolver?"

"No, sir; I did not say that I was certain. I said that, in my belief, it was fired from this revolver."

"Then you are not certain."

"No, sir; I am not."

"Why are you not certain?"

"Because this bullet was mushroomed to such an extent by impact with the skull wall of Dr. Cullen that it was impossible to make comparative measurements of the rifling on the bullet and the rifling of the revolver."

"In other words," said Gillian sharply, "this bullet might have been fired from any .38 caliber revolver?"

"I suppose it might have."

MR. YISTLE SPRANG up. "But you said, professor, that you firmly believed that it was fired from this revolver."

"Your honor," implored Gillian, "I am still cross-examining."

"You may proceed, Mr. Hazeltine. Mr. Yistle, you will take the witness, in your turn, for reexamination, if you wish."

"I apologize," said Mr. Yistle.

The next witness for the State was a policeman on an enforced holiday; a policeman in mufti who answered to the name of Cuthbert Lenihan.

Officer Lenihan raised his right hand and in a stuttering voice proclaimed his intention to abide by the truth.

Mr. Yistle: "Mr. Lenihan, on the morning of October 12, at about twelve forty-five, kindly tell the jury where you were and what you were doing."

"I—I was on me be—beat, sir. I was a walking down Dover Street from Summit toward the river. I was on me way down to the railroad yards, on the lookout for bums, sir."

"You were, officer, as a hired custodian of law and order, going your regular rounds, upholding the peace and dignity of the city. Is that right."

"Yes, s-sir; that is right."

"And while you were, in the performance of your duties, Mr. Lenihan, walking down Dover Street toward the river, shortly before one o'clock in the morning, did you see this man—this man over here who is accused of murdering Dr. Cullen?"

"Yes, sir; I saw him."

"Kindly tell the jury about it, Mr. Lenihan."

The policeman fixed bulging eyes of uneasiness on the jury.

"I was a-walking along, swinging my club, ladies and gents, when, all of a sudden, out of the dark this man came a-running. He didn't have on no hat. It was bright-like. I was, right then, underneath a street light, so I saw it all clear and plain.

"This man was running along, and when I saw he had a revolver in his hand I yelled at him to stop in the name of the law. But he didn't stop. He ran right on past me, faster than ever, and I started running right after him."

The court room was hushed. Mr, Lenihan's simple, direct narrative was dramatic. And he was scoring a telling point.

"This man, ladies and gents, when he saw I was after him, he ducked into an alley behind Homgarth's wholesale grocery warehouse. And I run in after him, still yelling at him to stop. I flashed on me pocket torch, but not in time to save myself from stumbling and falling down onto me hands and knees over an empty bushel basket. When I picked myself up, he was gone. I looked high and low for him, but I know now that he circled into another alley and went out on Summit Street and, as luck would have it, a taxicab was coming along and picked him up."

Mr. Lenihan stopped. The prosecutor went closer to him.

SAID MR. YISTLE: "Mr. Lenihan, when you were under the street light on Dover Street and saw this man running toward you, the light was sufficient for you to see quickly that there was a revolver in his hand, was it not?"

"Yes, sir. The light was good. It was a good light."

"The revolver this man had in his hand was dark, was it not? That is to say, it was a blue revolver?"

"Yes, sir; so it was."

"You have seen revolvers at night before, have you not?"

"Yes, sir; I have."

"So that you would say that the light must have been very good, or you would not have been able to see a blue or black revolver?"

"That's right. Yes, sir. The light was very good."

"It was good enough, in fact, for you to see the man's face clearly—so clearly that you would have no trouble in recognizing it if you saw it again?"

"Yes, sir."

"Very well, officer. Now. I want you to tell the jury what you saw in this man's face. I mean, what expression was on his face?"

Gillian was leaning back in his chair. He knew that Mr. Yistle was building up one of the most important points in his case. Gillian wore a grim smile.

"His face was pale—pale like death, sir," said Officer Lenihan.

"But his eyes—how about his eyes? Did you see them?"

"Yes, sir; I saw his eyes."

"Well, what kind of a look was in his eyes?"

"It was a murdering kind of look, sir—a cold, murdering kind of look."

"You wouldn't say that it was an insane look?"

"No, sir. Not at all. It was a cold, murdering kind of look. It was the kind of a look a man would have in his eyes if he was on his way to kill somebody."

There was a titter in the court room. Several of the jurors smiled. Gillian's smile widened. Mr. Yistle was not getting very far with his point. His witness was a little too eager to please.

Mr. Yistle frowned.

"I want you to be sure about this. Mr. Lenihan. I don't want you to exaggerate. We will confine ourselves to one thing only. Did this man Lally, when he came running toward you with the revolver in his hand, have an insane look in his eyes?"

"No, sir."

"There was nothing in his actions to suggest that he was an insane man?"

"No, sir."

"That will be all." Mr. Yistle bowed ironically to Gillian. Gillian leaned farther back in his chair.

"Mr. Lenihan," he asked, "how good are your eyes?"

The officer was immediately on the defensive. He answered defiantly: "They're all right."

"Ever have them examined by an oculist?"

"No, sir. The only time they were examined was when I went into the army for the war. They were good eyes then and they're good eyes now."

"Have you ever," asked Gillian, "been in an insane asylum?"

"No, sir!" snapped the policeman.

"Seen many insane people elsewhere?"

"Plenty!"

"So you consider yourself in a position to judge whether or not any man at whom you look is sane or insane?"

"I do!"

"And when Mr. Lally—this young man here—came galloping up Dover Street, you saw his eyes clearly enough to decide, from the look in them, that he was as sane as you or I?"

"Yes, sir."

"YOU WOULDN'T SAY that there was a terrified look in his eyes?"

"No, sir; there was not."

"Don't you think," said Gillian dryly, "that it is a little unusual for a man to run up a street, hatless, with a gun in his hand—"

"I object to that question," Mr. Yistle flared up. "It

presupposes a deduction, which is inacceptable as evidence."

"Question withdrawn," said Gillian pleasantly. "Mr. Lenihan, how many visits, since the murder, have you paid, to the prosecuting attorney's office?"

"Objection!" snapped Mr. Yistle.

"Sustained," ruled the bench.

Gillian smiled. "Mr. Lenihan, do you often see men with revolvers in their hands running through the streets?"

The officer grinned triumphantly. "I did once."

"You did once," said Gillian. "Once you saw a man running through the streets at night with a revolver in his hand. Was he on his way to commit a murder?"

"No, sir; he was just through shooting a man in the leg."

"You had better luck that time, didn't you? I mean, you didn't fall over a bushel basket and lose him?"

"No, sir: I got him." Officer Lenihan's face was red with anger.

"Did you take as good a look at that man as you did at the accused?"

"I did!"

"Did you see his eyes?"

"Yes, sir."

"What color were they?"

Officer Lenihan suddenly became thoughtful. "They were blue."

"They were not," said Gillian. "They were brown."

Mr. Yistle exclaimed: "Your honor, I object to the questions my esteemed adversary is putting to this witness. I object to this horseplay."

His honor was smiling. "Mr. Hazeltine, what are you proving?"

"That this witness does not see what he looks at, your honor; that this witness has been coached; that his testimony is therefore inadmissible."

Judge Simpson: "I do not see that you have proved your point, Mr. Hazeltine. Have you any further questions to ask the witness?"

"No, your honor."

Cuthbert Lenihan was excused.

Court was recessed for lunch. Outside the court room Gillian was surrounded by reporters. They reminded him of a pack of starving wolves. Cameras clicked in his face. Rude hands pawed at his lapels, plucked at his sleeves.

"What's your game, Hazeltine—are you trying to make a monkey out of every witness he puts on?"

"Are you going to put that redheaded sister of Lally's on the stand, Mr. Hazeltine?"

Gillian tried to push his way through the pack. They wouldn't let him.

"What about that Jap butler of yours, Mr. Hazeltine? Is he going to testify? Is he a dark horse?"

"Look this way, Mr. Hazeltine! Hold it! Give us a smile, Gill! Push your hat back a little."

Click! went a camera.

"When does the red-haired girl go on the stand, Mr. Hazeltine?"

Gillian put his head down and, like a football player, fought his way through the crowd to his car.

14

GILLIAN THROWS A BOMBSHELL

THE FIRST WITNESS of the afternoon was on Gillian's list of suspects, Benjamin Ashe, the butler. He was a dark-skinned man, with small brown eyes, bushy brows, thick red lips.

Benjamin Ashe walked heavily to the stand, seated himself, and faced the court room with an air of great self-assurance.

Mr. Yistle: "Mr. Ashe, what is your occupation?"

"I am a butler."

"Before you were a butler, what were you?"

"I entered the services of the Long Island Van Dorsetts as a second footman when I was seventeen. I became, in the course of six years, the Van Dorsetts' butler. When Commodore Van Dorsett died I went into the employ of Dr. Cullen."

"How long ago was that?"

"A little over ten years ago."

"You have been, then, Mr. Ashe, a faithful servant of Dr. Cullen's since 1919?"

"Yes, sir; I am proud to say that I have, sir."

"You served your master loyally and well?"

"To the utmost of my capacity, sir."

"Now, Mr. Ashe, I want you to tell the jury what you were doing between the hours of midnight and a little after one o'clock on the morning of October 12."

"I was in the kitchen, sir."

"What were you doing in the kitchen?"

"I—I was making some candy."

"Oh, you were making some candy. For whom were you making this candy?"

"For the doctor, sir. He loved candy. I was making some of his favorite candy."

"Was the door leading from the kitchen into the service pantry open?"

"It was, sir."

"And was the door leading from the pantry into the dining room also open?"

"Yes, sir; all the doors leading to the doctor's study were open. That door was closed."

"Why did you keep those doors open?"

"So that I would hear the doctor's bell in case he needed me and rang."

"This was not an electric bell, was it, but the kind of bell a school-teacher keeps on her desk?"

"Yes, sir; it was a little hand bell."

"Very well, Mr. Ashe. Between midnight and a little after one o'clock on the morning in question, you were in the kitchen making candy and waiting around in case the doctor summoned you?"

"Yes, sir; precisely, sir."

Most of the spectators were smiling. Even Judge Simpson was smiling a little. Benjamin Ashe, even on the stand,

was unmistakably the perfect servant—courteous, respect-
ful.

"Will you describe to the jury what happened in Dr.
Cullen's house at a few minutes past one?"

BENJAMIN ASHE, THE perfect servant, the perfect
witness, cleared his throat, drew his thick black brows
together slightly in an attitude of concentration, and gazed
at the jury.

"It was approximately one fifteen by the clock in the
kitchen when I heard a shot ring out. I remember the
time because, in making the candy, it was necessary for
me to boil a certain chocolate mixture a certain number of
minutes; no more, no less. I was glancing at the clock from
time to time—every few seconds, I suppose. At approximately one fifteen I heard a shot. It startled me so that I
dropped a spoon I held in my hand. As the sound of the
shot seemed to come from the doctor's study, I ran in there.
The door was closed but unlocked. I opened the door.

"My first impression was the smell of burned gunpowder. A whiff of it, rather a little pale cloud of it, was hanging in the air. To my utter horror and consternation, I saw
my beloved master lying on the floor. Standing over him
was this—this man!" He pointed his finger at Rufe. "There
was," went on the butler, "a revolver in his right hand. He
was standing there with the revolver in his hand and looking down at my beloved master. I seized the revolver from
his hand. I grappled with him. Then I telephoned to police
headquarters."

The perfect witness paused. Mr. Yistle was weighing a
coin in his hand, shaking his hand slightly.

"You came into the doctor's study, Mr. Ashe, and your

The piece of bullet-pierced cardboard was the silhouette of a face!

first impressions were the smell of gunpowder smoke, then the sight of gunpowder smoke, then you saw your dead master, with this man—this Rufus Lally—standing over him with a revolver gripped in his right hand?"

"Yes, sir."

"When you took the revolver from him, do you remember whether or not the barrel was warm?"

"Yes, sir; it was warm."

"Did any conversation take place between you and the accused?"

"Yes, sir. When I took the revolver Lally said: 'God, what have I done?' And I said: 'You've done enough; you've murdered the doctor.'"

"Was there anything further said?"

"Yes, sir. I asked him why he had shot the doctor. He said he did not know why."

"He said that, did he? 'I do not know why I shot him'?"

"Yes, sir; those were his words, as I recall them now, sir."

"Would you say that there was an insane look in his eyes?"

"No, sir; there was a cold, ugly look in his eyes, but I would certainly not call it an insane look."

"Merely the kind of look you would expect to find in the eyes of a man who had committed a murder a moment before?"

"I object to that," Gillian interrupted.

"On what grounds?"

"Has the witness any basis for comparison? Has he ever seen the eyes of any other man immediately after he committed a murder?"

The perfect witness looked narrowly at Gillian. He said: "No, I have not."

"The objection," ruled the bench, "is sustained. You may proceed, Mr. Yistle."

"I want the witness to tell the jury if the accused, after murdering Dr. Cullen—"

"Objection!"

"Sustained."

"Exception!"

"Exception noted. Kindly confine your interrogations to material evidence."

Mr. Yistle tried again. "I want the witness to tell the jury if the accused, after he—the witness—had come upon the accused standing over the dead man with a smoking revolver in his hand—"

"Objection!" snapped Gillian.

"It is sustained. I must ask you, Mr. Yistle," said the judge sternly, "to be more careful."

"—if the witness detected, when he looked into the accused's face, any indication of insanity."

"No, sir," answered Ashe. "He looked dazed—and tired."

"Yes!" cried Mr. Yistle. "Tired, fatigued, exhausted, as a man would look after committing a foul deed which he had carefully and deliberately planned!"

"STRIKE THAT OUT," the judge instructed the stenographer. "I hope you understand, ladies and gentlemen of the jury, that evidence which I hold inadmissible to the record is not to be weighed in your deliberations. You may proceed with your examination, Mr. Yistle."

The prosecuting attorney waved his hand in a gesture which indicated that he was through with his examination, and which further indicated that he was the victim of gross injustice. It was the gesture of a man wronged. But Mr. Yistle, resuming his seat beside Mr. Bullock, did not wear the expression of a man wronged. He had scored another important point; he had impressed upon the collective mind of the jury that the defendant had not appeared to be insane at, or shortly after, the time the crime was committed.

Gillian grimly approached the perfect witness.

How old are you?" he snapped.

"Thirty-three."

"Sure you're not thirty-nine?"

The butler's eyes were narrowed, His hands, which had been resting on arms of the chair, were now clasped in his lap. His attitude was one of weariness. He did not answer the question.

The stenographer said: "I did not hear his answer."

Gillian: "He didn't answer. Perhaps he is afraid to answer."

The witness: "I am thirty-three."

"You're not forgetting that you've sworn to tell the truth."

"I'm not forgetting."

"Have you ever been arrested on a criminal charge?"

The perfect butler's face lost what remained of its deep, warm color. Mr. Yistle had arisen. He looked anxious. Benjamin Ashe was possibly his most important witness.

"Have you?" barked Gillian. Ashe only stared at him.

"Isn't it true that between the time you worked for Commodore Van Dorsett and the time you went to work for Dr. Cullen, you served six years in Sing Sing on a manslaughter charge?"

The court room rippled with whispers. The bailiff brought down his gavel with a bang.

"Answer that question!"

"It was a trumped-up charge."

"Answer that question!"

"Yes. But it was a frame-up."

"It's always a frame-up," said Gillian. "You were given ten years, weren't you, and you got off with six, didn't you, for the murder of the Van Dorsett gardener?"

"It was in self-defense!"

"It was brought out at the trial, wasn't it, that you had ruined his daughter?"

"That was a lie!"

"They gave you ten years for it?"

"Yes."

"Where were you between the ages of fifteen and seventeen?"

"I don't know."

"I'll refresh your memory. You were serving two years in the Elmira reformatory for hitting another boy with a brick and putting him into the hospital for six months, weren't you?"

"It was an accident."

"But you threw the brick, didn't you?"

"Yes."

"You hit that boy in the head and nearly killed him, didn't you?"

Mr. Yistle had his fist half raised. He looked dazed. One of his best witnesses was being ruined Before his very eyes and there was nothing he could do to prevent the disaster.

"Isn't it true that Commodore Van Dorsett was in the habit of giving employment to men with criminal records?"

"I don't know."

"Isn't it true that Commodore Van Dorsett one time discharged you and later took you back because you stole a diamond-mounted wrist watch belonging to one of his house guests?"

"No!"

"It isn't true that you were discharged and taken back?"

"I didn't steal that watch!"

"But you were accused of it?"

"I say I didn't steal it!"

"Very well. We'll disregard the wrist watch."

MR. YISTLE MADE himself heard. "Your honor, I object to this attempt at bulldozing my witness. I object to these efforts at blackening his character!"

The judge, in spite of himself, smiled. "It doesn't seem to me, Mr. Yistle, to be requiring much effort. It is fully within the rights of counsel for the defense to refer in his questions to the past of any witness you produce. I see nothing out of the way in Mr. Hazeltine's very logical attempts to cast doubt upon the credibility of this witness It seems to me that the mistake was yours in having such a witness."

"But I didn't know he had a criminal record!"

"I am not accountable for that. Proceed, Mr. Hazeltine."

"I am very much interested in knowing," Gillian obliged, "what you were making in the kitchen at the time you heard the shot in the doctor's study."

"I said I was making candy, didn't I?"

"Did you?" Gillian was smiling his foxlike smile.

"Didn't I?" Gone was the perfect butler, the perfect witness; in his place sat a surly man with beetling brows.

"What a pretty picture," said Gillian ironically. "You were in the kitchen making candy while your master was being murdered—assailant or assailants unknown."

"I was making candy," the witness growled. He was clutching the arms of the chair, as if he were preparing to spring at Gillian.

"You have already perjured yourself," said Gillian. "I trust that it won't happen again."

"A man's age is nobody's business but his own!"

"We are talking about candy," Gillian reminded him. "You were out in the kitchen making candy—a picture of beautiful domesticity. What kind of candy were you making?"

"Chocolate candy."

"Ah, yes; chocolate candy. What kind of chocolate candy?"

"Chocolate creams."

"It fairly makes my mouth water, Mr. Ashe. If your skill as a candymaker extends to chocolate creams, you must be an expert indeed. How long did it take you to learn how to make chocolate creams?"

"I don't know. Maybe a year."

"No novice could make chocolate creams properly the first time, could he?"

The witness ignored this question. He merely grunted.

"I want to know, Mr. Ashe, if it isn't difficult to make a smooth, creamy chocolate coating for chocolate creams."

No answer.

Gillian: "Answer that question!"

"What's that got to do with the murder of Dr. Cullen?"

"You are on that stand to answer questions, not to ask them. Answer my question."

"I forget what it was."

"I asked you if it isn't difficult to make smooth, creamy chocolate for the outer shell, or overcoat, of chocolate creams. Yes or no?"

"Yes."

"In fact, isn't the most difficult point in the making of so-called homemade candy that of keeping the ingredients smooth and creamy? Yes or no?"

"Yes."

"That applies, of course, to making fudge, too, doesn't it?"

"I suppose it does."

"Don't you know?"

"I don't make fudge."

"But you have, of course?"

"Never. I never made fudge."

"Your honor," Mr. Yistle expostulated, "I object to this line of questioning. Mr. Hazeltine is, in accordance with his usual practice, making of this most solemn and dignified occasion a farce. All this nonsense about candy is irrelevant and immaterial."

Judge Simpson bent his glance upon Gillian.

"Will you answer Mr. Yistle's objection?"

"I am carrying out a definite plan, your honor," Gillian answered. "It is not yet necessary for me to stipulate the grounds upon which I will base my defense. It is within my rights to keep my intentions in the dark as long as I wish."

"That is true. Your objection, Mr. Yistle, is overruled. Proceed with cross-examination and, if possible, Mr. Hazeltine, omit any attempt at levity."

Mr. Yistle snorted, clearly conveying the impression that, to Gillian Hazeltine, the most sacred objects in life were open to ridicule.

"LET US," SAID Gillian pleasantly, "leave the candy-making and proceed directly to the scene of the murder. Certain points in Mr. Ashe's testimony arouse my curiosity. As I understand it, Mr. Ashe, you were in the kitchen making chocolate creams when you heard a shot. We agree on that, don't we?"

"Yes."

"Before you heard the shot, did you hear voices?"

"No."

"Had Dr. Cullen been in his study all evening?"

"Yes."

"From when to when?"

"He went into his study immediately after dinner—at about a quarter of nine. He shut the door and stayed there. That was the last I saw of him—alive."

"You have no idea, have you, what he was doing in his study?"

"I think he was working on a new book. A book on poisons."

"Did anyone call on the doctor to your knowledge?"

"No."

"Did any one call him by telephone?"

"Some one did, but I don't know who it was. He answered the extension in his study."

"You didn't listen in?"

"Certainly not! I never listen in!"

"You did not admit the accused to the house?"

"No. He came in by the side door into the little reception room which the doctor used to use when he was practicing."

"That door was unlocked?"

"It was always unlocked. The doctor liked to have his friends come and go informally."

"So that any one could have come in by that door and you would not have known?"

"No. I wouldn't have known."

"A hundred people might have come in that night and you wouldn't have known?"

The witness did not answer. He was staring sullenly at his hands.

"Was there any other access to the study except by the door through which you entered and the door through which all these visitors entered?"

"Yes. There is a flight of stairs leading upstairs from one end of the study—the south end. It connects with the upstairs hall."

"Aren't there windows, full length windows, opening on the side yard?"

"Yes. Two."

"Was not one of those windows open when you went into the study and found your master lying dead on the floor?"

"I think one of them was open."

"Aren't you sure?"

The witness sighed as if with boredom. "Yes, one of those windows was open."

"How high is that window from the ground? I mean, how high is the threshold from the ground?"

"I should say about a foot."

"You should say about a foot," Gillian murmured; reflectively. "In other words, hardly more than a short step up or down. Now, Mr. Ashe, when you entered the study and found your master lying dead on the floor, was this young man, this boy, facing that window?"

"I think he was."

"You aren't sure?"

"Yes. I'm sure. He was facing the open window."

"Did it occur to you to look outside that window?"

"No. I was too busy."

"Doing what, pray?"

"I grabbed him and held him until the police came."

"Did he offer any resistance?"

"He did! He offered a lot of resistance."

"Was it necessary for you to strike him, to knock him out?"

"No."

"Or to tie his hands?"

"No."

"And you say he offered a lot of resistance?"

"That's right."

"Then," said Gillian, "how were you able to telephone for the police?"

The witness flashed an ugly look at him. Gillian shot at him:

"Ashe, you aren't lying, are you?"

"No!" shouted the witness.

"Can you produce a witness—a single witness—who saw you out in that kitchen making candy? Can you produce a witness who can prove that you were not out in that side yard, and that you yourself did not fire the shot that killed Dr. Cullen?"

15

A STRONG CASE

THE COURT ROOM was in an uproar. The bailiff was banging with his gavel and shouting for order. Mr. Yistle was on his feet, violently gesticulating. The witness was staring at Gillian with eyes full of cold hatred. They were a snake's eyes.

The prosecuting attorney presently made himself heard. His objection was upheld. Gillian's last question and the witness's last answer were ordered stricken from the record.

In a tense silence Gillian resumed his cross-examination.

"Mr. Ashe, I do not want to bring perjury charges against you. But if you lie to me once more, I shall."

Adelbert Yistle made low moaning sounds in his throat and feebly waved his hands, but he did not object. Half of his witnesses could betray him, as Ashe had done, and he would still win the case. He merely hated being ridiculed. It seemed to him that he and Hazeltine never had fought a court room battle without Hazeltine, at some stage of the proceedings, making a monkey of him. He hated Hazeltine.

Gillian proceeded: "Prior to the night when Dr. Cullen was murdered, Mr. Ashe, was it or was it not known to you that you were a beneficiary under the doctor's new will?

Take your time to answer that question, Mr. Ashe. Did you know it or didn't you?"

The butler hesitated and said: "Yes, I knew about it."

"Knew that the doctor had bequeathed you ten thousand dollars?"

"Yes."

"Just how long before the doctor's death did that information come into your possession? Wasn't it the very afternoon preceding his death?"

"I think it was. Yes, it was."

"You seem uncertain."

"I'm positive."

"So that, on the afternoon immediately preceding the night of Dr. Cullen's murder, you learned that, at his death, you would receive the sum of ten thousand dollars?"

"Yes! But I didn't kill him for it!"

Gillian pounced upon that as an alert cat pounces upon a helpless stray rat.

"Then what did you kill him for?" he barked.

"I didn't kill him!"

"You said you did! You said, 'I didn't kill him for it!'"

"I didn't kill him at all!"

"I object!" roared Mr. Yistle. "The witness was trapped into making that answer. I request that the preceding question and answer be uttered again."

Judge Simpson decided crisply: "Overruled."

Gillian's nose was not six inches from the pale, bulbous nose of Benjamin Ashe. He said harshly:

"You admit that on the very afternoon of the night that Dr. Cullen was murdered you learned that his death would be profitable to you to the extent of ten thousand dollars."

"But that doesn't mean I killed him. I didn't kill him. I loved him." Benjamin Ashe was talking rapidly. "I wouldn't have harmed a hair of his head. I loved him, I tell you.

Several spectators snickered. The perfect butler, maudlin with self-pity, was not very convincing.

"That will be all," said Gillian, "But I want this witness held, your honor. I shall have more questions to ask him later."

The butler started to rise, but Mr. Yistle waved him back. His Humpty-Dumpty had fallen from the wall. As far as the interested jury was concerned, Benjamin Ashe's value as a witness was extinct. Mr. Yistle looked hopeless now. He looked dumb. Upon him devolved the delicate and difficult task of putting Humpty-Dumpty back together again.

SAID MR. YISTLE, sorrowfully: "Mr. Ashe, let us be frank; let us be candid."

The two men engaged eyes. Juror No. 8, a tender-hearted school-teacher, would have sworn that there were tears in the eyes of each.

"Yes," said the butler.

"Is it not true, Mr. Ashe, when you consented to give such information as you possessed to bring the murderer of your beloved master the punishment he richly deserved, that you realized that your past record would probably be pried into?"

Mr. Ashe looked at him. He said, returning magically to his old self: "Yes, sir; precisely, sir."

"You came to this city, did you not, Mr. Ashe, resolved to put your old life behind you; to build anew upon a solid foundation?"

"Yes, sir; exactly."

"You had served a sentence in a boys' reformatory; you had served a sentence in a penitentiary for a crime of which you were unjustly accused?"

"Yes, sir."

"You came to Greenfield and entered Dr. Cullen's employ, firm in your faith, determined to lead a fine, clean, useful life—hoping that no one would fling at you the unfortunate mistakes of your early youth?"

"Yes, sir."

"And in these ten years you have led a life of uprightness and probity, a life of which you can be justly proud?"

"Yes, sir; such, indeed, was my hope."

"And you took the stand to-day, out of the love you bore your master, wanting nothing but to bring the murderer of your dear master to justice, willing to sacrifice your peace of mind, willing—nay, eager!—to make any sacrifice so that that fiendish murderer might receive his just deserts?"

"Yes, sir. I knew that my past would be exposed to the world, sir; but I was willing to make that sacrifice for my beloved master."

Gillian gazed at the two of them with honest admiration. They had achieved the impossible. Mr. Yistle had put Humpty-Dumpty back together again. And Gillian realized that Mr. Yistle was improving; that Mr. Yistle was become a foeman worthy of his steel.

"I want you to know, Mr. Ashe," the district attorney went on eloquently, his voice deep and ringing, "that, speaking for the honest citizens in this court room, speaking for these twelve ladies and gentlemen of the jury, Greenfield, from the bottom of its heart, thanks you for your great sacrifice."

Mr. Yistle bowed. There was no applause. But Mr. Yistle bowed, as if in acknowledgment of a storm of applause.

"You are excused, Mr. Ashe."

"Not yet," said Gillian.

The expression of misty softness in the eyes of the witness was again replaced by a look of cold hatred. Humpty-Dumpty did not relish the thought of being knocked off again.

"I will not," said Gillian, "dwell upon the beautiful spirit of sacrifice you have displayed, Mr. Ashe, in taking the witness stand. There are a few further questions I would like to ask you. I want you to think harder than you have ever thought before. I want you to take pains not to perjure yourself again. I want to go back into the kitchen with you again."

Mr. Yistle had not seated himself. He stood beside his table wearing an expression of acute anxiety. He had restored the jury's faith in Benjamin Ashe. If Gillian Hazeltine attempted to destroy that faith, he, Mr. Yistle, would fight tooth and claw until it was restored and stayed restored!

"I want to ask you, Mr. Ashe," Gillian proceeded, "if you can't recall ever making fudge."

The court room burst into laughter. When order was restored, Gillian repeated his question, and Ashe replied:

"I don't remember."

"Think hard, Mr. Ashe. Didn't you, some time about the middle of September, make a batch of fudge and present it to the accused?"

"I think I did. Yes, I recall now that I did."

GILLIAN MERELY WISHED to establish that fact in the record. He said now:

"Will you kindly tell me, Mr. Ashe, who Dr. Cullen's most frequent visitors were?"

"There were so many, sir, it would be hard to give you a complete list of them."

"Then let me specify a few. Did Mr. Yistle, the district attorney, frequently call upon the doctor?"

"Yes, sir; frequently."

Mr. Yistle started to object, but restrained himself. He looked at Gillian narrowly, and there was a hard glint in his eyes.

"Was Mr. Bruce Pennyfeather a frequent caller?"

"Yes, sir. Mr. Pennyfeather supplied the doctor with many of the drugs and poisons he used. The doctor often wished to obtain certain chemicals in a pure state. Mr. Penny feather secured them for him."

"Were Mr. and Mrs. Dennis Van Zant frequent callers?"

"Yes, sir."

"Was Mr. Jeffery Whitaker a frequent caller?"

"Quite frequent, sir."

"How frequent a caller, Mr. Ashe, was Mr. Yistle?"

"I should say he called as often as two or three times a week."

"He and Dr. Cullen argued a great deal, did they not?"

The witness shot a quick glance at Mr. Yistle. Gillian turned in time to see Mr. Yistle briefly shake his head. He snapped:

"Your honor, my esteemed adversary is instructing this witness!"

Mr. Yistle shouted: "Your honor, I object to this line of testimony. It is irrelevant. I was shaking my head because I was bored."

Judge Simpson: "The witness will answer the question."

The witness: "No. They never argued."

"That will be all," said Gillian. "I may require this witness for examination later. He is excused for the present."

The State's next witness was Detective Sergeant Murdock, who had made the arrest. He testified that he had gone directly to Dr. Cullen's house on receipt of instructions from a telephone clerk in police headquarters; that he had found the accused seated in the doctor's study.

Mr. Yistle stressed his former point—that of the accused's presumptive sanity. Bill Murdock, a blond giant, made the best witness that Mr. Yistle had put on the stand so far. He had intelligent blue eyes. He spoke thoughtfully, as if endeavoring to tell the whole truth without prejudice.

Mr. Yistle: "Mr. Murdock, when you went into the doctor's study, where was the accused?"

"He was sitting in a chair near the desk."

"Did you look at him closely?"

"I did, sir."

"Did he look insane?"

"No, sir. He was white and scared. I would certainly say that he was not insane."

"Did you converse with him?"

"We had a long conversation. He claimed that he did not know whether he had killed the doctor or not. He said that he had been scared by ghostly sounds at the yacht club, and especially by a green light against a window in the trophy room. He said he remembered nothing from the time he fired a revolver at that window until he found himself standing over Dr. Cullen's dead body."

"Did you extract any further information from him, relative to the murder?"

"No, sir; he was hysterical. He babbled away about the ghosts and the green light."

"But you were convinced that he was not suffering from any mental derangement, aside from that professed loss of memory?"

"He didn't look insane to me, at any time. He was scared, as most people are who are caught after committing a murder—scared of the consequences."

Gillian snapped: "Objection!"

"Sustained," ruled Judge Simpson. "You will confine yourself, Mr. Murdock to direct answers."

Mr. Yistle: "Did you take the trouble, Mr. Murdock, to check up on the accused's claim that he had heard ghostly sounds in the clubhouse?"

"YES, SIR; LATER that night I went down there. There was some excitement there later. I got there just as it was ending. As far as I could gather, a number of other people went down there to check up on those ghosts. You were one. The others were Mr. Hazeltine over there, Mr. Bruce Pennyfeather, a Japanese who is Mr. Hazeltine's butler and a girl—the sister of the defendant. The Jap was arrested as an accomplice, but was released the next day because of insufficient evidence."

Judge Simpson interrupted: "I must ask you again, Mr. Murdock, to confine yourself to direct answers to questions."

Bill Murdock answered: "Mr. Yistle asked me if I had

gone to the clubhouse. What I found there was pretty interesting."

Judge Simpson: "Do you wish to know, Mr. Yistle, what he found at the clubhouse? I think we are wasting time. I don't want this trial to go on indefinitely."

Mr. Yistle: "What Mr. Murdock found at the clubhouse was very interesting. You will tell the jury, Mr. Murdock, what you found at the clubhouse."

Gillian had arisen. For the first time to-day he was really anxious. The district attorney, unless Gillian was mistaken, was preparing to use the very material on which Gillian had planned to base one premise of his defense. Mr. Yistle had cleverly anticipated him. More and more Gillian was realizing that Mr. Yistle was a dangerous foe. Rufe was in acute danger.

Gillian snapped: "I object to that question as leading."

Mr. Yistle flashed a grin at him. "Withdrawn." He opened a package and from it removed several objects. The first was a piece of cardboard of irregular shape. There was a round hole about a half inch in diameter in the center of it.

"I wish to introduce this," said Mr. Yistle, "as material evidence for the State." The stenographer marked it Exhibit C and Mr. Yistle handed it to the detective.

"Have you seen this before?"

"Yes, sir. I found it in the mud outside the trophy window at the yacht club on the night of the murder."

"Please hold it up in the proper position so that the jury can see what it is."

The detective did as he was instructed. He twisted the cardboard about and held it up to the jury. Several of the jurors gasped. The white piece of cardboard suddenly became the silhouette of a man's face—a caricature of Dr. Cullen's profile!

One of the jurors asked: "What is that hole in the center?"

"A bullet hole," said Bill Murdock.

"How," asked Mr. Yistle, "do you account for that bullet hole?"

"When I arrested the defendant," Bill Murdock answered, "he told me he had seen a silhouette of Dr. Cullen's face against the trophy room window, and that he had fired his revolver at it, I presume this hole would have been made by that bullet—if his story was straight."

Gillian barked: "Your honor, I strenuously object. Presumption is not acceptable evidence, nor is deduction which is not based upon material evidence."

Judge Simpson sustained his objection and added: "Mr. Yistle, can you prove that that bullet hole was made by a bullet fired by the defendant?"

"I can come very close to it, your honor."

The judge: "I believe that the jury may be in some doubt as to the purpose of this testimony. Do you wish to enlighten them? Otherwise, if the defense counsel insists, I will be compelled to hold this entire testimony irrelevant."

Mr. Yistle: "I am going to some pains, your honor, to establish that the defendant, in planning this crime of which he stands accused, deliberately planted obvious clews which would seem to indicate that he was mentally unbalanced."

Gillian: "I hold that that reasoning is absurd, and I request that the witness's testimony applying to his visit to the clubhouse be stricken from the record because of its irrelevancy."

Judge Simpson: "I cannot make a ruling on that point until further evidence is heard. It seems to me that Mr. Yistle is entitled to proceed with this witness's examination."

Mr. Yistle flung a grin of triumph at Gillian. And Gillian's anxiety increased. He did not believe that Mr. Yistle could prove his point, but he realized that he had made the mistake of underestimating his old enemy. Mr. Yistle was fighting as he had never fought before, and there was a growing possibility that he might succeed in sending Rufus Lally to the electric chair.

MR. YISTLE REMOVED another piece of cardboard from the package. This was marked Exhibit D and passed along to the witness.

Mr. Yistle: "Have you seen this piece of cardboard before?"

"Yes, sir; I have. I found it in the wastebasket beside the desk in the trophy room."

"Kindly hold it up so that the jury can see it."

Bill Murdock did so. From the center of the sheet of cardboard a piece had been cut—an irregular piece. At Mr. Yistle's request, the witness placed the Cullen silhouette into the hole; twisted it about. It fitted perfectly.

Exhibit E for the State was a length of rusty chain with links about an inch in diameter. Exhibit F was a pair of common cotton gloves, such as workmen use. Bill Murdock testified that he had found the chain and the gloves in the sail loft.

"The dust was pretty well trampled in the sail loft, but

I could plainly see the marks where the chain had been dragged. The defendant mentioned, when arrested, that he had heard sounds of chains being dragged about in the sail loft. This must be the chain."

"Did you go over those chains for finger-prints?" Mr. Yistle interrupted.

"Yes, sir. I went over everything for finger-prints. And it struck me that he had worn these gloves so that he would leave no finger-prints."

"Who?" asked Mr. Yistle.

"Rufus Lally."

"Wait a minute," Gillian barked. "I object to that assumption. You haven't satisfied me or any one else that Rufus Lally dragged that chain about the sail loft, or that he wore those gloves so that he would leave no finger-prints."

"I certainly am proving it!"

"Then prove it with material witnesses. Every scrap of your evidence so far is circumstantial."

"And convicting!" snapped the district attorney.

"Gentlemen," said the judge, frowning, "I will not reprimand you again for bickering. Address yourselves to this bench or to the jury."

"I am trying, your honor," said Mr. Yistle earnestly, "to establish a plot motive. I admit that I can produce no eye-witnesses. My entire case is based on what I consider to be irrefutable circumstantial evidence. With this witness I am trying to prove, as I stated, that the defendant was endeavoring, by planting these obvious clews, to prove that he was mentally deranged. I am trying to prove that he acted with scientific deliberation, that he was perfectly sane."

"Proceed."

Gillian seated himself beside the prisoner. Mr. Yistle was spiking his guns and there was nothing to be done about it. There was no longer any doubt about it. Mr. Yistle was building up a damaging case.

Bill Murdock answered more of Mr. Yistle's adroit questions. Yes; he had gone over every inch of the club property.

Mr. Yistle: "Did you find, in the kitchen, a small chest such as surgeons at sea use for keeping their medicines in?"

"Yes, sir."

"Would you recognize this chest if you saw it?"

"I think so, sir."

Mr. Yistle reached under the table. He pulled into the light a small iron-bound, green chest with the letters "R L" painted upon the lid in black. Bailiffs carried it over to the jury. Mr. Yistle, Gillian supposed, had had it moved into the court room during the noon recess.

"Is this the chest?"

"Yes, sir."

"I wish to introduce this chest, your honor, as Exhibit G for the State."

Gillian: "I object that that chest is not and cannot possibly be considered material evidence. It has no relation whatever to the death of Dr. Cullen."

Mr. Yistle: "I am introducing it, your honor, for the purpose of establishing a plot motive."

"THE CHEST," RULED his honor, "is admissible as material evidence."

"Exception is noted."

Mr. Yistle lifted the lid. Necks craned. The jurors in the back row stood up and saw that the green chest contained orderly rows of glass bottles and metal cans, all labeled.

"It will be established by a forthcoming witness," stated the prosecuting attorney, "that the contents of all these bottles and containers are correctly described on the labels. Each bottle, each container has been tested by the city chemist. I will pass these bottles around."

He began picking them out and handing them to the nearest juror.

"This contains muriatic acid. This, aconitine. This, arsenate of lead. This, blue vitriol. This, chloride of lime. This—arsenic. Here is a bottle of Paris green. Here is another bottle of arsenic. Arsenic! Arsenic! Arsenic! The man must have been infatuated with arsenic! I wish to show you, ladies and gentlemen of the jury, the sort of things that that fiend sitting at that table played with. Acids! Deadly chemicals! Poisons, a pinch of which would kill a strong, hale man! Arsenic! In bottle after bottle, we find this death-dealing white powder—arsenic! This case, ladies and gentlemen, if you will pardon my language, fairly stinks with arsenic! Wherever we turn—arsenic and yet more arsenic! Men in their graves, reeking with arsenic! Whisky reeking with arsenic! A chest in the defendant's kitchen containing bottle upon bottle of arsenic!"

"Your honor," Gillian interrupted, "I object. This is not testimony. It is summation."

"Sustained. Mr. Yistle, if you have questions to ask the witness, ask them."

"I am through with this witness."

Gillian took the witness. He said:

"Mr. Murdock, you say you spent eight hours going over the clubhouse, looking for clews?"

"I did, sir."

"In the vicinity of this cardboard silhouette of Dr. Cullen's profile, did you look for footprints?"

"I did, sir. There were any number of footprints. They were of all shapes and sizes."

"Did you make a thoroughgoing search for finger-prints on the desk in the trophy room?"

"I did, sir. I found no finger-prints but those of the accused."

"Did you make finger-print tests on this green chest?"

"I did, sir. There were only a few. The accused made them all."

"Did you find any proof, any kind of proof, that the accused had dragged that chain back and forth in the sail loft, or that he had deliberately fired a hole through that cardboard silhouette, or that he had worn gloves so that he would not leave his finger-prints? In short, did you find any material proof that the accused and not some one else had perpetrated these ghostly effects which have been described?"

"No, sir."

"Then you cannot say positively, from your knowledge and experience and observation, that the accused was responsible for the ghostly effects?"

"No, sir; I cannot."

"That will be all."

"Next witness," said Judge Simpson.

"Judge Woolwich," said Mr. Yistle.

16

ARSENIC

JUDGE CARSON WOOLWICH, a white-haired man of seventy, with finely-cut features and young blue eyes, made his way slowly to the witness stand. He testified, upon being sworn, that he had been Dr. Cullen's attorney and legal adviser; that he had drawn a number of wills for Dr. Cullen, the latest of which was dated a week before the murder.

Mr. Yistle introduced as material Exhibit H for the State the dead man's will. He then requested Judge Woolwich to read the eighth paragraph of the instrument. Judge Woolwich obliged, reading in a low voice.

" 'To my dear young friend, Rufus Lally, and to his sister, Eileen Lally, I hereby bequeath, free of all encumbrances, the sum of twenty-five thousand dollars in cash apiece.'"

"I should like to know," Gillian asked, "if this evidence is being introduced as a part of the State's intention to establish a plot motive."

"It is introduced," quickly answered the district attorney, "to establish a further motive for the murder. It is not connected with the plot motive. That is all, thank you, judge."

Gillian said: "Judge, will you read aloud paragraph fourteen of that instrument?"

Judge Woolwich complied: " 'To my faithful butler, Benjamin Ashe, I bequeath, free of all encumbrances, the sum of ten thousand dollars in cash.' "

"That will be all, judge. Thank you."

The judge retired. Mr. Yistle's next witness was Harry Zarrow, the city chemist. He took the stand with an air of indifference amounting to boredom. He yawned at the jury. He looked at the spectators and yawned again. Then he removed his gold-rimmed spectacles and carefully cleaned them with a snowy handkerchief.

"You are the city chemist of Greenfield, Mr. Zarrow?" Mr. Yistle asked.

"Yep."

"How long have you been in the employ of the city?"

"Ten years."

"Are you acquainted with Dr. Bartrom, the coroner?"

"Yep."

"On the date of October 15, did Dr. Bartrom bring to you labeled specimens of the linings of the livers cut from five corpses which had been exhumed from Maplewood Cemetery?"

"Yep."

"What did you do with them?"

"Tested for arsenic."

"Ah, yes—arsenic! It is strange, indeed, ladies and gentlemen of the jury, how, wherever we turn in this case, we find arsenic. Arsenic! Always arsenic! Mr. Zarrow, did you find arsenic present in the liver linings which were brought to you by the coroner?"

"I did."

"Arsenic present in every sample of liver lining?"

"That's right."

"Then what did you do with the liver samples?"

"I put each one in a bottle of alcohol, marked each bottle with the name of the dead man from whom it had been cut, and sent the bottles, with my analysis of each written on the respective labels, to your office."

"Would you recognize those bottles?"

"Yep."

Mr. Yistle uncovered five small glass bottles, each capped with metal and sealed with red wax; each labeled. Each of the bottles contained a clear colorless liquid in which floated a small, reddish-gray lump. The court room shuddered.

"I wish to introduce these bottles as Exhibits I, J, K, L, and M. for the State."

Mr. Yistle glanced at Gillian, but Gillian offered no objection. He was as anxious as was Mr. Yistle that those tested samples of dead men's livers be acceptable as material evidence.

JUDGE SIMPSON ACCEPTED them, but his nostrils quivered with distaste as he did so. Each bottle, upon being marked, was handed to Harry Zarrow. He had, in the interlude, skinned and placed in his mouth a stick of chewing gum. His jaws were now moving placidly.

Mr. Yistle: "Kindly read the comments on the label pasted on Exhibit I."

The city chemist did so. In his laconic voice, he informed the awed court room that the bottle contained a sample of the liver taken from the corpse of Jonathan Driggs, who died supposedly of cirrhosis of the liver on January 29, but actually of a cirrhosis brought about by chronic arsenic poisoning.

In turn, Harry Zarrow discussed the contents of each bottle until each of the five men was accounted for.

Gillian then interrupted: "I will gladly give my distinguished colleague permission to mention at this point, if he wishes, that no one suspected that these five men died from other than natural causes until after Dr. Cullen's death."

Mr. Yistle: "It is kind of you, I am sure."

Gillian: "Don't mention it."

His honor: "Please get on with your respective examinations, gentlemen. Time is flying."

Mr. Yistle: "I am through with this witness for the time being. He will be recalled later for another matter."

Gillian: "Cross-examination waived."

His honor: "Your next witness, Mr. Yistle."

"Gertrude Bixby."

A comely young woman of twenty-seven or eight took the stand. Under examination, she stated that she had been employed by Dr. Cullen as his private secretary. She had been in his employ four and a half years up to the time of his murder.

Mr. Yistle picked up from his table a loose-leaf notebook with a black imitation leather cover. He held it up for Miss Bixby to see, then said:

"Do you recognize this notebook, Miss Bixby?"

"Yes, sir," she said in a clear voice.

"I wish to introduce this notebook, your honor, as Exhibit N for the State." When the notebook was tagged and given to Miss Bixby, Mr. Yistle went on:

"Will you tell the jury, Miss Bixby, what this notebook contains?"

"It contains," the girl replied, "all sort's of typewritten data which were compiled from stenographic notes I made of the doctor's dictation. It was my custom to assemble all of his scientific notes, regardless of its relation, in weekly books of this sort. Later, he would go over the typed notes and rearrange them or act upon reminders I had taken down."

"For what week is this book, Miss Bixby?"

"It is for the week ending October 10."

"For the week ending two days before the doctor's murder?"

"Yes, sir."

Mr. Yistle placed his thumbs in the armpits of his vest, drew a deep breath, frowned, gazed long at the jury and then back again at Miss Bixby.

"Miss Bixby, will you read aloud the very first paragraph on the very first page in that book?"

Miss Bixby obliged. In a clear voice she read:

" 'Mystified by these frequent cirrhosis deaths.' "

Mr. Yistle: "One moment, Miss Bixby. I want the jury to understand clearly that what you are reading is matter that was dictated to you by Dr. Cullen—matter which you first took in stenographic form and later transcribed, in typewriting, to that page. Is that correct?"

"Yes, sir. Shall I read on?"

"If you will, please."

" 'Mystified by these frequent cirrhosis deaths. Their periodic occurrence is suspicious. Why was no autopsy ordered in any of these cases? I suspect arsenic. Find from

Dr. Bartrom—the coroner—if examination was made of livers of Jonathan Driggs, Marshal Fox, Robert Sandover, Vail Hendricks and William Andrews.'"

"Is that all, Miss Bixby?"

"That is all."

"Now, Miss Bixby—" Mr. Yistle paused and glanced at Rufus Lally who sat, pale and tense, looking at the girl. Some of the newspapers had rumored that he was in love with her. The tabloids had gone so far as to intimate that they were secretly engaged.

"Now, Miss Bixby, will you tell the jury whether or not this man—this man who is accused of the brutal murder of your employer—had access to this book?"

THE GIRL HESITATED. She was looking sadly at Rufe. She said "Yes" in a voice hardly louder than a whisper.

"He had access to that notebook?"

"Yes, sir."

Mr. Yistle demanded with rising emotional excitement: "You say, that Rufus Lally could go into the doctor's study at any hour of the day or night, unwatched, unobserved, and could have read the sentence you have just spoken aloud?"

The girl hesitated longer. "Yes, sir, he could have."

"He could have read the names of those five men, who, we have since proved, died of arsenic poisoning; he could have learned that Dr. Cullen would shortly investigate those horrible deaths?"

"Yes, sir."

"This book was lying within easy reach on the doctor's desk?"

"Yes, sir."

"It was lying there during the two days preceding the doctor's death, was it not?"

"It was. Yes, sir."

"And this ruthless fiend, this man who so loved to play with arsenic, could have learned, by merely peeping into that book, that Dr. Cullen was shortly to investigate the deaths of these five men who had died of arsenic poisoning?"

Mr. Yistle glared at Gillian. But Gillian did not object to that rousing inquiry. He sat in his chair, faintly frowning, gazing at the witness, slowly twirling between two fingers a lock of his black hair.

"Yes—sir."

"That will be all, Miss Bixby. Thank you."

Miss Bixby looked at Gillian. He got up slowly and smiled.

"Miss Bixby, you didn't see this boy—the defendant— look into that notebook, did you?"

"No, sir."

"Were you usually present when he came into the office, or the study?"

"Sometimes."

"He came and went as he pleased, did he?"

"Yes, sir."

"Why?"

The girl's eyes became round. "Well, he—he and the doctor were very good friends. The doctor thought he would become a great toxicologist. He was encouraging Mr. Lally. He wanted Rufe—I mean Mr. Lally—to use all his books and his notes that he wished."

Mr. Yistle didn't like this. He was frowning darkly.

Gillian said: "Was this young man the only person who had access to the doctor's books, who could come and go as he wished?"

"No, sir; there were a number of people who came and went. Doctor had so many friends."

"Among his most frequent callers, Miss Bixby, do you remember seeing Mr. Bruce Pennyfeather, Mr. Jeffery Whitaker, Mr. and Mrs. Dennis Van Zant, and Mr. Yistle, the district attorney?"

"Yes, sir; all of them were frequent callers."

"Did any of them ever quarrel with the doctor?"

Miss Bixby bit her lip. The question seemed to embarrass her. She lifted her chin and looked defiantly at Mr. Yistle.

"Yes, sir; the doctor and Mr. Yistle often quarreled."

"Over what?"

"Over some property they owned together in the new Riverside Manor development."

Mr. Yistle's scowl was now black. One fist was clenched.

"Did they ever come to blows, Miss Bixby?"

The girl looked frightened now. She said breathlessly: "Yes, sir; they did. Rather, one time, after a most heated quarrel, Mr. Yistle struck the doctor with his hand."

"Objection!" roared Mr. Yistle. "Irrelevant and immaterial."

"Overruled. Proceed, Mr. Hazeltine."

"So," said Gillian cheerfully, "Mr. Yistle one time struck the doctor, did he?"

"Yes—sir."

"And when, Miss Bixby, did this happen?"

"On the morning before the night of doctor's murder."

"I SUPPOSE," MR. Yistle furiously burst out, "you'll be laying the murder on my doorstep next!"

"It might be placing the foundling where it belongs!" cried Gillian. "No! It isn't beyond the realm of possibility that you murdered Dr. Cullen! That might explain why you are hounding and persecuting this poor boy!"

"Gentlemen!" thundered the judge. "One more word of this argument and I will hold both of you in contempt. Silence in this court. Bailiff, if you cannot, enforce silence, I will have this court cleared."

When order was restored, Gillian said:

"Miss Bixby, did you hear, on that or any other occasion, Mr. Yistle making threats?"

"I did. He said he would beat the doctor black and blue if the doctor did not give in to him."

"Did the words 'kill' or 'murder' occur in Mr. Yistle's conversation?"

"Yes!" the girl gasped. "Mr. Yistle said he would like to kill the doctor for being so stubborn."

"Objection!" panted Mr. Yistle.

"Overruled!"

"And he struck him with his fist?"

"Yes, sir; in the jaw. It almost knocked the doctor out of his chair."

"Thank you, Miss Bixby. That will be all."

She started to arise, but Mr. Yistle fairly shrieked: "Oh, don't go; don't go. I'm not through with you, Miss Bixby. Not by any means!" He was breathing noisily. His color was purple. His eyes were flashing. Mr. Yistle looked exceedingly dangerous. And he promptly proved that he was not nearly so dumb as he often pretended to be.

"Miss Bixby," he said, in a crackling voice of indignation, "you are not in the least anxious to see that man, that pale, cowering man over there—that Rufus Lally—go to the electric chair, are you?"

She answered firmly: "I certainly am not!"

"Why not?" Mr. Yistle roared.

"Because I do not think he is guilty."

"Oh! Is that so? You do not think he is guilty! How extremely interesting! How Christian! How noble! Miss Bixby"—the prosecutor flung out a hand at her so vigorously that the girl shrank back as if she feared he would strike her—"isn't it true that you are in love with this man, this Rufus Lally?"

"It is true."

"Ah! How tremendously interesting! You are in love with the man accused of a fiendish murder. You do not believe he committed the murder. No! Of course not! You are excused."

Miss Bixby, pale and distressed, looked quickly at Gillian. He only smiled and waved his hand. She went from the witness stand with hanging head and faltering step. Gillian glanced at the press table. There, heads were lowered. Pencils were flying. He pitied the soft-voiced, gentle Miss Bixby. What a morsel she would be for those wolves of the tabloids!

"Next witness!"

Mr. Yistle snapped: "That distinguished barrister, that noble defender of the wronged and the downtrodden—Gillian Hazeltine!"

17

A THRUST DRAWS BLOOD

GILLIAN WAS NOT surprised. He had been duly notified that he would be summoned as a witness. Grave and composed, he walked to the witness stand and seated himself. The light from the north window fell upon his tired face. He crossed his knees, folded his arms comfortably and gazed with a half-smile at the jury.

His name, he responded to the clerk's perfunctory question, was Gillian Hazeltine. He swore to tell the truth, the whole truth, and nothing but the truth. He presumed that Mr. Yistle would take advantage of this opportunity to bait him.

"What," the district attorney politely inquired, "is your occupation?"

"I am a lawyer."

"So you are a lawyer! Is it true, Mr. Hazeltine, that whenever an under dog appears in the public prints accused of this crime or that, that you, out of your great nobility, rush to his rescue in an approved legal manner?"

"Sometimes," said Gillian.

"Is it true, Mr. Hazeltine, that you one time stood trial for bribing a judge?"

"I object to that question."

"Your objection is sustained," said Judge Simpson. "Mr. Yistle, I consider your line of questioning irrelevant to any issue."

"I am merely endeavoring to establish the witness's credibility as a witness or lack of the same, your honor."

"I will not tolerate horseplay, Mr. Yistle," said the court sternly. The court room wore a wide smile.

"My purpose in having you take the stand, Mr. Hazeltine," the district attorney went on, "is to further my contention that the man you are defending is guilty of a plot; that he murdered Dr. Cullen out of fear that that plot was to be discovered."

"I understand your purpose perfectly," said Gillian. "I will gladly give you any information within my power to further that purpose."

The two enemies exchanged smiles. They were challenging, hard smiles. Mr. Yistle, after a moment, said:

"Will you kindly tell the jury, Mr. Hazeltine, whether it is true that you are in the habit occasionally of drinking Scotch whisky?"

"It is true that I drink an occasional Scotch highball."

"Just how occasionally?"

"On the average, I should say, I drink four or five Scotch highballs a week."

"Yes, Mr. Hazeltine. And within the past three years from whom have you been purchasing your Scotch whisky?"

"Until the time of his arrest, from the defendant."

"I see. Ah, yes. Then the defendant was a bootlegger?"

"He was. Yes."

"Do you know where he procured the Scotch whisky which he sold to you?"

"I believed he purchased it from a rum-runner."

"A smuggler?"

"Yes. A whisky smuggler."

"Was it good whisky?"

"It tasted like good whisky."

"Did it react like good whisky?"

"I'm afraid I did not, on any occasion, drink enough to be able to give you a scientific answer."

"And this good-tasting whisky you bought from the defendant?"

"Yes."

"In case lots?"

"In case lots. Yes."

Mr. Yistle rubbed his hands. "Now, Mr. Hazeltine, I wish you would describe to the jury the state of your health, beginning about a month before the death of Dr. Cullen."

"My health," Gillian answered, "beginning about the middle of September, was not of the best. A feeling of lassitude came over me by such imperceptible degrees that I cannot name when it began. But I should say about the middle of September. The condition gradually became worse. I felt sleepy most of the time. I lost my pep. My mental powers suffered. It was on the very night that Dr. Cullen died that a person, familiar with such symptoms, suggested that I might be suffering from an ordinary cirrhosis of the liver or a cirrhosis induced by arsenic."

"Who was that person?" Mr. Yistle snapped.

"I seem to forget," Gillian answered.

"By any chance, was it Eileen Lally?"

"My brain," Gillian gravely responded, "was in such a sluggish state that I cannot remember."

"VERY WELL. PROCEED, Mr. Hazeltine. You discovered that you had some form of cirrhosis of the liver. Did you have the usual kind of analysis performed by a doctor—urinalysis, to be exact—to determine whether or riot your cirrhosis was ordinary or arsenic?"

"I did," answered Gillian. "The analysis showed that I was harboring considerable arsenic."

"Arsenic!" cried Mr. Yistle. "Ever and forever we are meeting that leering name! Arsenic! Found in the liver linings of five dead men! Arsenic! Found to be present in the body of the living! Arsenic in green chests! Arsenic hidden in the kitchen! Where won't we find arsenic!"

"Let us hope," said Gillian, dryly, "that we will not find arsenic in your liver lining."

"Yes!" cried the district attorney. "You would joke about arsenic. But let me warn you, Gillian Hazeltine, the time will arrive when you will cease to laugh! The time will come, and soon, when these twelve intelligent men and, women—"

"I object, your honor," Gillian interrupted. "I am not on trial for murder. I am, just now, a mere witness."

Judge Simpson bent toward him. "Do you wish Mr. Yistle's remarks stricken from the record?"

"No, your honor. I object merely to his soap-box oratory. What were you about to ask me, Mr. Yistle?"

"This tasty Scotch whisky which you bought from your bootlegging client, Mr. Hazeltine— Tell me, on the night of Dr. Cullen's murder, did you have any of this whisky in your possession?"

"Yes, sir. I had, I believe, four or five full bottles of it."

When had that lot, that case, been delivered to you?"

"About three weeks previously."

"And on the night of the murder, what happened to those unused bottles of Scotch whisky?"

"My suspicions that they contained arsenic were aroused by the fact that several of my friends were complaining of the same symptoms that I was suffering. One of them, Mr. Dennis Van Zant, had had whisky obtained from the same source analyzed by Mr. Harry Zarrow, the city chemist. So I sent my whisky down to Mr. Zarrow to be analyzed."

"And did he find arsenic in it?"

"He did."

"Arsenic!" cried the district attorney. "I can hear that word even in my dreams! Arsenic in the lining of dead men's livers! Arsenic in green chests! Arsenic in whisky! May I ask you," he went on, "if your health has improved since you stopped drinking this arsenic-poisoned whisky?"

"It has, indeed."

"That will be all. You may take yourself for cross-examination."

"Thank you." Gillian smiled faintly. "I should like to ask myself if I or any one else has yet found a scrap of material evidence linking the defendant with five dead men poisoned with arsenic. My answer is unqualifiedly 'No.'

"I should like further to ask myself if it has been proved that the defendant placed arsenic in my whisky or any one's whisky. My answer is again 'No.' That is all. Am I excused?"

"Not yet," barked Mr. Yistle. "I should like to ask you whether any men other than those to whom the defendant was selling whisky have died of arsenic poisoning?"

"Who knows?" answered Gillian. "Have you exhumed the body of every man who has died in recent years of cirrhosis of the liver and made tests for arsenic?"

"You are excused."

"Not yet," said Gillian. "You have furnished not even the slimmest kind of circumstantial evidence to uphold your inference that the defendant brought about the deaths of these five men."

"The arsenic in that chest at this moment would kill a hundred men!"

"But did any arsenic ever used by the defendant find its way into the bodies, the livers, of those particular five men?"

"Yes!" shouted Mr. Yistle.

"Prove it!"

"I have proved it. You are excused."

"Not yet," Gillian grimly repeated. "You are slanderously blackening the character of an innocent young man. I wish to re-cross-examine this witness. I want to ask myself how long I have known the accused. I answer: 'Five years.' I ask myself if, in all that time, I have detected any flaw in his moral character. Answer: 'No!' I ask: 'Have I observed his habits?' I answer: 'I have!' I ask: 'What are his habits?' I answer: 'Honest, steady, decent—those of a student who is seriously preparing himself for a career in one of the most important branches of medicine.' Am I excused?"

"Yes!" roared Mr. Yistle.

GILLIAN DESCENDED FROM the stand and took his place beside Rufe. A little color had entered the face of the defendant.

Gillian stopped smiling when the name of the next

witness was uttered. He sat up warily and reached for a folder, which he opened. He gravely consulted the contents.

Bruce Pennyfeather, tall, gaunt, worried-looking, took the stand. His eyes were eerie lights set deep in his skull. He was manifestly ill at ease.

Mr. Yistle put questions to him similar to those which Gillian had answered. How much Scotch whisky was he in the habit of drinking? Where did he secure this whisky?

In his deep voice, Pennyfeather answered: "From the defendant."

"Were you aware recently of certain symptoms of ill health?"

"I was. My mental processes slowed up. I lost interest in life. I was dopey."

"On the night of Dr. Cullen's murder did you send samples of this whisky which you had been securing from the defendant to the city chemist?"

"I did."

"Did you ascertain whether or not this whisky you had been drinking contained any poison?"

"Yes, sir."

The stenographer interrupted: "Will the witness please speak more loudly? I can't hear him."

Mr. Yistle: "What poison did the city chemist find present in this whisky of Rufus Lally's which you had been drinking?"

"Arsenic."

"Arsenic!" repeated Mr. Yistle triumphantly. "Once again we meet our old friend. Mr. Pennyfeather, on the night of Dr. Cullen's murder; rather, at about four in the morning, did you pay a visit to the Greenfield Yacht Club?"

"I did."

"Why?"

Pennyfeather hesitated. "Curiosity, I suppose."

"Will you describe to the jury what happened to you there?"

"I drove down there," the witness answered, "directly from Gillian Hazeltine's house. I parked my car beside a pile of lumber. I switched off my lights and was preparing to climb out when a pair of hands seized me from behind."

"Where did those hands seize you?"

"By the neck. Powerful hands. I—I was terrified. I struggled. I tried to turn about, to strike my assailant, but my wind was cut off. Presently I lost consciousness. When I came to myself again I was lying on the floor of the sail loft, surrounded by policemen. You were there, Mr. Yistle. So was Mr. Hazeltine. Also an evil-looking Japanese and a red-haired girl who, I believe, is the accused's sister."

"You do not remember being dragged into the sail loft?"

"I remember nothing from the time I lost consciousness at the automobile until I regained my senses in the sail loft."

"You have no idea who your assailant may have been?"

"No, sir. Unless it was that Jap."

"You were aware, of course, that that neighborhood is infested with dangerous characters—railroad hoboes, river rats and the like?"

"Yes, sir. It may have been one of them."

"Were any of your valuables stolen?"

"A gold watch and chain. I had only a few cents in my pocket. I had left my wallet at home."

Gillian raised no objection to the irregularity of this

questioning, although Judge Simpson glanced at him inquiringly. He was curious to see how the district attorney would tie up this very loose end. Mr. Yistle, Gillian thought, had done it very neatly.

WHEN THE DISTRICT attorney gave way for cross-examination, Gillian arose with the alacrity of a cat. Bruce Pennyfeather watched him with misgivings. His eyes narrowed. He seemed to shrink back into the chair. His fingers were nervously fumbling with one another.

"Mr. Pennyfeather," said Gillian vigorously, "what is your business?"

"I am a wholesale druggist."

"Did you ever sell drugs, chemicals, poisons to Dr. Cullen?"

"Yes"—a whisper.

"Did you ever sell drugs, chemicals, poisons to Rufus Lally?"

"Yes"—more faintly and hesitantly than before.

Judge Simpson said crisply: "Mr. Pennyfeather, you will have to raise your voice."

Gillian: "Mr. Pennyfeather, when you sold poisons to Rufus Lally, did you require a prescription or an order of any sort?"

"No."

"Why not?" Gillian shot at him.

"Because Dr. Cullen had vouched for him."

"Dr. Cullen told you that Rufus Lally was seriously studying to become a toxicologist and that he was a responsible, trustworthy young man?"

"He said something of the sort."

Gillian walked slowly toward the wholesale druggist. Bruce Pennyfeather looked worried.

"Mr. Pennyfeather, between the hours of twelve midnight and one thirty on the morning of October 12, where were you?"

"Driving my car."

"With whom?"

"I—was alone."

The color had faded from Pennyfeather's long, horselike face. It became an unwholesome yellow. He wet his lips. His head sagged forward as if he were about to faint. With an obvious effort he lifted it and fixed his deep, melancholy eyes on Gillian.

"Where did you drive?"

"From my house to Millbrook, across the river to Esty and back by the same route."

"Can you produce any witness, Mr. Pennyfeather, who saw you at any time during that drive?"

"No."

"If you were accused of having murdered Dr. Cullen, you would have no alibi?"

Bruce Penny feather opened his eyes. They were fiery with hate.

"I did not kill Dr. Cullen!"

"Your honor," panted Mr. Yistle, "I object. This witness is being bulldozed and insulted."

"I am attacking nothing but his credibility, your honor," Gillian explained.

"Every witness I have put on the stand," Mr. Yistle expostulated, "he has, directly or indirectly, accused of murdering Dr. Cullen. I most strenuously object to his procedure."

Judge Simpson ruled: "I cannot sustain your objections, Mr. Yistle. It would appear that Mr. Hazeltine is convinced that some one other than the defendant was guilty of the crime of which he is charged. It seems to me that by attempting, as you are doing, to establish a plot motive, you have given Mr. Hazeltine a wide target. He is certainly entitled to attack the credibility of any witness you put on the stand. You may proceed with cross-examination, Mr. Hazeltine."

"IS IT NOT true, Mr. Pennyfeather," Gillian complied, "that you have been paying a great deal of attention to Miss Gertrude Bixby, the doctor's secretary—taking her to dinner, to the theater?"

"Yes."

"Is it not true that you were aware that she was, at that time, the fiancée of the defendant?"

"Yes."

"Is it not true that, on more than one occasion, you threatened to 'fix' the defendant?"

"I don't remem—"

"Didn't you call the defendant a presumptuous young squirt in the hearing of several men in the City Club smokeroom, one afternoon early in October?"

"What if I did?"

Gillian said grimly: "We'll let that pass. Mr. Pennyfeather, you are reputed to be a good cook, are you not?"

"People have said that, yes."

"You live alone, don't you?"

"I do"—faintly.

"Mr. Pennyfeather, have you ever made fudge?"

"I don't remember."

"Come! Think hard!"

"Oh, God. I don't—"

The witness suddenly collapsed. He went limply forward and would have sagged to the floor if Gillian had not been there to catch him.

18

A DRAWN BATTLE

THE COURT ROOM was in a hubbub. The district attorney came running over to Gillian and seized him by the arm. He burst out: "You know damned well, Gillian, that that poor devil has been sick since the night of the murder. Why did you annoy him with those utterly pointless questions? It was brutal!"

"The man who murdered Dr. Cullen didn't stop at brutality," Gillian answered.

The bailiff could be heard above the clamor of voices demanding order. "Order in the court! Order in the court!" His gavel was beating a tattoo.

When quiet was restored, Judge Simpson said: "Let's have your next witness promptly, Mr. Yistle."

"Your honor," Mr. Yistle protested, "I am only too anxious to get this over with. It is not I who am trying to delay the case. That white-faced wretch is guilty. All these underhanded attempts on the part of the counsel for the defense to sidetrack—"

Judge Simpson: "Mr. Yistle, the jury will decide in due course on the guilt or innocence of the defendant. Call your next witness."

Mr. Yistle's next witness was Jeffery Whitaker, who

came striding to the stand as if he were indignant over some wrong. His square face and his bald head were redder than usual. He took the stand and glared about the court room.

In his crackling voice, he answered Mr. Yistle's questions about the poisoned whisky. Yes: he had detected symptoms of chronic arsenic poisoning. Yes; he had sent several bottles remaining from a case he had purchased from the defendant to Dr. Zarrow, the city chemist. Yes; it had proved to contain arsenic.

Gillian's first question, in cross-examination, was:

"Mr. Whitaker, where were you between the hours of midnight and two o'clock on the morning of October 12?"

"In my office!"

"Where is your office?"

"Tenth floor, Marple Building."

"Can you produce a witness to prove that you were at your office between those hours?"

"No," snapped the witness.

"You mean, the night watchman did not let you in and out?"

"I did not see the night watchman. I let myself in and I let myself out."

"How did you reach the ninth floor?"

"I used an elevator. I ran it up to the ninth floor and when I left I ran it down."

"No one saw you doing all this?"

THE WITNESS ANSWERED angrily: "I told you, didn't I, that no one saw me?"

Gillian smiled grimly. "I only wanted to make sure. What business are you engaged in, Mr. Whitaker?"

"Toro! Where in the devil have you been?"

"Stocks and bonds."

"You are a broker?"

"That's what I am."

"You knew Dr. Cullen well, did you not?"

"Yes. I knew Dr. Cullen."

"Is it true that you handled some or all of his funds for investment?"

"I handled some of his funds."

"Isn't it true," Gillian whipped at him, "that you have been borrowing money steadily from Dr. Cullen for a period of over two years—that you are in debt to him for approximately fifty thousand dollars?"

The witness glared at him. He barked: "No. No. It is not true!"

"Isn't it true that he lent you this money, from time to time, without the formality of anything but your unsecured notes?"

"He did not lend me any money!"

Mr. Yistle: "Objection. This is absolutely immaterial testimony, your honor."

"Overruled."

"Your honor," said Gillian, "I would like to have a former witness recalled to prove that this man is lying—Miss Bixby. Before you step down, Whitaker, I want to ask you two more questions. Isn't it true that Dr. Cullen's death would have been advantageous to you?"

"Objection!" roared Mr. Yistle.

"Sustained!"

"Exception," said Gillian grimly. "I want that in the record, your honor."

"Exception is noted."

"The other question," Gillian went on, is: "Was your father engaged, during ten years of your boyhood—that is, from the time you were ten until you were nineteen—manufacturing various kinds of candy?"

"He was."

"And you were an apprentice candy maker?"

"I was."

"Did you learn how to make fudge?"

"I don't remember."

"Step down, please. I am through with this witness, your honor, but I want him held for further examination later."

"It is so ordered," the judge complied.

Gertrude Bixby, pale and nervous, came in. She looked anxiously at Gillian and took the stand. Gillian asked her:

"Miss Bixby, were you ever present when Dr. Cullen lent sums of money to Jeffery Whitaker?"

"Yes, sir," huskily.

"Did you see Mr. Whitaker sign and give to Dr. Cullen his notes for the money borrowed?"

"Yes, sir. On several occasions."

"What happened to these notes?"

"The doctor put them in the upper left hand drawer of his desk."

"Did he keep that drawer locked?"

"No, sir. He never locked anything."

"Did you ever clean out his desk?"

"Yes, sir; I put everything in order once a week."

"When was the last time, prior to his death, that you cleaned it?"

"The 10th of October."

"Were those notes that Mr. Whitaker had signed in the upper left hand drawer then?"

"Yes, sir."

"When was the last time, to your knowledge, that Mr. Whitaker visited the doctor?"

"The morning of the eleventh."

"The morning before the doctor was murdered?"

"Yes, sir."

Gillian slowly walked toward her. His expression was kindly. Mr. Yistle was watching him with alertness.

"Where are those notes now, Miss Bixby?"

"I don't know, sir."

"Aren't they in that upper left hand drawer?"

"No, sir."

"Are you sure?"

"I looked through the desk the morning after the murder. The notes were gone. I looked very thoroughly."

"YOUR HONOR," MR. Yistle broke in ironically, "all of

this is interesting—tremendously interesting. But what, I should like to know, has it to do with the issue at stake?"

Judge Simpson looked at Gillian; said: "Do you care to answer that, Mr. Hazeltine?"

"It seems to me, your honor," Gillian answered, "that the facts are self-evident. I am attempting to discover who really murdered Dr. Cullen."

"You mean," said the district attorney angrily, "you are attempting, in every possible way, to befog the issue, to drag in irrelevancies! You are resorting to your old tricks— attempting to prejudice the jury against every witness."

"That is within my legal right," snapped Gillian.

Judge Simpson interrupted: "For the last time, I will request you gentlemen to address this bench. Are you through with this witness, Mr. Hazeltine?"

"Yes, your honor."

"Do you, Mr. Yistle, wish to reexamine her?"

"Your honor," said Mr. Yistle wearily, "this girl is obviously anxious to save the life of the accused. I consider her testimony therefore worthless. I have no questions to ask her."

"You are excused, Miss Bixby," said the judge. "Call the next witness."

The next witness was Cornelia Van Zant. When her name was called, Gillian looked at Mr. Yistle and grinned. Mr. Yistle returned his grin with a look of defiance. Gillian well knew why Cornelia was serving as a witness. She had bullied Bert Yistle into it.

Gillian's grin widened as she appeared. She was more smartly dressed than any woman in the court room. In a tight-fitting blue felt cloche, a smart blue-tweed suit and stockings of a subtle gray shade which showed off the perfection of her legs, she looked the part that she longed to play—the aristocrat. Cornelia bowed to Gillian, as she swept past him. It was a haughty little bow accompanied by a haughty little smile. Gillian bowed formally in return.

When she seated herself in the witness chair, Cornelia struck an attitude that made Gillian chuckle. Her air was that of a queen seating herself on her throne.

Mr. Yistle questioned her gently. Did she occasionally indulge in a Scotch highball with her husband? Yes—occasionally. Had she observed any peculiarly ill effects from that indulgence? Indeed she had. What were they? Headaches, lassitude, and a tired feeling.

"Did you ever see your husband and the accused together?"

"I did. The accused came to my house and delivered whisky. I saw him delivering it three times."

"Did you take steps to discover whether or not your symptoms were those of chronic arsenic poisoning?"

"I did."

"What was the result?"

"I was poisoned with arsenic!"

Mr. Yistle bowed to her, "That will be all."

Gillian arose and hooked his thumb between two top buttons of his vest.

He barked: "Cornelia Van Zant, did you murder Dr. Cullen?"

Cornelia uttered a small shriek. Rosy color flooded her face. Her eyes snapped angrily.

"Gillian Hazeltine, I think you're dreadfully rude!"

"So do I!" snapped Mr. Yistle.

"I apologize," said Gillian. "The question is withdrawn."

He knew that he'd never hear the end of this from Cornelia. Well, she wanted publicity—and he wanted time.

"Mrs. Van Zant," he said gently, "will you tell me whether or not you are, in your own opinion, a good cook?"

"I am an expert cook," Cornelia flashed at him. "Furthermore, I make perfectly delicious fudge! That was the next question, wasn't it?"

"It was. Thank you. You are excused."

Flushed and with sparkling eyes, Cornelia descended from the witness stand. In passing the press table, she glanced over shoulders. Her fleeting expression of disappointment was perhaps due to her discovery that, as far as she could see, no sketches were being drawn of her.

THE STATE'S NEXT witness was Dennis Van Zant. Upon his round, pink face was an expression of eagerness and anxiety that caused Gillian to smile again. Dennis, of course, was a necessary witness—and how he loved it!

His testimony bore out Bruce Pennyfeather's, Jeffery Whitaker's, Gillian's and Cornelia's. Yes, he had bought whisky from the accused. Yes, he had quaffed of it liberally. Yes, he had had symptoms of chronic arsenic poisoning. Yes, he had taken whisky to Harry Zarrow, the city chemist, for analysis.

Cross-examining him, Gillian asked: "Have you any reason to suspect that the accused bore a grudge against you?"

"No, sir. I paid him cash on the spot when he delivered whisky to me."

"You know of no reason why he should have wanted to poison you?"

"None, whatever. I think he's crazy."

Gillian fixed stern eyes upon him. "Mr. Van Zant, where were you on the morning of October 12, between the hours of midnight and one thirty?"

"I was in Zarrow's laboratory, watching that whisky being analyzed."

"You saw Mr. Zarrow run off the arsenium trisulfide precipitate test?"

"I don't know the name of it. He held a porcelain disk in a hydrogen flame and a yellow spot formed."

"That will be all. Oh, just a moment. Do you know how to make fudge?"

The court room burst into laughter. Dennis Van Zant vigorously shook his head and retreated, pink with confusion.

Harry Zarrow was now recalled. He was asked to testify, merely for purposes of record, that he had analyzed the whisky and found arsenic present. A long, tiresome chemical analysis was read into the record.

Mr. Yistle's next witness was Tom Murphy, of the homicide squad. He testified that he had been present when the accused dictated and signed a confession.

"Did you sign that confession as a witness?" the district attorney asked him.

"I did," said the detective.

"I wish," said Mr. Yistle, "to introduce the statement as material evidence." He handed a sheet of paper to the stenographer, who marked it. The signed confession was accepted as Exhibit O for the State. Tom Murphy, in a firm voice, read it aloud:

"I, Rufus Lally, being of sound mind, do hereby state that at the hour of one fifteen on the morning of October 12, 1928, I did enter the premises of Dr. Horace G. Cullen, that I did enter his study, and that I did, with due deliberation and consideration of the consequences, shoot him dead with a thirty-eight caliber bullet. I make this statement of my own free will and accord, because I wish to confess my crime before my God. I further state and declare that this statement was obtained without duress, without pressure of any kind being brought to bear upon me.—Signed, Rufus Lally, Fourth Precinct Jail, October 12, 1928."

Gillian snapped: "I object to the acceptance of that statement as material evidence, your honor; and I request that it be held inadmissible to the record."

Judge Simpson asked his grounds.

"It was obtained under duress, your honor."

Mr. Yistle fixed a hard look upon Tom Murphy, but the detective was looking at Gillian.

Judge Simpson: "I will withhold decision until the witness has been cross-examined. Are you through with examination, Mr. Yistle?"

"Yes, sir."

"You may take the witness, Mr. Hazeltine."

Gillian said: "Mr. Murphy, were you in the Fourth Precinct jail when the accused was brought in?"

"No, sir. I was at headquarters, I went up to the jail immediately."

"WILL YOU KINDLY tell the jury what you observed there between the time of your arrival and about five o'clock that morning?"

Mr. Yistle stared at the detective, but Tom Murphy was now gazing at the jury. He began:

"They had this kid in the warden's office when I got there."

"Who were 'they'?" Gillian interrupted.

"Murdock, of the homicide squad, and a traffic officer named Fogarty."

"What was happening, Mr. Murphy?"

"They were trying to get him to make a confession. They had a big thousand-watt light in a nickeled reflector on his face. Murdock was standing behind his chair and Fogarty was standing in front of him. The kid was hysterical. He was blubbering that he hadn't killed the doctor."

Tom Murphy paused.

"Go on, Tom. Tell the jury what they did to him."

Mr. Yistle's look of anxiety had become one of indignation. But he made no objections.

"The kid was thirsty and wanted a drink of water. He fainted a couple of times. Every few minutes Murdock would go out and get a glass of water with ice in it. He made the ice tinkle."

"Did he give the boy a drink?"

"No, sir. He—that is, Murdock—kept making that tinkling sound every time the kid asked for a drink. It kept up all night long. I sat down close to the kid and kept asking him if he didn't want to sign a confession. And he kept saying that he didn't kill the doctor."

Again the detective paused.

"What else did they do to the accused?"

Mr. Yistle barked: "I object to that question as leading." Mr. Yistle was perspiring. It was a certainty that Tom

Murphy would not long enjoy his present occupation, if the district attorney's office had anything to say about it.

"Sustained. Rephrase your question, Mr. Hazeltine."

"Did any one, at any time that night, hit, slap or kick the defendant?"

"Yes, sir. Murdock slapped him three or four times in the face and once he kicked him in the shins."

"Was the hot end of a lighted cigar pressed against his face or his hands?"

"No, sir. But Murdock held it so close to the back of his neck one time that I smelled singed hair."

"When did the defendant sign this confession?"

"At a little after five. The district attorney came in about four thirty, and took my job away from me."

"What do you mean—took your job away from you?"

"I had been sitting in front of the kid. I got up and Mr. Yistle sat there."

"What did he say?"

"I object!" roared Mr. Yistle. "This witness is lying, your honor. It's a wonder he isn't black in the face!"

"Overruled," snapped Judge Simpson. "The witness will answer."

Gillian said: "The question was: 'What did Mr. Yistle say?'"

"He told the kid that he'd better sign the confession, because if he didn't sign it his sister would be involved."

"That's a black lie!"

Judge Simpson frowned. "Mr. Yistle, I must ask you to restrain yourself. You may reexamine this witness if you wish."

Gillian: "What else did Mr. Yistle say, Tom?"

"That's all. He kept saying it over and over again until the kid finally broke down and cried. Then Mr. Yistle and Murdock went to the typewriter and framed up the confession, and the kid signed it."

"Did he read it before he signed it?"

"No, sir. He couldn't. That light had blinded him."

"That will be all, Tom. Thank you."

Mr. Yistle cried: "Take him away. I don't want to reexamine him—the perjurer! Bring Murdock back here."

BILL MURDOCK PRESENTLY walked down the aisle and took the stand.

Mr. Yistle, in an imploring tone, said to him:

"Bill, we want the truth about this confession. You were right there all night, weren't you?"

"Yes, sir."

"Were any methods of torture employed, such as tinkling ice in a glass behind the accused, or slapping or kicking him, or holding the hot end of a cigar near his neck?"

"No, sir! Certainly not!" Bill Murdock exclaimed.

"Was a powerful light held close to his face during the time he was being questioned?"

"No, Mr. Yistle."

"Did you hear me or any one else say to the accused that if he did not sign a confession his sister would become involved?"

"No, sir! Nothing like that happened while I was there, and I was there every minute."

"Except when you went out to get a drink of water or something like that?"

"Yes, sir. But I was never gone very long."

Mr. Yistle wiped his sweating brow. He had, he was certain, pulled his chestnuts out of the fire.

"That will be all."

"Cross-examination waived," said Gillian. "Your honor, I respectfully request that that signed statement, admitted as Exhibit O for the State, be held inadmissible as material evidence, and that all of the testimony relating to it be stricken from the record. Perjury has obviously been committed."

Judge Simpson pursed his lips and frowned. His tanned face was troubled. He presently shook his head.

"I cannot grant that request, Mr. Hazeltine. The point you raise is not one of law, but of personal opinion. It will be for the jury to decide whether or not that statement was obtained under duress. You may, if you can, call further witnesses to testify."

Gillian accepted defeat with a grim smile. Mr. Yistle beamed.

Judge Simpson said: "Call your next witness, please."

"I have no further witnesses, your honor. The State rests."

Gillian promptly said: "Your honor, I should like to have a postponement of forty-eight hours, for the purpose of securing a witness who has thus far been unavailable."

Judge Simpson said firmly: "Petition is denied. Defense will open tomorrow morning. Ladies and gentlemen of the jury, we are about to take a recess until to-morrow morning at ten o'clock. The court admonishes you not to speak about this case among yourselves or permit any one to speak to you about it. You will keep your minds open until the case is finally submitted to you. The defendant will retire."

Gillian: "Your honor, I should like to obtain your and the

State's attorney's permission to have finger-prints taken from all of the witnesses who have testified to-day. They are in the witness room."

Judge Simpson looked at Mr. Yistle. "I have no objection. Have you, Mr. Yistle?"

"It's all right with me," said Mr. Yistle affably. He grinned at Gillian. "Going to string it along with experts, eh? Go to it!"

"Thank you," said Gillian.

"The court," Judge Simpson declared, "will take a recess until tomorrow."

19

THE RETURN

GILLIAN LEFT THE courthouse by a back door, thereby hoping to escape the reporters. But ten or twelve vigilant young men were waiting there to pounce upon him. Questions came popping at him.

"We'd like to know, Mr. Hazeltine, what all these references to poisoned fudge are about. Did somebody get a box of poisoned fudge?"

"I can't answer that."

"Are you going to put the Lally girl on the stand?"

"I haven't decided."

"What's happened to that Japanese butler of yours?"

"I wish I knew. He vanished immediately after his release."

"Do you think Bruce Pennyfeather murdered the doctor?"

"I don't know."

"Do you know who did murder him?"

"I won't answer foolish questions."

"Then you do know?"

"I won't answer."

"Whether or not you know, Mr, Hazeltine, have you any basis for suspecting what the motive was?"

"Yes."

A dozen voices chorused: "What was it?"

Gillian smiled grimly. "I won't tell you."

"I've got a good guess," said a tall, earnest-looking young man who wore a bright green felt hat cocked over one eye. "It was the doctor's butler. That guy had a mean eye. And what a record! Am I right, Mr. Hazeltine?"

"I agree with you," said Gillian, "that he had a mean eye."

"The butler didn't do it," burst out another reporter. "It was Pennyfeather. Where was he when the murder was committed?"

"You're crazy," broke in another. "What motive did Pennyfeather have? Jeffery Whitaker is my guess. He had a motive. What became of the fifty thousand dollars' worth of bum notes? Am I right, Mr. Hazeltine?"

"One guess," said Gillian, "is as good as another."

"How about that Jap butler of yours, Mr. Hazeltine?"

"What was his motive?" Gillian countered.

"Well, those yellow bellies are funny people."

"You're all full of bull," growled a thick-set young man with a pugilistic cast of countenance. "Lally himself did it. He killed off the doctor so the five arsenic deaths wouldn't be hung on him. Mr. Hazeltine's going to pull an insanity defense. Do you know what they're betting on the verdict now, Mr. Hazeltine? Twenty-five to one for first degree murder!"

Gillian broke away from them and ran to his car. As far as he was concerned, the odds against an acquittal were a thousand to one. And if he did not hear from the red-haired girl before morning, they would be a million to one.

Gillian stopped at the Herendon Arms for dinner, then drove home. There was a full night's work ahead of him.

The telephone began to ring before he had arranged the contents of two thick brief cases on the desk in his study. He answered it. A strange voice at the other end angrily demanded why he didn't have the guilty man arrested.

"What guilty man?"

"The real murderer of Dr. Cullen!"

"Who is he?"

"Any fool would know that the district attorney is the real murderer!"

"Can you prove that?"

"I don't have to prove it! It's written all over his ugly face!"

Gillian gently hung up. That call would be, he knew, a fair introduction to a long evening of them. Cranks, newspaper reporters, well-intending strangers. He would have ignored the phone entirely except that he feared to miss Eileen Lally's call.

AT TEN THIRTY Cornelia called. It appeared that she was still indignant over his rudeness of the afternoon. She was provoked over the operator's reply of "the line is busy" when she called him on the telephone.

"I've been trying to reach you since seven o'clock. Gillian, I think you were unspeakably rude."

"Darling," Gillian chuckled, "a child who puts his finger into a buzz saw must expect to see blood drawn. Will you do me a favor?"

"No," said Cornelia, petulantly. Then: "What is it?"

"I'd like you to be one of my witnesses."

"Yes! And have you humiliate me!" A hurt pause. Then: "What do you want me to testify to?"

"I want you to testify as a domestic science expert on some fudge which I will introduce as material evidence. Will you?"

"Of course I will! But you've got to promise not to be rude—or funny."

"I'll promise, Cornelia, if you'll promise to be punctual."

He returned to his work—and to the continually ringing telephone. It was nearly midnight when he picked up the receiver to hear the tired but thrilled voice of the red-haired girl.

She was so excited that she stammered. "Mr. H-Hazeltine, you were right! And I found the can with at least two ounces of arsenic in the bottom!"

"Good girl! Where?"

"In an ashcan in the cellar! It was full of old tin cans and rubbish."

"When did this happen?"

"It just happened! I'm phoning from the Riverside drug store."

"But wasn't anybody home?"

"A wild party was going on. Shall I bring you this arsenic?"

"No. Take it down to Colton Thorpe, the finger-print expert. Tell him to go over it with a microscope. Then go home and go to bed. Tomorrow may be a hard day. Meet me at my office at nine. Good night."

"Good night."

Gillian hung up the receiver. As he did so he heard a faint scuffling in the hall.

He presumed that it was his new houseman, a sullen, inefficient creature who answered to the name of Mullins.

Toro entered—a thin, shabby, aged Toro. His clothes were rumpled and dusty. His face was gaunt. There were half moons of purple under his eyes.

Gillian swung around from his desk and glared at him.

"Where in the devil have you been?"

The Japanese sighed. "I have, alas, been seeking the gold of truth in the desert of despair. In the dark hour of my life I ran away from myself. I have returned."

"Why did you run away in the first place?"

"Fear," groaned the penitent Jap.

"What were you afraid of?"

"That my part in this dreadful murder case would be discovered!"

20

ANOTHER MOTIVE

"OYEZ! OYEZ! OYEZ! The Superior Court, Part One, Criminal Term, is open and in session! Judge Simpson presiding!"

An odor of soggy humanity permeated the court room. It had been raining since dawn. Crowds of the curious, packed in the streets about the courthouse, had endured the downpour for an opportunity to catch a brief glimpse of the leading performers in the Cullen trial. A comparative handful had found seats.

The State's attorney and his assistant, Mr. Bullock, were whispering together at their table. It was their opinion that Gillian Hazeltine would resort to any tactics to befog the facts which they had so cleanly established in yesterday's long session. They were certain that he would base his plea of not guilty on insanity. The State's attorneys were despondent over this project. An insanity defense meant days and days of wrangling, of hearkening to the long-winded testimony of alienists.

Most of the jurors looked sleepy. Most of the men at the press table looked bored.

Gillian Hazeltine spread out a dozen sheets of paper on the table before him. Off to one side was a cardboard box.

Beside it were two round tin cans, one large, one small. Near-by, in a small pile, were greatly enlarged photographs of finger-prints—black swirls and whorls on shiny paper.

Judge Simpson asked: "Is the defense ready?"

Gillian arose and answered: "Your honor, the defense is ready."

"The defense may proceed."

Gillian walked thoughtfully over to the jury. His face was gray. He appeared to be fatigued. But he spoke crisply.

"Ladies and gentlemen of the jury, you heard the prosecuting attorney make the statement yesterday that the defendant entered this court room presumptively innocent of the charge against him. By means of witnesses and the introduction of material evidence you saw and heard the prosecuting attorney attempt to prove that the defendant is guilty. By means of witnesses and material evidence, you heard and saw the prosecuting attorney attempt to prove that the defendant is guilty of a plot by which five citizens of Greenfield were murdered with arsenic. It is the State's contention that Rufus Lally killed Dr. Cullen in an attempt at concealing the crime of murdering these five men.

"On one point I am in wholehearted agreement with the prosecuting attorney: that Dr. Cullen was killed so that no investigation into the death of the five men would be made. But it is my contention that the wrong man has been brought to trial to answer to this grave charge. It is my contention that Rufus Lally has been made the victim of a plot; that the actual murderer has yet to be apprehended.

"That is my contention, and that is what I shall, with witnesses and suitable material evidence, set out to prove. I claim that Rufus Lally did not commit any murder. I claim that the actual murderer, with diabolical cleverness, made it appear that Rufus Lally was the murderer. And I claim that the motive behind these various murders is one which has, so far, not been advanced in this court room. I will prove to you beyond reasonable doubt that Rufus Lally has been most unjustly accused. I will support the State's attempt at proving the existence of a diabolical plot. And I will attempt to place the blame where it belongs. First witness: Bruce Pennyfeather!"

The wholesale druggist took the stand. He walked heavily. His shoulders drooped. Seating himself, he sighed gustily. His long, horselike face had the waxen yellowness of lemon rind.

When he was seated, Gillian picked up from his table a yellow document bound in faded blue paper. Mr. Yistle watched him suspiciously.

"This," Gillian explained, "is the original charter of the Greenfield Yacht Club, and it contains the sundry amendments which have been since added. I wish to introduce this instrument as material Exhibit A for the defense."

Judge Simpson glanced at Mr. Yistle. The stenographer marked the club charter and it was handed to Bruce Pennyfeather.

"Mr. Pennyfeather, will you read to the jury paragraph one of section one under the articles of incorporation?" asked Gillian.

THE WHOLESALE DRUGGIST glanced down the first page and turned to the second. Finding the paragraph Gillian referred to, he read:

It is agreed that membership in the Greenfield Yacht Club

is not transferable, nor is it transmissible by inheritance. And
it is furthermore agreed that the assets, properties, fixtures
and all real estate owned by the Greenfield Yacht Club shall
be owned, share and share alike, by surviving members in
good standing. In case of the sale of the properties, fixtures
and real estate of the Greenfield Yacht Club, such moneys
as are derived from such sale are to be distributed share and
share alike among surviving members in good standing."

Bruce Pennyfeather stopped reading and looked up.

Gillian: "Mr. Pennyfeather, are you not the secretary of
the Greenfield Yacht Club?"

"I am."

"And Dr. Cullen was, I believe, the president?"

"He was."

"Will you tell the jury, Mr. Pennyfeather, who the surviving members of the club are?"

"The surviving members," Mr. Pennyfeather obliged,
"are yourself, Mr. Jeffery Whitaker, Mr. Dennis Van Zant,
and myself."

"And the five men whom the defendant is inferentially
accused of murdering with arsenic—were those five men
members of the Greenfield Yacht Club?"

"Yes, sir."

"It would seem then, would it not, that the actual
murderer of Dr. Cullen may have been motivated by a
desire to eliminate from the membership rolls as many
members in good standing as possible, so that—"

"I object to that," snapped Mr. Yistle. "It is summation."

"I am merely elaborating the point I raised in my prelim-
inary address."

"The objection is sustained," ruled the court.

Gillian: "Mr. Pennyfeather, you testified yesterday under cross-examination that the defendant purchased quantities of drugs, chemicals and poisons from you."

"Yes, sir."

"Did it strike you, at the time he made these purchases, that he was using extremely large amounts of arsenic for his experiments?"

"Yes, sir."

"Do you know how he was using, or planning to use, the arsenic?"

"Yes. He was carrying on some elaborate experiments in killing insect pests. He was trying to formulate a dusting powder."

"Was he interested in exterminating any particular insect?"

"Yes. The cutworm."

"That will be all. You may cross-examine, Mr. Yistle."

"The State waives cross-examination." But Mr. Yistle wore a worried look. He went into a whispered conference with Mr. Bullock. It was obvious to them that Gillian was up to some of his tricks. The Silver Fox was preparing to perform!

Gillian's next witness was James Carpenter, a white-haired man of sixty. In response to questions, he stated that he was the president of the Greenfield Real Estate Board, that he had been a real estate operator in Greenfield for the past thirty years.

"You consider that your knowledge of Greenfield real estate values is thorough, do you, Mr. Carpenter?"

The witness smiled. "I suppose it is."

"Isn't it true that you are always called upon to appraise real estate when its value is doubtful?"

"Not always, but generally."

"Have you ever appraised the property owned by the Greenfield Yacht Club?"

"I have."

"For whom did you make this appraisal?"

"The Western and Southern Railroad."

"When?"

"About fourteen years ago. The Western and Southern was putting in a storage yard by the river. The real estate department of the railroad requested me to make an appraisal of the yacht club property and to make inquiries to determine whether or not the land could be purchased. I had the land surveyed. In my report to the railroad, I appraised the property at five hundred thousand dollars. The Western and Southern made the yacht club officials an offer slightly less than that, but it was declined."

"HAS THAT PROPERTY increased in value since then?"

"Very materially. Since the new channel has been dredged, it is probably the most valuable piece of water front property in the city. I should say that it is worth, conservatively, two and a half million. It might go as high as three million."

"Thank you, Mr. Carpenter. Are you taking this witness, Mr. Yistle?"

Mr. Yistle arose and his air was combative.

"Your honor, I object most strenuously to the admission into the record of these two witnesses' testimony. Counsel for the defense has made a discovery in regard to the value of the yacht club property that is beside the issue. I should like to know," he inquired with heavy irony, "if the Greenfield Yacht Club or Rufus Lally is on trial for the murder of Dr. Cullen."

Judge Simpson replied: "Counsel for the defense is entitled to examine witnesses to support his contention that the accused is the victim of a plot. It seems to me he has succeeded ably in establishing a plot motive paralleling, but opposed to the State's. Was this charter introduced at the grand jury hearing?"

"No, your honor."

"Do you wish to withdraw your objection?"

"No."

"It is overruled."

"Exception!"

"Exception noted. Mr. Hazeltine, had you finished with this witness?"

"Yes, your honor."

Mr. Yistle looked angry and bewildered.

He said: "The State waives examination, but requests that all of the defense witnesses be held for recall."

Judge Simpson nodded. "It is so ordered. Who is your next witness, Mr. Hazeltine?"

"Mrs. Cornelia Van Zant, your honor."

Cornelia Van Zant was called. Mr. Yistle looked disgusted. He was certain that Gillian did not have a case. He believed that Gillian would introduce every shred of evidence on any grounds whatever, and examine every witness available, merely to drag out the trial, to dim the brilliance of the State's efforts, to confuse the jury. He felt Gillian would, in short, stoop to any device, resort to the lowest court room trickery, to bring about a disagreement.

Mr. Yistle looked at Cornelia, when she came in, with the expression of a man whose breakfast is not properly digesting. She sailed queenlike to the witness stand.

"Mrs. Van Zant," Gillian began his examination, "will you kindly tell the jury whether you were, prior to your marriage, a high school-teacher?"

Cornelia gave the ladies and gentlemen of the jury her patronizing smile.

"I was. Yes."

"In what subject, or subjects, Mrs. Van Zant, did you instruct?"

"I taught English for awhile, then domestic science."

Gillian picked up the larger of the two tin cans from his table.

"In teaching domestic science, you taught, among other domestic activities, cooking, did you not?"

"I did."

"You taught your pupils how to broil steaks, make good coffee, how to bake cakes and pies and so on?"

"I did."

"In the course of your experience as a domestic science instructor, you cultivated the ability. I presume, to judge the cooking skill of hundreds of pupils?"

"I did. Yes."

"So that you became, in the course of time, an expert judge of all kinds of culinary skill?"

Cornelia Van Zant looked at Gillian archly, as if to say: "Are you going to make fun of me again?" Her spoken answer was: "I suppose I became an expert judge."

"Would you say, Mrs. Van Zant, that your ability as a

judge extended to the commoner kinds of home made candy?"

"Fudge!" murmured Mr. Yistle disgustedly. And in a whisper to Mr. Bullock: "Is this a murder trial or a candy contest?"

The witness answered: "Yes. Of course."

"You instructed your pupils in the making of candy?"

"Yes."

"Of fudge?"

A titter was audible in the rear of the court room. Bailiffs glared. Some of the morning newspapers had made humorous references to Gillian's interest in fudge.

"Yes."

GILLIAN PULLED THE top off the tin can.

"This can," he explained to Cornelia, "contains a number of pieces of fudge. They are several weeks old. It is, in fact, difficult to put an exact date on this batch of fudge, but I should say that it was made two or three days prior to the murder of Dr. Cullen."

Mr. Yistle interposed: "I beg to ask if it, by any chance, has anything to do with the murder of Dr. Cullen."

"Perhaps it has," Gillian answered.

"I object to this fudge," said Mr. Yistle, "on the grounds that it has no possible connection with the issue at stake. Your honor, I must request that counsel for the defense be instructed to confine his examinations and his evidence to the issue."

"I am merely trying, your honor," Gillian explained, "to prove a conspiracy against the accused. My methods may seem roundabout; but I will, step by step, build up an argument that I am certain you will find unshakable. I beg the State's tolerance for a few minutes longer."

Judge Simpson looked inquiringly at Mr. Yistle. "Will you withhold your objection until Mr. Hazeltine has submitted further evidence?"

"Yes, yes, yes!" complied Mr. Yistle in a groaning voice. "Time is flying. The calendar, as you are aware, your honor, is crowded. Other cases are being held back while we decide whether or not fudge is fudge or sealing wax sealing wax. Perhaps we might investigate whether or not it is true that birds fly and fish swim."

Judge Simpson smiled. "You may proceed, Mr. Hazeltine."

"I wish," said Gillian, "to introduce this can of fudge as material evidence for the defense."

Amidst broad smiles and some giggling in the rear of the court room, the can of fudge was marked Exhibit B for the defense and, at Gillian's request, handed to Cornelia.

"This fudge," Gillian resumed, "was sent to me anonymously. It was fresh when I sealed it in this tin. It should not be dry or stale. Mrs. Van Zant, will you select any piece of fudge in that can and examine it?"

Cornelia selected a piece of fudge and looked at it.

"Do not taste it!" Gillian said hastily. "Because it contains arsenic."

Mr. Yistle sprang up as if some one had prodded him with a pin.

"Arsenic?" he echoed.

"But don't be afraid of it!" Gillian hastened to reassure Cornelia. "I ate pounds of it, and it didn't kill me. What I want, Mrs. Van Zant, is your expert opinion of it. Does it look like good fudge? Does it feel like good fudge?"

Cornelia was looking at him dazedly.

"Do you mean—"

"I mean, can you tell by the feel of it whether it has the qualities of fudge that has been made by an expert—creaminess, smoothness. You can crumble it between your fingers. Will you do so?"

Cornelia did so, and her expression was distasteful.

"Is it smooth? Does it feel smooth? Does it feel like fudge that was made by an expert?"

"Yes."

"Is it true that fudge made by non-experts is apt to be grainy, gritty, rough?"

"Yes."

"That will be all. I merely wanted your opinion as an expert. Do you wish to cross-examine this witness. Mr. Yistle?"

"What I want to know is, who made that fudge?" Mr. Yistle demanded.

"I will attempt to establish that later."

"If that fudge contains arsenic, as you claim, why wasn't it brought to my attention? Why wasn't it brought to the grand jury's attention?"

"Because I was basing the defense upon that batch of fudge. That fudge was a kind of octopus that I had been nursing unknown to my bosom. I found, little by little, that its long arms enfolded not only me, but that they reached out in many directions. They reached into dead men's graves.

"They reached into Dr. Cullen's study; they reached

down into the innocent life of this young man who stands charged with the murder of Dr, Cullen. I wish to call another expert—Harry Zarrow."

MR. YISTLE BRUSQUELY waved his hand to indicate that he had no questions to ask Mrs. Van Zant.

She retired. Harry Zarrow came strolling in, looking more bored, if possible, than usual. He seated himself and slowly began to knead the gum in his mouth.

Gillian said: "Mr. Zarrow, at about six thirty on the morning of October 12, you performed in your laboratory an arsenious trisulfide precipitate test on some samples of fudge I brought to you, did you not?"

The city chemist nodded. "Yep."

"Did your test prove that arsenic was present in that fudge?"

"Yep."

"When you had tested that fudge, what did you do with it?"

"I sealed it up in a tin container and wrote out my analysis on a label which I pasted on the tin."

"Is this the tin?"

Harry Zarrow examined Exhibit B.

"Yep. This is it."

"That will be all. Mr. Yistle?"

"Cross-examination waived. Let's hear some more witnesses." Mr. Yistle spoke sarcastically. He looked sarcastic. He asked: "Who sent you that fudge?"

"Don't be impatient," said Gillian pleasantly. "Perhaps I don't even know who sent it."

"Perhaps no one sent it! Perhaps you sent it to yourself and put arsenic in it to clog up this trial!"

Judge Simpson: "Address your remarks to me, Mr. Yistle."

"I beg your honor's pardon."

"Your next witness, Mr. Hazeltine."

"Mr. Frederick Lonsdale."

Mr. Frederick Lonsdale took the stand amidst murmurs of interest which were subdued by bailiff's glares.

Gillian: "You are the postmaster of Greenfield, are you not, Mr. Lonsdale?"

"I am, sir." Mr. Lonsdale was a stout, gray-haired man with worried brown eyes.

"Will you tell the jury, Mr. Lonsdale, how long it would require, under ordinary circumstances, for a small package, dropped in the package box on the corner of Elm and Hadley Streets to be delivered to any house in Riverside Heights?"

"At what hour," the postmaster inquired, "would the package be dropped into the box?"

"Between seven and eight in the evening."

"It would be collected at nine," answered Mr. Lonsdale. "It would be delivered to any house in Riverside Heights next day before noon, except perhaps around the Christmas season."

"Normally, then," said Gillian, "a small package—like a pound box of fudge—if dropped into the package box at Elm and Hadley before 7 P.M., would be delivered to my house in Riverside Heights next morning?"

"That's right."

Said Gillian: "That's all."

Mr. Yistle snorted. "Trying to trace it, eh?"

Gillian smiled and asked him if he wished to cross-examine. Mr. Yistle did not.

"My next witness," said Gillian, "is Toro Sukawa."

21

THE MURDER PLOT IS UNMASKED

THE COURT ROOM buzzed with whispers. Heads turned. Even the bored occupants of the press table turned and looked.

Toro, refreshed by a night's sleep, but still looking worn and weary, walked on tiptoe to the stand. Gillian asked him routine questions in regard to his nationalization. Then:

"What is your employment?"

"I was, until October 12, a butler."

"In whose employ?"

"In yours, sir.

"On the 12th of October, you ran away from Greenfield, did you not?"

"I did, alas!"

"Why did you vanish?"

"Because I feared that my slight part in one of the complications growing out of this dreadful affair might be apprehended. And because I was once accused of complicity in drug smuggling."

"Were you brought to trial for drug smuggling?"

"I was indeed."

"Were you acquitted?"

"Thanks to your efforts, I was, sir."

"Toro, I want you to tell the jury just what you mean by the slight part you played in Dr. Cullen's murder,"

"He who holds by the tail a tiger fears to release that hold," said Toro. "Until I was a boy of twelve, I lived in Japan and China. Many regrettable customs were imposed upon my formative young mind. Among them was the custom of what, in Asia, we call squeeze, which is directly related to the Oriental custom of cumshaw."

"Explain what you mean—and do it briefly."

"In a business transaction," Toro explained, "a third party who has little to do with the transaction or who may possess information injurious to either of the two transacting parties may demand a stipend. That is called squeeze or cumshaw. How often," Toro moaned, "our conception of the ocean is limited because we are well frogs! What a fool any man is to pause under a plum tree to adjust his hat, or in a melon field, stoop down to tie a shoelace! In your law courts, prosecuting attorneys, gifted in the use of circumstantial evidence, would declare that the innocent man had paused to steal a plum or a melon! So it was, alas, with me. I was demanding and obtaining squeeze, or cumshaw, from the luckless defendant in this lamentable trial—because he was engaged in the illegal practice of selling Scotch whisky! I threatened to inform the prohibition officers. I visited the luckless defendant regularly—weekly, oftener, and collected my squeeze."

"How much squeeze did you collect?"

"Four dollars a week," answered the Japanese.

The court room burst into laughter. But no smile appeared on the wan face of the witness. Nor was Mr.

Yistle smiling. His expression was one of contemptuous disbelief.

"And you ran away because of that?" Gillian demanded.

"I ran away because it was discovered that arsenic was in the Scotch whisky. That made my friendship with the luckless defendant open to great suspicion, because I often helped him unpack the whisky."

"Does that explain your frequent visits to the yacht club?"

"My squeeze was small, yet a gnat may obscure one's contemplation of an ocean. Rotten wood cannot be carved. I fear that I am constituted of rotten wood."

"WHAT WERE YOU doing at the yacht club in the hours following one thirty in the morning of October 12?"

"I went there to procure a pair of shoes and a pair of trousers which I kept there."

"Why did you keep trousers and shoes there?"

"Because I sometimes waded about in the mud of the river, seeking a certain crawfish which is indigenous to the river mud of my native land and which is employed in the concoction of one of my favorite dishes."

"Did you procure your shoes and trousers?"

"The trousers I procured and threw into the river. The shoes I could not find. They were being used."

"Toro, when you were at the yacht club on the morning following Dr. Cullen's murder, did you see Mr. Bruce Pennyfeather?"

"Yes, sir."

"Describe the circumstances."

"I had just returned from the river, after throwing my trousers in, when I was leaped upon by a number of strong policemen. They urged me upstairs to the sail loft. It was there that I saw Mr. Bruce Pennyfeather, lying unconscious on the floor."

"You were not, were you, responsible for Mr. Pennyfeather's hanging by a rope from the rafters?"

"Oh, no, sir."

Gillian turned to the jury. "In case you may not be informed, perhaps I should say that this witness was arrested that night in the sail loft and held as an accomplice to the murder. He was released next morning because of insufficient evidence. Now, Toro, I want you to tell the jury about ghosts. Do you believe in ghosts?"

"Yes, sir."

"On any of your evening visits to the yacht club, did you ever hear sounds which led you to believe that the clubhouse was haunted?"

"I did, indeed, Mr. Hazeltine. I heard chains clanking and voices moaning."

"When was this?"

"On the night of October 10."

"What did you do when you heard the clanking chains and the moaning voice?"

"I went away."

"Toro, do you recall that boxes of fudge were occasionally sent to me anonymously through the mail?"

"Yes, sir."

"How often did those boxes of fudge arrive?"

"Always on Tuesdays, sir."

"I will want to question you again later. You may leave the stand now, unless Mr. Yistle wishes to cross-examine you."

"I'll cross-examine him later," said Mr. Yistle. "I want you to finish tracing that fudge."

"My next witness," said Gillian, "is Miss Janet Fly."

A pretty, blond, blue-eyed girl came to the stand and looked nervously at Gillian. She was, she stated in response to questioning, the chief night operator of the Greenfield telephone exchange.

Gillian: "Some time ago, Miss Fly, I asked you to prepare for me a report on the calls which were put through to my house on the night of October 12. Did you prepare that list?"

"Yes, sir," in a shaking voice. "I have it here."

"It seems to me," broke in Mr. Yistle, "this is entirely irrelevant. What have telephone calls to do with fudge?"

"I am working back," Gillian answered, "along one of the long arms of that octopus I referred to. Miss Fly, will you kindly read off that list of calls?"

"There were three of them," the nervous girl answered. "The first call to your house was from River 9743—the Greenfield Yacht Club. The second call was from Main 7265—the office of the city chemist. The third call was from Hillside 7120—a pay station in the Stacy All Night Drugstore at the corner of Elm and Hudson."

"I WISH," SAID Gillian, "to submit that list of telephone calls as material evidence, your honor. I will prove, if possible, that one of the conspirators in the plot of killing five citizens of Greenfield, in murdering Dr. Cullen so that those other murders would not be discovered, and in placing the blame for said murders upon the defendant—I will prove, if possible, that one of the conspirators used the telephone in the Stacy All Night Drug Store."

Judge Simpson glanced at the district attorney. "Does the State object to the admission of this list of telephone calls as material evidence for the defense?"

Mr. Yistle shook his head. There was a puzzled look about his eyes as he whispered to Mr. Bullock: "I wonder if Gillian has something up his sleeve!"

And his yes-man echoed: "Yes, sir; I've been wondering the same thing!"

"Cross-examination is waived," Mr. Yistle said to the court. "But I should like to ask the esteemed counsel for the defense some questions, with your honor's permission."

"You may proceed, Mr. Yistle."

"What I want to know," said Mr. Yistle brusquely to Gillian, "is this: is it your theory that whoever sent you that box of poisoned fudge killed Dr. Cullen?"

"It is," said Gillian.

"And how about the poisoned whisky?"

"I will take that up in due course," Gillian answered.

"Your theory," Mr. Yistle went on, "is that the murderer's motive was to eliminate as many members from the yacht club rolls as possible—every one of them, except himself, if possible—so that when the property was sold, he would become rich?"

"That," Gillian said, "is my theory."

"In other words, the theoretical murderer must be either yourself, Bruce Pennyfeather, Dennis Van Zant or Jeffery Whitaker?"

Gillian only smiled. It was a grim smile.

"If you can fasten the murder on one of them you're a wonder!" breathed Mr. Yistle. "If you can even cast suspicion on any one of them, you're a wonder, because you know it will bring about a disagreement of all the foxy, smooth, underhanded methods of defense you've ever used in a court room—"

"Gentlemen!" the judge snapped. "You are holding up this trial. Are you through with this witness?"

"Yes, your honor," said the two lawyers in chorus.

Miss Fly retired. "My next witness," said Gillian, "is Mrs. Cornelia Van Zant. Recall Mrs. Van Zant, please."

Cornelia Van Zant reappeared. This time when she took the stand her smile was somewhat bored.

Gillian said: "Mrs. Van Zant, on the night of October 11 or the morning of October 12—say between the hours of 11 P.M. and 2 A.M.—you were extremely worried, were you not, over the fact that your husband had discovered that there was arsenic in the whisky that you and he had been drinking?"

"Yes. I was terribly worried."

"And when he stayed so long at the city chemist's, having that whisky analyzed, you became almost hysterical with worry, did you not?"

"I may have. I know that I was dreadfully worried. The very thought that he—"

"You were so upset, were you not, that you telephoned me and insisted that you were coming to my house to meet your husband when he came from the city chemist's? Is that true?"

"Yes. I remember."

"Do you recall where you were when you telephoned to me?"

"Of course I do! I was at home."

"You did not, by any chance, telephone me from Stacy's

All Night Drugstore? I mean, you are quite sure that you telephoned me from your house?"

"Quite sure! Quite!"

"You may step down for a moment, Mrs. Van Zant. Please sit over here. Your honor, I should like to have a bailiff attend this witness—she may become hysterical again."

MR. YISTLE BURST out:

"What are you driving at? Are you accusing—"

Judge Simpson: "Gentlemen!"

"But, your honor, this man has already shown you that he will go to any lengths to divert suspicion from the accused!"

"Mr. Hazeltine will proceed," ordered the court.

"My next witness," said Gillian, "is Eileen Lally."

The court room was humming now. The humming rose and fell in waves of all but inaudible sound, as if many hearts were beating loudly, becoming still, beating more loudly.

The red-haired girl entered the court room. She was so white that her appearance was startling. In a silence that was painful, the *tap-tap-tap* of her high heels echoed and reechoed.

Miss Lally seated herself and lifted large brown eyes. She lifted her right hand, to be sworn, as if she were limp with fatigue. In a low, husky voice she answered perfunctory questions.

Gillian, in a gentle voice, asked:

"Miss Lally, will you tell the jury what you have been doing since this trial began?"

The white-faced girl looked at the jury. "I have been

trying to find out who sent poisoned fudge to Mr. Hazeltine."

"Tell them, Miss Lally, just how you went about this investigation."

"I worked under Mr, Hazeltine's orders. His belief was that the person or persons who had been sending the poisoned fudge had also been responsible for the deaths of the five other yacht club members and for the death of Dr. Cullen. It was also his belief that the murderer or murderers had wanted to kill off all the yacht club members and acquire control of that property. That limited my investigations to Bruce Pennyfeather, Jeffery Whitaker, and Dennis Van Zant."

"How about Gillian Hazeltine?" Mr. Yistle barked. "He'll make nearly a million himself out of the sale of that property!"

Judge Simpson frowned. "Mr. Yistle, I am tired of your constant interruptions.

"Proceed with your examination of this witness, Mr. Hazeltine."

"Go on, Miss Lally."

"I made a thorough examination of the premises of all three men," the red-haired girl continued. "And until last night I had no luck. But last night I finally found what I was looking for. I found an old man who lives on the corner of Elm and Hadley. Shall I tell about him now, Mr. Hazeltine?"

"Go right ahead!"

"His name is Jacob Wolff. He has been so ill with arthritis for the past two years that he has not been out of the house. He lives with his son, Jacob Wolff, Jr., in the house on the northwest corner of Elm and Hadley. About six months ago the son had the porch inclosed with glass and a heater put there so that the old man could sit there and watch the traffic go by. That seems to have been the only pleasure he had.

"Mr. Wolff—the old man—cannot come to court to testify. To obtain his testimony it would be necessary for everybody to go to his house. I am saying just what he said to me. You can verify every word of it.

"I finally found him after I had canvassed dozens of houses. I was looking for some one—any one—who had seen any one of the three yacht club members mailing boxes. There was a chance that the boxes had been mailed from the main or a branch post office, but there was a fair chance they had been dropped into a package box. So I was exhausting that possibility.

"Mr. Wolff told me that, every Monday evening, some time after seven o'clock, either a man or a woman came and dropped a package into the package box in front of his house. As there is a street light there, he saw them plainly. Sometimes the two of them came together to mail the package."

Gillian snapped: "Who were this man and this woman?"

"Mr. and Mrs. Van Zant."

Cornelia Van Zant was staring at the red-haired girl. The high color had left her cheeks. Her lips were parted, Her eyes were like bits of glass.

"Wait a minute!" shouted Mr. Yistle. "What are you trying to prove here? Do you want us to believe that the Dennis Van Zants were mailing you poisoned fudge?"

GILLIAN PAID NO attention to him. He said: "All right Miss Lally. What else happened that night?"

"As soon as I heard that—from Mr. Wolff—I went back to the Van Zant house. Oh, I'd been there before, a number of times. There was a party in progress. I had been in the cellar before, but I wanted to search it once more. I finally found what I was looking for in a barrel of old tin cans and rubbish."

"This?" Gillian snapped, as he picked up the smaller of the cans which had been on his table.

"Yes, sir—that."

"What is this, Miss Lally?"

"It is a can containing arsenic."

Cornelia Van Zant uttered a choking sound. She was leaning forward now, staring at the girl on the witness stand as if fascinated.

"Have you an idea where this can came from?"

"Yes, sir. It came from my brother's green chest."

"How do you know?"

"When I had found that can last night and had telephoned you, I took it down to Captain Thorpe, the finger-print expert. Mr. Thorpe had taken finger-prints last evening of all the witnesses, including those of the Van Zants. I waited in his office until he had dusted this can with some sort of powder and gone over it with a magnifying glass. He found three distinct sets of finger-prints—my brother's, Mr. Van Zant's, and Mrs. Van Zant's."

In the hush which followed this disclosure Gillian said:

"Your honor, I am expediting matters by not calling certain witnesses. It seems to me that this case should be referred again to the grand jury. I will proceed, if you wish."

Mr. Yistle brought his fist banging down upon his table under Mr. Bullock's nose.

"Your honor, I am astonished that you permit this travesty to continue! This girl would lie herself black in the face to save her brother from the electric chair. Not one witness has proved that poisoned fudge was actually received by Gillian Hazeltine. No one but that lying Japanese, who, to say the least, at one time was arraigned on a charge of dope smuggling. I claim that this fudge poisoning story is a cock-and-bull story. I claim that it was cut from whole cloth, merely to divert suspicion from the accused.

"Your honor, this is not the first time that the counsel for the defense has resorted to trickery to save the life of a red-handed murderer. I demand a retrial. I wish to secure further witnesses for this case."

Judge Simpson answered: "I must reserve decision on your petition until further evidence is submitted by the defense. Then I will hear you."

"But, your honor, this man is dragging the fair names of a decent and honorable man and woman through the mud!

"Look upon that woman—that gentlewoman—and dare to tell me that she could be guilty of such hideous crimes!"

Judge Simpson said severely: "I repeat, I will decide later upon your petition."

"But, your honor," the frantic district attorney cried, "the evidence against the accused is absolutely convicting. Consider the one point: the poisoned whisky! That lethal beverage! Was it not proved conclusively that that whisky was delivered to the club members by Rufus Lally, and that it was found to contain arsenic?"

"Your honor," Gillian broke in, "I was preparing to take up that point next. Will you permit me to have several witnesses recalled at once?"

Judge Simpson nodded. "Yes."

"Then I want Dennis Van Zant, Bruce Pennyfeather and Jeffery Whitaker."

The three men named presently filed into the room.

"Miss Lally," said Gillian, "may retire. Mr. Van Zant will take the stand."

Dennis Van Zant could not be described as pale. His skin was gray. His lips were blue or green. His bulging eyes were more than ever reminiscent of a gorged puppy's.

Judge Simpson said: "Mr. Pennyfeather and Mr. Whitaker will come and stand near this witness, please."

"ON THE NIGHT of Dr. Cullen's murder," Gillian said to Van Zant, "you telephoned to me from the yacht club, shortly after twelve thirty, disguising your voice and threatening to 'get' me if I touched this case. Isn't that true?"

"N-no!" stammered the witness.

"You had just finished frightening the accused out of the clubhouse by making ghostly sounds, had you not? You had been working on his imagination night after night, had you not, until finally, with an ingenuity that surpasses the ordinary imagination, you terrified him into running to Dr. Cullen's house, gun in hand? Isn't that so?"

"I don't know. I don't want—"

"Then you took samples of whisky, which you had loaded with arsenic, to the city chemist's. And from there you telephoned me again. Is that true, or isn't it?"

"Y-yes, I did. But I didn't—"

"Then you came to my house, collected an armful of

bottles from me, another armful from Bruce Pennyfeather, and still another load from Jeffery Whitaker, and you took them down to the city chemist's, after you had injected an arsenic solution into each bottle with a hypodermic needle, did you not?"

"No. Oh, no! I didn't do that! I tell you—"

"Before that—months before that—didn't you deliver little jars of homemade jellies and boxes of candy and other delicacies to each of those five men who were exhumed and found to have died of chronic arsenic poisoning?"

"I can't think. I don't know what you mean. Look here—" Dennis Van Zant was, or seemed to be, strangling. The grayness of his face had become purple. Some one cried. "He's going to have a stroke!"

"You killed these men," Gillian relentlessly proceeded. "You attempted to kill Bruce Pennyfeather, Jeffery Whitaker, and me, so that you would possess that property! You telephoned your wife at Stacey's Drugstore, where she was waiting to go over and kill Qr. Cullen—the moment Rufus Lally entered his study! Isn't that true? Didn't she shoot Dr. Cullen? Answer that question!"

The witness was shaking uncontrollably. He burst out: "Cornelia, Cornelia, I can't stand it! What shall I say?"

GILLIAN LASHED AT him: "You wore those cotton gloves at the yacht club, and those shoes of Toro's you found in the kitchen—so that you'd leave no mark. Didn't you?"

"Yes, I did!"

"Then you phoned your wife, didn't you?"

"Oh—God! Yes, I did!"

"And she ran down the street to the doctor's, and stood in the window, and the moment Rufus Lally entered the doctor's study she shot the doctor through the brain with the .38 caliber revolver you gave her! Later that night you went back to the yacht club. You tried to kill Pennyfeather, didn't you? Answer me!"

Gillian glared at the witness while awaiting his reply.

Dennis Van Zant did not answer. Silently he pitched forward and fell to the floor.

Bailiffs might shout for order now. Bailiffs might bang with gavels. Judge Simpson had risen. He was trying to make himself heard by the jury. But the jury paid no attention to him. Mr. Yistle was shouting at Cornelia Van Zant; but she was not listening. She was staring, staring at the witness stand, as a sleepwalker stares.

A reporter, not remembering how Lally's shots had been fired at the silhouette, was roaring at Gillian Hazeltine:

"Well, does that explain why only one shot was heard by the doctor's butler?"

But Gillian was too busy shaking Rufus Lally's hand to hear him. It had been the hardest day Gillian had ever spent in court—and the most successful. Those clews had been so fragile! He was glad for a number of reasons. Glad that he had cleared Rufus Lally of that dreadful charge. Glad that he had triumphed over his superstitions about red-haired girls.

He heard a man say: "Van Zant must have been dead when he hit the floor."

And Gillian reflected that he was not sorry. Dennis Van Zant deserved to be dead.

www.ingramcontent.com/pod-product-compliance
Lightning Source LLC
Chambersburg PA
CBHW031151020726
47499CB00002B/328